Rebecca hugged the edge of the Bentley to balance.

Below her, in the open car, was the body of a girl. She lay face-down on the floor, wedged between the seats. She was bent over, kneeling with one arm outstretched, fingers curved like a ballerina's in first position. Her other hand disappeared under her body. Black hair spilled across her shoulders concealing her face. She could have been a dancer waiting for her music, poised to unfold and begin the routine.

If it weren't for the blood.

Blood saturated the thin chiffon covering her thighs. It pooled around her knees. Rivulets streaked away from the body like electricity seeking an easier path. It ran under the footrests, toward the door sills, seeped through the carpet, soaked into the floorboards, dripped onto the bed of the trailer. The metallic stench, intensified by the heat, rose in waves. Rebecca could taste it in the back of her throat. Again.

So much blood. Drained from the body of a girl too young to die.

"Rebecca Moore is not your average sleuth—an investigative journalist turned classic car restorer, all to flee a past that catches up with her faster than a Formula One Racer on a slick track . . . Judith Skilling is a fresh new voice in the mystery field."
Robin Burcell

Books by Judith Skillings

DANGEROUS CURVES
DEAD END

Dangerous CURVES

JUDITH SKILLINGS

AVON BOOKS
An Imprint of HarperCollinsPublishers

AVON BOOKS
An Imprint of HarperCollins*Publishers*
10 East 53rd Street
New York, New York 10022-5299

Copyright © 2005 by Judith Skillings
ISBN 0-06-058319-3
www.avonmystery.com

First Avon Books paperback printing: March 2005

Avon Trademark Reg. U.S. Pat. Off. and in Other Countries, Marca Registrada, Hecho en U.S.A.
HarperCollins® is a registered trademark of HarperCollins Publishers Inc.

Printed in the U.S.A.

10 9 8 7 6 5 4 3 2 1

This book is dedicated to

Lucille M. Benning
and
Richard C. Perkins

for being such supportive fans

Acknowledgments

All the characters in this book are fictitious and bear no resemblance to persons living, dead, or freshly killed. However, the cars really do exist. So, my sincerest thanks go to Ken and Keith Sherper for allowing me to show off 3BU86, their magnificent Phantom III; and to the past and current owners of LSCX853—I hope I didn't embarrass you too much.

Many thanks also to those who contributed inspiration, support, and technical advice: Dr. John Skillings, Mike Farrell, Rick Mullin, B.J. Jefferson, Mermie Karger, Bert and the guys at The Frawley Company, especially the president. And special appreciation to Greg Albers of Bentley Zionsville (a.k.a. Albers Roll-Royce) and Dale Powers of Powers Parts, Inc., for allowing their business names to be used in this book.

Although writing is a solitary activity, the encouragement to write comes from those around us. I would be remiss if I did not remember three remarkable women who, at various stages in my life, greatly influenced my desire to write: Barbara Owen, best English teacher I could have had; Patricia Harker Janis, who really was a "breath of fresh air in a stifling room;" and Elizabeth Farrell, honorary president of my Scranton-area fan club. You are missed.

Author's Note

At present, there is no Washington Vintage Grand Prix. The event depicted in these pages is based on the Pittsburgh Vintage Grand Prix, which takes place each year near the end of July. It's a grand three-day event for the whole family—part car show and part race, sanctioned by the Vintage Sports Car Club of America. Set in Schenley Park, in the heart of the city, the track winds past lush shade trees and round low stone walls where spectators can picnic while enjoying the race. It is a not-for-profit event. Since its inception in 1983, all proceeds have gone to the Autism Society of Pittsburgh and the Allegheny Valley School for the mentally retarded and severely handicapped.

Dangerous
CURVES

In the dream I drift
float to a gentle motion outside my control.
Unaware of my surroundings. Unafraid. Until
the first touch.
A wisp tickles my face. Clammy.
It recedes.
Drifts back. Wraps like an eel around my neck,
slithers down my arm.
I shiver as
it caresses bare flesh with a slimy finger.
Tendrils lash my ankles. Drift over calf, thigh. Slither
  between my legs.
I thrash, flail. At nothing.
Elusive strands float away, return. Thickening. Clinging.
Entwining.
Dank fronds cover my face, fouler than night.
I open my mouth to scream.
I inhale death.

Part One

Broke in Istanbul

One

Prufrock measured out his life in coffee spoons.

Rebecca sympathized with the compulsion. She would have delighted in counting out days of productive work, cars delivered on time, payrolls met. Nights of uninterrupted sleep. Or borrowed books of poetry read and returned.

Instead her life was littered with dead bodies.

Val's panicked call had come around eleven o'clock on what had been a normal Tuesday morning. His cackle echoed through the line, competing with the background voices of men at work, the buzz of official activity. Rebecca's first fear had been a logistics mix-up at the docks. Val giggled, said no. Her second fear was worse—a twisted fender, shattered headlamps, a wire wheel bouncing along the berm of the Washington-Baltimore Parkway.

She closed her eyes. "Tell me you didn't wreck the Bentley."

The day before, she'd received a package from Todd Shelley—a prayer rug he'd haggled for in some Turkish bazaar. Pinned to it had been a four-color postcard of the interior of Santa Sophia with the message: "Pray for the Bentley. 'Something that made the car go broke. And it must have been important 'cause now it don't go at all.' " The quip was from NASCAR driver Michael Waltrip. Shelley was trying to be funny. Rebecca had not been amused. Especially when she read the postscript saying that the 1925 3-Litre would arrive in Baltimore on July 22.

Three days ago.

Val, her youngest mechanic, had begged a flatbed from his cousin's wrecking yard. That morning, he took Paulie and left Vintage & Classics at seven for the Dundalk docks in Baltimore. Instead of being on their way back with the car, they were being hassled by District police.

Val yelled into the phone to be heard over a siren coming closer. Cops wanted to search the 3-Litre. Said they had probable cause, didn't want to wait. Wanted him to sign a consent form. No way was he letting them near the car. That wasn't his call. And, no, he couldn't contact the owner. The guy was schlepping around China in a Hispano-Suiza.

Then an officer had come across Rebecca Moore's name on the transit papers. He said she'd do.

Rebecca had pressed the phone to her ear, sagged against the rough edge of a workbench and stared at a splat of oil on her steel-toed boots. Palms sweating, she heard Val screech that blood was dripping through the floorboards of the Bentley.

Rebecca downshifted, flicked the turn signal and exited the Capitol Beltway at Route 214, Central Avenue. She was in the easternmost point of the District of Columbia, a far cry from the Capitol. She poked along until she reached Division Street, took it north. With each turn the per capita income dropped, as did her spirits. Midway down Fifty-sixth Street she squeezed the MG against the curb behind a station wagon with four flat tires. She was out of the car before Jo Delacroix, her friend and lawyer-in-need, could locate the pull cord to open his door.

Across the street, the Bentley baked in the sun. It was chained to a flatbed, draped with yellow scene-of-the-crime tape. The green paint was streaked with fingerprint powder. The tonneau was unsnapped and flung back, falling over the tail end of the car like a serape. The rear door was open. An amorphous bundle hugged the floor.

Emergency medics wheeled a gurney toward the car. A large man in a polyester suit stopped them. One nodded; the other bounced on the balls of his feet. A gust of wind slapped the wrapper from a Whopper against the leg of her jeans. She bent to peel it off, reluctant to take her eyes from the Bentley. It was déjà vu all over again. Last crime, the car had been in her restoration shop with a splatter of blood on the door edge. This time it was parked in a run-down city neighborhood, drenched in the stuff. There was no sign of either Val or Paulie.

What was the car doing here?

Chained to the rollback, it squatted in front of Naomi's Boutique like an automotive hunchback, shadowing a display window already obscured by orange plastic to protect Naomi's goods from sun fade. The surrounding block was littered with abandoned vehicles, emaciated row houses branded with graffiti, storefronts boasting metal grilles for after-hours protection. Derelicts huddled amid garbage cans. One balanced on a lid, stared at the Bentley like the lookout in a crow's nest. Next door an Hispanic pretended to restack produce while he watched the policemen. A homeless woman, layered in cast-off clothing too warm for the day, stepped on and off the curb, mumbling.

Val had complained about a stupid bag lady. Said that while they were in the store, she'd crawled onto the flatbed to nap in the sun. Beat cops spotted her. Crossed the street to roust her. When she rolled off and stood up, her backside had been covered in blood that wasn't hers.

Rebecca sensed Jo standing an arm's length behind her.

He waited for her to turn before informing her that the employees had been taken to the Sixth District Police Headquarters on Forty-second Street for questioning. An officer would drive him there. Rebecca nodded. She would follow the transporter to the impound lot and see the car safely stowed, then join them. Val Kearny was just eighteen; Paulie Antrim was a naive rich kid, amused at life. She fretted over what they'd already said to the police. They needed their lawyer.

She needed her workers.

Rebecca started across the street. The man in the shapeless suit glared as she advanced, blocked her progress midway. He was the size of an average football tight end, six-two, maybe six-four if the hunched shoulders ever straightened. He introduced himself as Lieutenant Theodore Schneider. He flashed his badge, widened his stance to center his bulk.

He asked for identification. His eyes bounced from her face to the plastic likeness, trying to match her shaved hair and smudged eyes to the woman in the photo. The picture had been snapped at the height of her days as an investigative reporter: eighty dollar haircut skimmed the collar of an Ungaro suit, cocky gray-green stare, lips smug at an insider's joke.

Schneider shoved the license at an underling, wrapped his hand around her upper arm and leered down at her.

"You faint?"

Rebecca shook her head. Probably not. She hadn't the last two times she'd seen a body.

The detective propelled her toward the car. He elbowed a medical technician aside. With one hand he hoisted Rebecca up onto the bed of the rollback. She hugged the edge of the Bentley to balance.

Below her in the open car was the body of a girl. She lay facedown on the floor, wedged between the seats. She was bent over, kneeling with one arm outstretched, fingers curved like a ballerina's in first position. Her other hand disappeared under her body. Black hair spilled across her shoulders, concealing her face. She could have been a dancer waiting for her music, poised to unfold and begin the routine.

If it weren't for the blood.

Blood saturated the thin chiffon covering her thighs. It pooled around her knees. Rivulets streaked away from the body like electricity seeking an easier path. It ran under the foot rests, toward the doorsills. Seeped through the carpet, soaked into the floorboards, dripped onto the bed of the trailer. The metallic stench, intensified by the heat, rose in waves. Rebecca could taste it in the back of her throat. Again. So much blood. Drained from the body of a girl too young to die.

Rebecca didn't realize she'd swayed until a technician asked if she was okay. She held onto the door with both hands, said she was fine.

Schneider told him to cut the crap.

The medic's mouth hardened into a frown. He leaned in from the opposite side and gripped the body under her arms. He gently pulled the torso erect. With latex fingertips he raked back strands of matted hair, then raised the elfin chin of the too-white face of an alabaster angel.

Someone on the ground inhaled a gasp, turned it into a short cough. As if that were a cue, the corpse's arm extended, her hand easing away from her body. Graceful fingers remained curled, frozen in the act of clutching the knife embedded in her flesh. One drop of blood trickled down her finger, quivered, then plopped onto the ivory chiffon shielding her lap.

Rebecca forced herself to look up. The teen's soft lips

were parted over small even teeth. Her dark almond eyes were wide. They stared directly at Rebecca, slightly perplexed. As if asking how her life could have been cut so short. Asking who had thrust the blade into her stomach. Why had they done such a senseless thing?

Two

Val ranted that the girl had been a stowaway. A runaway belly dancer. Probably slipped aboard the boat in Turkey and hid out. One of the seamen must have discovered her when they docked. Threatened to turn her in at knife point. They'd fought and she was stabbed. He planted her body in the 3-Litre.

Rebecca stopped pacing. She leaned across the table.

"Val, the girl was not killed in Istanbul. The car has been in transit for a month, sealed in a container. If she had stowed away, she would have died from dehydration and been decomposed. You were hauling a fresh corpse."

Rebecca dropped into a plastic chair. She was confined in an interrogation room with Paulie and Val. They were spouting nonsense. She was losing patience, fast. Lieutenant Schneider was treating the case as a homicide. Naturally, her employees were his prime suspects. He was sure they were lying. She suspected the same.

The guys had been somewhere they shouldn't have been, dragging a corpse they claimed they knew nothing about. And they refused to talk to anyone but their lawyer—who had disappeared. Jo Delacroix was somewhere outside, do-

ing whatever lawyers do when their clients are going to be in-
terrogated in a suspected homicide. The guys weren't under
arrest yet. Unless they came up with a better story, they
would be.

So far, Rebecca had coerced only three sensible admis-
sions from them.

One: There had been no blood on the Bentley when they
picked it up at the docks.

Two: Neither of them had killed the girl en route.

Three: They hadn't stopped anywhere between the docks
and Naomi's Boutique.

Paulie sat upright at the table, hands folded in front of him.
His unlined face was whiter than his button-down shirt. He
cleared his throat, looked at Val, but addressed his boss. "Do
they know who she was?"

Rebecca shook her head. Schneider had asked her the
same thing: Did she recognize the victim? There was no
identification.

Val tipped his chair back, trying to act cool. He was a re-
formed criminal, ex–drug user and, still on probation for a
botched B&E, but he was far from hardened. His wide blue
eyes tried to match her stare, couldn't.

"We didn't do anything. We didn't know there was a body
in the car. We just picked it up like you asked. Why aren't the
cops hassling the dock guys?"

"Why, Val? Because she died while you were hauling the
Bentley."

Jo Delacroix's voice—less deep than James Earl Jones's
but just as mellifluous—boomed from behind Rebecca. He
had entered the room as silently as a panther. His suit jacket
was buttoned, tie smoothed, white sleeves shot the requisite
three-quarters of an inch. Only in the set of his jaw could Rebecca read his annoyance. He moved around to the end of the
table, patted Val's shoulder in passing.

Behind him, framed in the doorway Jo had vacated, stood Lieutenant Michael Hagan.

Rebecca flashed a glance at her lawyer. *What the hell is he doing here?* Jo shrugged. She squeezed her eyes shut. She didn't have to look at Hagan to see him. Thick dark hair contrasted by brilliant blue eyes, etched with laugh lines. Head tilted to one side as if viewing life slightly off-kilter. Taut chest muscles, tight jeans, restless hands. A man with an edge. And the charm to pull you over it with him.

Detective Hagan was high on the list of people she was better off without. They shared too much history. First the suicide of his stepbrother. Then the murders of Graham and Vera Stuck. Plus a physical chemistry that had fizzled down if not out—thanks to time, distance, and the dead stepbrother. Rebecca wasn't prepared to meet up with Hagan again. Not today. Not over another dead body.

It looked like she didn't have a choice.

She walked around the table and extended her hand. Hagan held it a second too long. Or maybe she imagined it. She didn't imagine the deliberation with which he checked her out: starting with her scuffed boots, faded jeans, polo shirt, and shorn hairdo. He slid a toothpick to the other side of his mouth. Said nothing.

Which was what he'd been saying for the past month.

After the Stucks's murders, Hagan had returned to the District. At first he'd kept in touch. They met twice for dinner at points midway between. Romantic evenings, electric with promise. Just not enough spark to bridge the distance or overpower everyday demands. New homicide cases were added to his workload. The trial of Alonso, postponed by the death of Justice Reiske, finally began. Hagan was testifying. For her part, Rebecca had inherited three former customers of her murdered rival, all of them with deadlines. So the shop was operating ten hours a day, six days a week. Neither she nor Hagan was good at phone conversations. Their relationship was too tenuous. Their flippant banter was too easily misconstrued when not backed up by a smile or a touch. Gradually, the calls had dwindled. Then ceased.

Paulie broke the silence. Standing, he held out his hand and thanked the detective for coming. Jo raised an eyebrow. Val looked bored. Rebecca was perplexed.

Paulson Antrim III was unquestionably her best-dressed employee and, until now, the only one without a police booking sheet in his résumé. He was also the son of Head Tide's wealthiest widow. A battle-ax in cashmere twin sets who would have rushed to the District flanked with the kind of lawyers old money can buy. If Paulie had asked. Instead he'd called Hagan.

"Mick helped us before. No reason he won't again."

An optimistic sentiment, though Paulie looked more somber than hopeful. Rebecca didn't blame him. She could think of several reasons why the DC detective would be of little use, starting with the fact that this mess didn't happen in his district, so it couldn't be his case.

Jo must have reached the same conclusion. He asked Hagan to leave while he spoke to his clients. Hagan went without comment, taking his toothpick and much of the tension with him. Once the door latched shut, Rebecca sank into the chair beside Val. Jo remained standing, eyes on both men.

"As I was saying, from his preliminary exam, the coroner believes that the girl exsanguinated in the hour before she was discovered, between ten and eleven. She died after you left Baltimore, before you arrived at Fifty-sixth Street. Are you positive you stopped nowhere else—for gas, a soda, to use the rest room?"

Paulie studied his belt buckle. Val picked at a cuticle on his thumb.

Their lawyer removed his glasses. "How very perplexing. If you went directly from the docks to the store in DC without stopping, then *where* was the girl murdered and *by whom?*"

Jo flicked Rebecca a glance over their bent heads. He let the silence settle for a long count of thirty before he slapped the table. Both heads jerked to attention.

"Gentlemen, you have one minute to revise your story. Or, I promise you, I will abandon you to the police."

Three

Damn. Moore looked good.

It hit Mick each time he saw her. How the woman could look that seductive without makeup and a low-cut dress was a mystery he kept exploring, like a tongue prodding a loose tooth. It had to be the cheekbones. Or the delicate shoulders, so straight they seemed to hold her body suspended, allowing her hips and legs to move unburdened by her torso.

He didn't know what to do about her. Extraction would be too painful. The constant dull ache wasn't much fun either. The return to police work had been a daytime analgesic. Until this happened.

He should have stayed away. Might have, but Antrim had sounded so needy on the phone.

In Head Tide, Antrim had seemed a fish out of water, a priss playing with wrenches. He wore a starched shirt, tie, and clean shop coat to work every day. Drove a 1960s baby blue Cadillac. Fussed with fancy coffees and was annoyingly congenial. A word Mick couldn't apply to many people. Kind of refreshing. In short, not a stereotypic murderer. But here he was, sequestered with his sidekick in interrogation room number four, being championed by Moore.

Mick leaned against the wall opposite, shutting out the racket of police business buzzing from the squad room. Through the one-way glass he watched Moore pace inside the ten-by-ten cell, her energy bouncing off the grimy green walls. When she leaned across the table toward the guys, the tension in her body telegraphed her concern, etched a frown line between her eyes. He longed to smooth it away, touch her cheek, make her smile. What he should do was leave.

He pushed away from the wall. He had to get back to the courthouse. He'd used up the lunch break. But instead he leaned closer, a moth to her flame, compelled to stand outside and watch.

Then Moore straightened, headed for the door.

Hagan pivoted abruptly, moved down the hall away from the interrogation room.

She called out his name. He stopped. She closed in, standing behind him, not quite close enough to touch. She waited. He turned.

Her mouth was set in that Mona Lisa smile, hands stuck in her back pockets, like she didn't know what to do with them. The resulting pose was appreciated by two cops loitering in the hallway. She half smiled at Mick.

"Any chance you could help on the case officially?"

Mick shook his head. "Schneider caught it. It's his district. I'm spending most days in the courtroom."

"Right. Alonso. How's the trial going?"

Mick wanted to say, *I'll tell you over dinner.* He settled for "So-so. Reconvenes at two."

Moore glanced at the wall clock. She asked if they could talk in private. Off the record. Mick motioned her forward.

From inside the interrogation room the lawyer and his clients watched them move off.

"For Christ's sake. They stopped at some strip joint over in Prince Georges County, dragging the Bentley behind them? Then hauled it into the city to buy dancing shoes? What were they thinking?" Mick kicked at the leg of a chair, caught it and sat.

Moore fluttered her hands. "Val was thinking about a diamond for Juanita. He'd heard that the bartender at the club could put him in touch with a wholesaler."

"Hot merchandise, no doubt. What if the bartender's got a record? The kid knows what buying stolen goods from a felon will do to his parole?"

"Of course. That's why he refused to level with the detective."

Moore ran both hands through hair that was no longer there. Mick was momentarily distracted. He grinned at the futile gesture. "Looks good."

Her hair had been shoulder length when they'd first met. Gleaming waves streaked with auburn. The left side had been singed off when she'd set fire to a murderer. She must have decided to shave it, start again. Clipped sides, tousle of lazy curls on top—she looked like everybody's kid sister. *Yeah, right.* Mick extricated a toothpick from a back pocket.

"My advice? Come clean with Schneider, though be prepared. He's a pain in the ass about ex-cons."

Moore started to say something in defense of her friendly felons, then shut her mouth. Prudent. Instead, she let her gray-green eyes beseech him. They were brighter than high beams on a straight stretch of country road. Mick broke the toothpick in half, dropped it on the floor, sighed as he leaned back in the chair.

"Tell me what you know."

Moore hunched forward. "They arrived at the club around eleven-twenty. It wasn't open so they waited in the parking lot until eleven-thirty."

"Details, Moore. I know you grilled them. I know you know how. How close did they park to the building? Any other cars? People milling about? Give."

Moore scowled, but switched into reporter mode. She drew the scene with precise words. The picture came alive. As she spoke, her thumb rubbed up and down the length of her index finger. She stared off into space. Mick stared at her.

He'd heard of Gentlemen Only, but had never been there. A new club across the line in Maryland, it was north of Andrews Air Force Base, not far from the sports complex and just twenty minutes east of the city. It pulled in a mixed crowd.

Per Antrim's description, it was an oasis. You reached it via a half-mile drive that ended in the parking lot. Kearney had driven the flatbed across the lot, circled, parked it parallel to the front door, spanning the first row of spaces. There were a half-dozen cars, most huddled close to the trees for shade. In an alley running alongside the building, there was a black Silver Shadow. They'd joked about it—if it belonged to a dancer, she was making impressive tips.

They'd waited in the cab of the rollback. After a few minutes they heard a noise in the alley. From his seat, Val watched a janitor throw trash into the Dumpster. He'd braced the alley door open and returned inside. A minute later the bartender unlatched the front door, ready for business.

"They know he was the bartender then, or find that out later?"

"Paulie knew. He mentioned it to Val at the time."

"So Antrim's been to the club before?"

Moore shrugged. "Surprisingly, yes."

Mick didn't respond. He had too many years on the force to raise an eyebrow at the discrepancies between a person's private behavior and his everyday appearance. Moore was only taken aback because Antrim worked for her, hurt that she didn't know all his secrets. Mick motioned for her to continue.

Once inside, they'd gone to the bar. Antrim had introduced Kearney to bartender, Vince Lambesco, who poured the guys sodas. Then Antrim heard music in the main room. He left Val, carried his drink in to watch the girls practice their routines.

Mick jotted down the bartender's name. "No one else around?"

"Not at first. Val was chatting up the bartender. Swapping stories. Then all at once Lambesco clammed up. Val thought it was because the sound system set up a racket, started screeching. Until he realized someone was standing behind him. He didn't turn. He played with the ice in his Coke. He heard a man ask the bartender to get someone named LeClerc. Lambesco nodded and yelled in the direction of the hallway behind the bar for 'Ozzie,' saying that Mr. D wanted him. A short man with thick glasses and a paunch emerged from the hallway wiping his brow. He walked away with the unseen 'Mr. D.' Val finished up and went off to find Paulie. As they recrossed through the bar area on the way out, the short guy was downing a drink. Lambesco was rinsing glasses behind the bar. There was no one else around."

"They see the victim while they were there?"

"Both denied it."

"Kearney buy the diamond?"

"No. No money changed hands."

Mick leaned across the table, close enough to count the threads in the logo embroidered on her chest. He said he'd do what he could. Unofficially. But Kearney and Antrim would have to come clean with Schneider. Tell him everything. Beg for mercy. Delacroix could coach them. Mick was willing to accept that the girl had crawled—or been stashed—in the car at the club, while the guys were inside drinking sodas. He'd try to peddle the story to Schneider.

"Why not? Should be easy pickings. If Schneider can't find a criminal in a strip joint, he should turn in his badge. Of course, if the girl was killed outside the city, he'll have to share jurisdiction. Schneider won't like that. Never did play nicely with others."

Four

Rebecca strode out of the police station. She sucked in the muggy air as the afternoon heat hit her like the blast from a pizza oven. She slid into the MG, avoided touching bare skin to anything metal and fished in the open glove box for sunglasses.

Jo was a heartbeat behind. He folded himself in half and eased into the car. It was not an easy fit for a well-proportioned man six-foot-two. It was more Rebecca's size: half a foot shorter and lean through the hips. The '57 was a relic from her teenage years, disreputable like an old pair of jeans. It needed paint, but at least it ran. Jo's Saab was in the shop for repairs.

Delacroix wriggled, searching for a seat belt. "I feel like I'm sitting on the ground."

"Then you don't have far to fall."

The lawyer grunted. "A fall from grace is an easy step, it seems, for your employees. Unwittingly they've gotten themselves accused of knifing a dancing girl, stuffing her into your customer's Bentley and transporting her inert body across state lines while she bled to death."

Rebecca peered at the glare bouncing off Jo's glasses. "Tell me you're joking?"

"Lord, I hope so. Charges haven't been filed yet, but the lieutenant is salivating." Jo tugged on the door to make sure it was latched. "Please remember, Rebecca, I'm not a criminal defense attorney. Nor am I licensed to try cases in the District of Columbia."

"Then keep my guys out of court."

They sped down the freeway to Head Tide, Maryland, in silence. Wind noise, the traffic exiting the capital, and the rumble from a leaking exhaust gasket made conversation difficult. Fortunately, their relationship made it unnecessary.

The friendship had begun just months before, when Rebecca found the body of a business rival dead in her shop and Jo signed on to give legal advice. Frank Lewis, her head mechanic, had needed the lawyer when he'd been arrested for two homicides. He was released the night the real killer tried to add Rebecca to his pile of victims.

Rebecca had recovered from her burns. The cracked ribs had healed. Her shoulder where the bullet had gone through only bothered her on damp days. The scar was fading. She missed having hair but the short cut was comfortable for summer. Practical when driving the topless MG. Jo said it made her look like an adorable pixie.

She'd take his word for it. He'd been right about so much. About the strategies for getting the shop out of debt. Right about the therapist he recommended to help her deal with the nightmare. And caring enough to see that she kept her appointments.

When the nightmare refused to go away, Jo had made her keep paper and pen by the bed. Instructed her to put the terror into words when it woke her in the dark. During an early morning thunderstorm with lightning flashing over the back fields, she'd done what he asked. Scribbled uncensored phrases across a blank page.

When she had hesitantly handed him the notes the next morning, he exclaimed that her description was a haiku, that she was a natural poet. He'd loaned her the *Complete Plays and Poems of T. S. Eliot* the same day. She'd struggled through the first poem, not read any farther. Still, she appreciated his efforts to overcome her literary shortcomings while trying to quell her fears.

Until he'd handed her the dog-eared volume, Rebecca hadn't known that Jo liked poetry. It didn't surprise her. Jo Delacroix had more contradictions than a prism has facets. Glimpsed in town, he was a deliberate attorney in boxy Brooks Brothers suits, removing his glasses to offer gentle advice to needy clients. At the all-county baseball finals, pared down to shorts and a sweaty tee, he was a toned athlete. With daring and more speed than he ever showed in a courtroom, Jo had captured the season's MVP award. He accepted it with grace, then stashed it in the closet along with his bat.

Jo wasn't quite a charlatan, though there were days when Rebecca wondered if his eyeglasses were only a prop. She was convinced he was honorable, a man she could trust with her life. She was equally convinced that the sum of his complex parts exceeded the flawless whole he presented.

Rebecca dropped Jo at his office. It was a tall brick house from the Federal period. The last building in the town center before the spit of water that came and went with the tide. Head Tide had been named for the occasional stream. A narrow stone bridge arched above the damp grasses. The tide was out.

She revved the MG, blipping the accelerator to keep it from stalling while Jo went over what little they could do at this juncture. He promised to contact a colleague, a DC criminal lawyer. He would review the case with her, as a precaution. He ruffled Rebecca's windblown curls and told her to go home. Rest. Try not to worry. He would call her the minute he knew more.

Rebecca drove to Vintage & Classics.

She parked in front of her shop and let herself in. She dropped her keys on the desk, disturbing Maurice, who was asleep in the in basket. The cat raised his head and meowed for attention. She obliged, then strode into the car shop, hopeful that her senior mechanics had made progress in her absence.

Frank and Billy Lee were bent over the front left hub of a Phantom III. Frank cocked his head when the door opened. He motioned her over, pointed at the brake assembly.

"Mr. Carroll going to drive this thing on Sunday?"

"Three laps around the two-and-a-half-mile course."

"Imagine he'll have to slow for the curves? Maybe want to stop at the end?"

"Frank, are you saying the brakes are shot?"

"You doubting me?"

Rebecca examined the left brake shoe. The copper rivets were through the liner, which explained Thom Carroll's complaint that there was an occasional squeal when he stepped on the pedal. *Occasional, my foot.* The condition of the brakes would be reason enough to have murdered Graham Stuck, if he weren't already dead. Frank concurred. When you're dealing with a vehicle nearly nineteen feet long, weighing over thirty-five hundred pounds, and sporting a massive V-12 engine—you better have good brakes.

Rebecca ran her hand over the sensuous fender. 3BU86 had been ordered new in 1937 by His Highness the Nawab of Bhopal, Bhopal State, Bhopal, India. Rebecca grinned every time she envisioned the ruler and his entourage descending on Thrupp & Maberly's showroom in Devonshire House in

London's Mayfair district. There, he would have selected the appointments for the car: the paint colors, fittings, uphol-stery, lamps, luggage. Rebecca suspected that Rolls-Royce, Ltd. had the easy job in supplying the engine and chassis. The salesman at Thrupp's would have had to wear kid gloves when dealing with the royal owner's tastes and requirements.

The current owner was unveiling the freshly restored car at the Washington Vintage Grand Prix weekend. As befitted the marque, it would be displayed on the hill under shade trees. As a patron, Thom Carroll was encouraged to parade around the winding track before the races on Sunday. As a soft-spoken perfectionist, he expected the car to be fully prepared for both activities.

Frank said it would be, once those brakes were relined.

"You better call your brake buddy see if he can do them to-morrow. And get that estimate done for what's-her-name. Notes are on your desk."

Frank was referring to Dorothea Wetherly.

After Val's frantic call, Rebecca had grabbed up her purse and bolted for the front door. She'd nearly collided with a stranger about to knock. The man had yanked back his fist as if in fear of contamination. He was delicate, in his early thir-ties. Receding, bland hair was compensated for by wiry eye-brows and the hint of a stiff mustache. He introduced himself as M. L. Talmadge, pushed forward a narrow hand with buffed nails holding an engraved calling card.

Rebecca had squinted at the card, trying to place him.

Talmadge tapped his watch. "We had an appointment. Eleven o'clock. Or rather, Mrs. Wetherly did."

He smiled, confident that no one could forget a meeting with Mrs. Wetherly. He gestured to the Silver Cloud III parked in the shade.

Weeks earlier, Rebecca had agreed to inspect a 1963

Cloud. Like the owner, the car was becoming a bit tatty. Mrs. Wetherly didn't want it restored exactly, just propped up, running better and looking more presentable. Which Frank interpreted to mean that the old broad was hurting for cash, prepping the car to sell to some sucker. Despite his suspicions, Rebecca had agreed to go over the car.

That was before a body had been discovered in the Bentley.

Rebecca had handed Talmadge over to Frank, explaining that he would perform the inspection. She would call Talmadge later with the figures. His eyebrows bristled. Before he could protest, Frank distracted him by wrestling open the nearside bonnet of the Phantom III.

Rebecca had retraced her steps through the office and jogged from the building.

As she slammed the door, a woman who could only be Mrs. Wetherly had emerged from the back seat of the Rolls. Good posture in a lavender dress and pearls. Wisps of white hair, deep-set eyes behind frameless glasses. Both arthritic hands gripped the window pillar for support as she stared in Rebecca's direction. Transfixed. She moistened her lips, fluttered a hand impatiently.

"Wait. Please wait."

Rebecca hadn't had the time. She'd gunned the sports car out of the parking lot, south onto Main Street, to collect her lawyer.

Billy Lee pulled the wheel from the hub and rested it against the wall next to the curled-up Doberman. Wonder raised one eyebrow at his master. He wasn't about to move. Billy Lee didn't make him.

Frank depressed the locking plate, then wiggled the retaining clip from the front hub. He handed it to Rebecca. She dropped it on the workbench. Work as normal. The blood in the Bentley seemed totally unreal, the guys determined to ignore the tragedy. Since they couldn't do anything to help, that was fine with her.

Rebecca tapped Frank on the shoulder. "How did you get along with Talmadge?"

Billy Lee chuckled. "Like peanut butter and jelly. With a little help, that'll be a mighty fine car again. Even if the old lady's elevator has shorted out south of the penthouse."

"You spoke with Mrs. Wetherly?"

"Couldn't avoid it. Her shuffling after me asking all those questions about you. Where were you born? What was your father's name? Any living relatives? Hell, I asked her if I looked like a genealogist. That shut her up for a bit."

"Why would she care about my antecedents?"

"If that means parents, I can tell you. She thinks you're her granddaughter, misplaced as an infant."

"What?"

Billy Lee laughed until he coughed. He wiped the corner of his mouth and winked at Rebecca.

"I told you—Mrs. Wetherly is three steps around the bend and heading out of sight."

Five

Rebecca shooed Frank and Billy Lee out of the shop at six-thirty. They had been working hard. She'd been moving parts from one bench to another, listening for the phone to ring. She could be just as nonproductive at home. She hoisted Maurice onto her shoulder, locked the shop and headed up the hill.

Once home, she plopped Moe on the bed, showered, changed clothes, reshelved a book on symbolism, marked her place in a paperback biography of Eliot. She puttered in the kitchen. Waited for the phone some more.

She gave up and dialed Jo. The taped message said the office was closed and gave an emergency number. She knew the number at his farm. But this wasn't an emergency. Not really.

She dialed Hagan. He wasn't in. She didn't leave a message.

Moe scratched at the back door. She let him outside and joined him on the flagstone patio.

The evening was muggy. Haze painted the sky a soft rose as the sun faded. Across the field, two does grazed at the edge of the woods. The fawn had white specks on her back. The elder raised her head to contemplate Rebecca, twitched over-sized ears and went back to munching. Moe dove into the border of unruly phlox, nosing after a rodent, black fur wriggling amid the pinks.

She should fetch a glass of wine, kick off her sandals and collapse on the wrought-iron love seat. Lounge around in shorts and a damp tee, watch the sun set while her hair dried. Instead she paced to the herb border and ground at the Corsican mint with her toe. The pungent fragrance hung in the air.

Too much irritating tranquility. She dropped into a chair under the umbrella, jabbed fingers at her head to detangle the curls. She needed to act. To get the guys out of jail. Retrieve the Bentley before its owner returned next week. Finish the P III by Friday. Persuade this Mrs. Wetherly that they weren't related. And decide what to do about Hagan—which presupposed that she knew what she felt for him. Or had any say in their relationship.

She leaned back. The metal of the chair was cool against her bare arms. Clammy like bars of a jail cell.

Val and Paulie were being held pending results of some forensic tests. Preventing them from being charged with murder was critical. Both for their well-being and for the shop's survival. They wouldn't kill anybody. They wouldn't have hidden a bloody body in the 3-Litre. The girl had to have been killed at the club, by a stranger.

They had been in the wrong place at the wrong time, a folly they'd compounded by lying to the detective. It was stupid, but how could she chide them? Being suspected by the police was demoralizing and intimidating. You opened your mouth and babbled anything you thought would get you away from them.

She should know. Her final investigation as a reporter had resulted in a botched sting, the loss of her credibility as a journalist, her resignation from the *Post* and the suicide of her lover. Her nonprofessionalism had brought on the wrath of SEC officers as well as District cops. Eight months later, Stuck's murder had the constabulary knocking at her door again. The local sheriff, plus a renegade from the District— Michael Hagan.

In the case of her lover, David Semple, Rebecca accepted that her meddling had been to blame. In Stuck's homicide, her inaction. Her reluctance to investigate Graham's death had resulted in Frank's incarceration. And possibly had cost Vera Stuck her life. *Flip a coin: Heads they win, tails you lose.*

Rebecca snatched up a twig from the table and flung it at Moe. He ignored it, remained fixated on the flower bed.

When Walt died, he'd left her an easy way out and she'd clutched at it. Buried herself in Head Tide, overseeing a group of ex-cons while they restored obscenely expensive classic cars for the rich and infamous. It turned out to be an ostrich's dream of safety. Her employees attracted trouble the way a charismatic attracts followers.

Or the way a fox lures the hounds.

Fox and hounds. That was how Peter Hayes viewed investigative reporting. The story was an elusive quarry to be cornered. She and Hayes had argued over too many glasses about the *who* versus the *why* of a story. Who was enough for him.

Would it be enough to motivate him in this case? If she was too numb to act, could she convince Peter to follow the scent, track down the killer of a sweet, young dancer? Sniff around the nightclub to see whose scent he could pick up?

She pushed off from the chair.

Hayes owed her. His article on the Stucks's murders had heaved him up a couple of rungs at the paper. Longer hours, better assignments, more stress—he wallowed in it. With luck, he would still be typing his fingers raw at the *Post*. She ran up the stairs.

Managing her uncle's business had convinced Rebecca

that her investigative drive to know why was genetic. Walt never replaced a component if he could fix it. He insisted you didn't learn anything by just swapping parts. He'd work until midnight to disassemble some unit, then repair all the pieces. He had to see why it had failed, where it had gone wrong. So did she.

She was so much like Walt. They had the same values, spoke the same language even when discussing different subjects. Growing up, she had always been at ease around him—just the opposite of being with her parents. Even after she'd gone away to college, Walt was the one she called for comfort. Like sophomore year when she'd nearly been caught illegally buying liquor for a dorm party. Walt was the person she told first when she'd been hired by the *Washington Post*. He would have been the person she could have turned to for advice on handling the current mess.

Upstairs, Rebecca e-mailed Peter Hayes from the study that until a month ago had been Juanita's bedroom. Juanita Whitt was another stray Walt had befriended, nurtured and given a new start. Since the girl had moved out, the room contained only a secondhand Mission table, a rack of glass-fronted bookshelves and Rebecca's new laptop. While she luxuriated in having an office at home, the silence of the hot-pink walls was oppressive. She missed Juanita's constant chatter, the slapping of her feet running up and down the stairs.

As Rebecca pushed back to leave, Hayes's reply flashed on the screen: If she wanted background on Gentlemen Only, he'd get right on it.

His phone call came less than an hour later. It was a welcome distraction from two unproductive activities—thinking about Hagan and rummaging in the refrigerator for leftovers that weren't growing enough penicillin to qualify as a science experiment. Rebecca dumped a blob of pinkish-green baked beans into the sink.

"No, Peter, this isn't research for a front page story. You're just satisfying my curiosity. What have you uncovered?"

He snorted. "Not much, just some small nuggets, which may need polishing, but I know they're shiny."

Rebecca nodded to herself. Nuggets—the juicy bits that were often left out of a news story, questionable "facts" omitted to avoid lawsuits. Tidbits shoved into a file drawer, too suggestive to throw away.

In the newspaper morgue, Peter had located an article on Gentlemen Only from 2000, the year of its grand opening. The club was owned by a businessman of Egyptian extraction, Sergio Dohlmani. It was his second operation in the area. In the interview, Dohlmani had billed the club as upscale entertainment for the sophisticated male. More Vegas revue than inner city raunch. He claimed it was tastefully provocative. While he believed in the importance of family values, he recognized the need for many men to relax outside of the home. He was pleased to provide a suitable environment.

Rebecca muttered, "Dohlmani. As in Val's mysterious Mr. D?"

"Guy sounded way too sanctimonious. Got my antenna quivering. I looked up the stringer, Sydney—" Peter shuffled papers. "—Sydney Holt. She still does an occasional assignment on spec. She remembered Dohlmani because someone from the paper called her up and initiated it, she didn't have to hawk it. Also, she says Dohlmani's something of a hunk, if you like the smooth, Mediterranean type. A do-gooder. Naturally, that got me salivating. Not his looks. The fact that the owner of a strip joint was trying to pass as virtuous."

Hayes had chipped away at Dohlmani's varnish, only to find another shiny surface underneath. The man didn't just sound holier-than-thou, he acted it. Influential in his community; involved at his church; philanthropist, giving mostly to causes for children. Wife died a few years back. No kids.

Sponsors young people from his home district in Egypt to come to the U.S. By all accounts, low-key, modest, successful. Pillar of his community.

"Low-key? He was savvy enough to get the opening of a suburban nightclub written up in the *Post*." Rebecca unwrapped the foil from a petrified chunk of French bread, pitched it into the garbage can. Peter talked over the thunk.

"True. But, according to the stringer, Dohlmani declined to be photographed. He kept the interview factual, not promotional. Behaved himself. As well he should have. Per my contact on the police force, he needed favorable media coverage.

"The opening of Gentlemen Only corresponded with the demolition of Dohlmani's previous club, Back Room. Located inside the District, Back Room was several notches lower in terms of location, clientele and merchandise. It burned one night. Arson was suspected, but not proved. Dohlmani had cancelled his insurance on the place just weeks before the fire. Never complained to the insurance company, took his losses and went on. Ha. No one's that saintly."

Rebecca sniffed at a plastic tub containing cold lima beans. Congealed butter, but no mold. She rooted in the refrigerator for the Tabasco.

Peter rattled on. The Back Room was no gentlemen's club. It was an old-time strip joint with few pretensions and fewer amenities. Beer was cheap, liquor watered. The strippers—women trying unsuccessfully to rise above a life dependent on pimps and junkies—were bored, but they delivered what the patrons wanted. That occasionally included services on the side.

No surprise that the Back Room had been raided for prostitution. Big bust was in the spring of '99. The manager of the club had hosted an after-hour's party for special customers. Dohlmani hadn't been there, but he did the bosslike thing.

Bailed out the manager. Hired an expensive lawyer who got the guy off on a technicality. Then Dohlmani had fired the slob. Canned all the girls who had attended the party. Ran a tight ship for the next ten months as he began construction on a new club over in Maryland.

Rebecca put down the limas. "What's your problem? Sounds like Mr. Dohlmani was feeling sullied. Wanted to wash his hands of the sordid mess. You think it's worth locating the ex-manager? See if he has a different take?"

"Probably won't have any bearing on the current operation. I'll dig up a name if you want to check him out, and an address." Peter sighed. "You realize, Bec, it's possible that Mr. Dohlmani really is a decent citizen who has a talent for making money in a shoddy business. It's possible." He paused, waited for her to contradict.

She didn't. He imitated a drum roll. In unison they said, "Then again . . ."

Rebecca laughed for the only time that day.

Six

The doorbell rang as she was saying good-bye to Hayes.

Paulie Antrim was out of jail and standing on the far side of the screen. Eyes downcast, hands clasped at his waist, a penitent in a button-down shirt and Jerry Garcia tie. Delighted as she was to see him, Rebecca frowned. Paulie never came to her house without calling first. She held the door wide.

"Paulie. How—"

"Lieutenant Hagan called my mother. I wish he hadn't. Not that I could adapt to the life of a criminal. Though it was interesting in a macabre way. Mother's lawyer had me 'sprung' by teatime. She insisted we go to Bis in the Hotel George for a bite. I could barely eat the snails I was so worried." Paulie listed against the doorframe. "Rebecca, what are we going to do?"

She dragged him inside toward the kitchen. She assumed Paulie was concerned for Val, who had not been released. The police were holding him until they consulted with his parole officer about the violation of consorting with a known felon. Lambesco had a record—naturally.

She uncorked a bottle of sauvignon blanc and handed Paulie a wineglass.

He held it without seeming to notice.

"It's not Val. It's the girls I'm worried about."

Rebecca raised one eyebrow. *Girls?* She'd never heard Paulie mention a girl younger than his mother's seventy-year-old bridge cohorts. He'd never mentioned a guy, either. Paulie didn't seem to have many friends. At least not ones he talked to her about.

Paulie sat. The object of his concern was called Serena. She sounded like a rosy-cheeked twin to the dead girl: young Middle Eastern dancer at Gentlemen Only. Paulie was convinced she was in dire trouble.

Serena had been responsible for their detour to Naomi's Boutique. All the dancers shopped at Naomi's. Mostly a mail-order business, it supplied performers—ballet artists as well as drag queens—with natural hair wigs, stiletto heels, and everything in between. Paulie had ventured there to purchase a pair of sparkling ruby slippers for Serena. She was working on a new number based on Dorothy from the *Wizard of Oz*. The club's theme was old movies.

"You should see her, Rebecca. She moves like a willow. Total grace. Her skin is so smooth it almost shimmers. And she has long, expressive fingers, like—"

Rebecca held up a hand. "How long have you known her?"

She was buying time. Adjusting to the image of the over-bred, overly polite Paulie frequenting a seedy nightclub. He must. He knew the bartender's name and was aware that the man had a side business in gems. Plus, he was so infatuated with this dancer that he knew her shoe size. For her, he had driven thirty miles out of his way, dragging a vehicle worth five years' profits. *Too bizarre.* Rebecca reached for her wine.

Paulie stopped fiddling with his. He interlaced his fingers and confessed that he went to the club several times a month.

Usually on Thursday night when his mother played bridge. Sometimes he went with a friend, often alone. He had met Serena in April. She'd been in America for less than a year and was lonely. Now that Shauna was dead, he might be her only friend.

"Shauna?"

"The body. In the car."

"The body? Christ, Paulie, you're saying you knew—"

"Yes. But I couldn't admit that without telling them we'd been to the club, which we'd already lied about. Later, when we confessed to being there, well, it seemed simpler to say nothing."

Rebecca buried her face in her hands. Simpler, maybe. Maybe even smarter. But definitely not good.

Paulie tapped on her arm. "That's why I have to go back to the club, to break the news to Serena in person."

Rebecca jerked her head up. "No."

Paulie was hurting. He pleaded with her to understand. She did. She understood the knight-in-shining-armor impulse only too well. It was right up there with tilting at windmills on the list of top ten most useless endeavors. She wanted to scream. Instead, she reasoned with him. Just because the police released him didn't mean they'd eliminated him as a suspect. If Paulie returned to the club, and they found out about it, they would be convinced he was mixed up in the girl's death.

Paulie squared narrow shoulders.

"If they're suspicious, they will have already flashed my picture around the club. Someone will have recognized me. Going back won't incriminate me further. Besides, how can you stop me? Are you going to fire me?"

Rebecca rolled her eyes in frustration. He knew she wouldn't fire him. His mother had given Uncle Walt a ten-thousand-dollar, four-poster lift in exchange for permanent employment for her rudderless son. Besides, with Val in jail, she needed Paulie at work.

He touched her hand. "I must go to her."

After lunch, from the back seat of his mother's Town Car, Paulie had called the dancer to tell her about the shoes. "She sounded petrified, Rebecca. She spoke in a whisper, one-word answers. She thanked me, told me to keep the shoes. She didn't seem to care. She was anxious to hang up. Until I asked her if the police had been there.

"She grew so quiet I thought she'd put the phone down and walked away. Finally she says, 'I think so. We were told to stay upstairs, speak to no one. Is it about Shauna? Why do the police come? Is she hurt?' Then she lowered her voice to a breath: 'Is she dead, too? Dead like the others? Am I to be next?' "

Seven

A sound. Rebecca jerked awake. The nightmare flicked off like someone had hit the remote. But the afterglow lingered. The specter was still there. Kneeling, a dead girl floated at the bottom of her bed. Her arms were flung wide, blood trailed down her white skin, pale lips pursed in a moue of dismay. Instead of a knife in her stomach there was a smooth hole the size of a soda can, through which Rebecca saw clouds building on the horizon over a slate-colored sea.

Six A.M. Someone was knocking at the door. She flung back the bed sheet and dropped her legs over the edge. She hollered "Coming," and tripped down the stairs.

Juanita waited on the doorstep, a warmly human spirit. She was clutching a thermos of coffee, biting her lip to keep from crying.

Juanita had blossomed from the malnourished teenage runaway who'd come to the shop door, pregnant and begging for work. Walt had given her a job, paid the medical bills and provided Juanita with an uncritical haven. After she'd lost the baby, she kept house for him and finished high school, as he insisted. She would have still been living in his home with

Rebecca if she hadn't fallen in love with Val Kearney. After graduation, with Rebecca's qualified blessing, the girl had moved into Val's trailer.

The tears on her lashes said Juanita was questioning the wisdom of the move.

Over two strong cups of coffee laced with cocoa, Rebecca assured Juanita that the police had no real evidence against Val. He'd done nothing wrong, so they couldn't hold him long. They would probably keep the Bentley a lot longer.

Rebecca had not revealed the gist of her lawyer's early morning call.

Jo suspected that Lieutenant Schneider was dragging his feet about investigating Gentlemen Only, content that he had the guilty parties. Schneider would hold Val until after the autopsy, ostensibly to check out the kid's police record, though more likely he was stalling, hoping that more evidence would surface. In other words, Schneider was suffering from bird-in-hand syndrome. It was making Jo nervous.

Rebecca had compounded Jo's nervousness by telling him that Paulie had lied to the police about knowing the dead girl.

"He said her name was Shauna. Did you know Paulie frequents Gentlemen Only?"

Jo frowned. "No. But then he has to have more of a life than we see on the surface. A most reserved young man."

"Downright secretive. Another of my employees about whom I know nothing."

When Juanita rose to go, she was still sniffling, her chocolate eyes brimming with tears. Rebecca relented. She told Juanita that the reason Val had been at the club was to buy her an engagement diamond.

Juanita blinked. The tears stopped. A toothy grin consumed her face. She knew he had a good reason for being there. She just knew it. Juanita hugged Rebecca, then bounded

out the door and down the steps, off to work. Such was the re-
silience of youth.

Rebecca had barely finished itemizing the repairs for
LSCX853 when the Silver Cloud swung into the lot. She went
outside to meet Talmadge. Mrs. Wetherly wasn't with him.

In the shade of a maple that predated Prohibition, they
conferred like surgeons at a patient's bedside. Rebecca
opened the bonnet and pointed to cracked hoses and corroded fittings. Talmadge bent stiffly toward the engine, nodded occasionally. He was marginally more pleasant than
yesterday, until Rebecca handed him the estimate. He read
the bottom line. He blanched—on Mrs. Wetherly's behalf,
naturally.

"The entire brake system?"

"Master cylinders, servo, lines, hoses. The car hasn't been
serviced regularly."

Talmadge sniffed. "The car hasn't been driven regularly."

Rebecca had heard it before. An owner shelled out a small
fortune for one of the finest cars in the world, then was reluctant to drive it. Fretted about bad weather. Worried about
paint chips, a fender bender, mileage depreciating the value
of the car. Or the image it sent to one's neighbors.

Not driving it was the kiss of death for a car like that. The
Silver Cloud III was an eight cylinder, designed to cruise high-
ways in excess of today's speed limits. Big and heavy, it liked
an adequate braking distance. But could cause whiplash fast
enough to delight the most jaded personal injury lawyer—if
the brakes functioned properly. Most didn't because the cars
sat in garages being pampered. When not driven regularly, the
seals dried up, fluid leaked out, air seeped in and the stopping
power evaporated. Then the owner heard repair figures like
five to ten thousand dollars and decided he could live without
driving his Rolls-Royce motor car.

Inside the garage the phone rang. Frank took a message.

Talmadge patted at the left side of his mustache as he continued down the list of ailments.

"Transmission seal is leaking as well?"

"You have fluid puddling on the garage floor?"

Talmadge brushed at his lapel, dismissing the offending stain. He plucked a Cross pen from an inside pocket, twisted it to expose the nib. "Mrs. Wetherly has owned it since new. She's very keen on using it again. Now that she has me to drive."

Rebecca steadied the clipboard for him as Talmadge signed the contract. The legal-sounding document was Jo's idea. It bothered Rebecca, but none of the customers had blinked. She handed Talmadge his copy. He took his time folding it.

He stated that Mrs. Wetherly was very sorry she had a prior commitment scheduled for today. She wished to meet with Rebecca.

Rebecca hesitated, then promised she'd set aside time when the car was dropped off, two weeks from Friday. That wasn't good enough for Talmadge. Mrs. Wetherly requested Rebecca's presence at the house today. Tomorrow at the latest. Talmadge's chin went up. He expected Rebecca to be suitably honored. And to dress appropriately.

Rebecca begged off, saying that this week was full, which was an understatement.

"Thank Mrs. Wetherly for her invitation. And assure her I'll call her about a convenient time."

"Tomorrow?" Talmadge had his appointment calendar out and pen raised.

"I'll call tomorrow." More than that she wouldn't promise.

Rebecca and Billy Lee stood in the open garage door and watched Talmadge drive away. The pale blue car floated like the receding tide on a bright summer's afternoon. Light dancing on water. Not the cold dankness of the sea in her dream.

"Been repainted," Billy Lee said, pulling the garage door down behind Rebecca.

"You can tell from forty paces?"

"From the colors. Silver Mink over Caribbean Blue. Shadow colors. Introduced about three years later than the Cloud. Looks good, though. Better than on a Shadow. Hell, in primer a Cloud looks better than a Shadow any day."

Billy Lee's chortle dissolved into a cough. He coughed a lot since being released from the hospital and coming to work at Vintage & Classics. His sixty-nine-year-old lungs had been damaged by smoke inhalation when he tried to rescue Vera Stuck from her burning house. Wasted gallantry. Vera had been killed before the blaze broke out. Billy Lee wasn't one hundred percent yet, but he was fitting in nicely.

"Talmadge want the work done?"

"Mrs. Wetherly does. You want to head up the project?"

Billy Lee grinned. "Why not? I've dealt with crazies before."

"Speaking of crazies," Frank said, dangling a pink memo slip over her shoulder. "Your buddy Hagan called. I imagine you know the number."

Eight

Mick had five minutes until court reconvened. The hordes had returned from lunch break. The hallway was claustrophobic with lawyers toting briefcases, eager beaver reporters carrying tape recorders jostling curious onlookers. Half the corridor wanted to see justice done: watch a reputed mob boss get put away for some serious time. The cynical half was shaking its collective head, positive that the fix was in and Alonso would walk. From where Mick sat, it didn't look good for the lady with the blindfold. He wasn't confident that anyone was listening to his testimony, let alone buying it.

He bent over the water fountain, slurped some water. Straightening, he glanced toward the doorway. Backlit by bright sun, a slender woman with short hair and dangling earrings slipped through the metal detector and retrieved her purse. White sundress showed off well-toned arms, lots of leg. She glowed in the dim corridor, floated toward him through a sea of dark suits, hips moving gracefully, strappy sandals tapping on the stone floor. She stopped a foot away, removed her sunglasses. It was Moore.

He grinned. He couldn't help it.

She smiled in return. "Sorry I missed your call. Sergeant Batisto told me where to find you."

"He didn't tell me. Just hung up on him."

"Am I too late to take you to lunch?"

"On my way back in." Mick gave her the once-over, stopped short of whistling. "Didn't know you owned anything white."

"Only wear it when I'm not carrying my wrenches. Any progress?"

"You're following Alonso?"

She hesitated. Mick snorted. Of course not. Moore wasn't asking about his trial. Her only concern was the case involving her employees. She'd left work, come to the District dressed to kill, hunted him down just to pump the sap detective for every crumb of information. What did he expect? She'd been a reporter. Old habits never die and all that. He scowled.

"You want news about the dead dancer, ask Schneider. It's his case."

"You must know something, Mick."

"Schneider says I have no need."

Mick checked the clock on the wall above her head. Three minutes. He should turn, walk into the courtroom, reclaim an aisle seat. Leave Moore to her own devices. She didn't have to know that he'd driven to the Sixth District before coffee, curious to see if Schneider was making any progress. The lieutenant had been away from his desk. On it was the case file: new folder, neatly labeled. Inside was the preliminary autopsy report, notes from the interrogations of Antrim and Kearney, and handwritten transcription of a conversation with someone named LeClerc. For a slob, Schneider penned neat notes.

Mick had very nearly gotten away with perusing the entire folder before Schneider caught him bent over the desk.

Schneider had snatched the file away and shoved past Hagan. His blotchy red face said he was miffed. Once he calmed down, he admitted that the dead girl had been a live-in dancer at Gentlemen Only. Well-liked kid. According to the manager, bartender, and janitor, the girl had been away in the morning at some appointment, but as far as they knew she was planning to work the evening shift, same as always. Schneider's partner, Stall, was tracking down the taxi driver who drove her back. There was no indication that she'd been killed in the club. None.

As a result of that early morning sortie, Mick did have news he could impart to Moore. And enough time to do so, if he were in the mood to share.

He wasn't. He nodded good-bye, started to leave.

Moore snagged his arm. "Fine, Hagan. I'll ask Schneider myself. If he won't talk, I'll send my lawyer. Paulie thought you were a friend. I knew better."

She swung away. Mick grabbed her waist.

"Don't go ballistic. You can have the *Reader's Digest* condensed version. It's all I've got."

He slipped his hand to the small of her back, propelled her to a vacant spot out of traffic. He leaned his shoulder against the wall. Watched her while he talked.

"The manager, LeClerc, identified the dead girl as Shauna Aziz. Good girl from a good Egyptian family. Niece to the club's owner, maybe. Came to the U.S. about eighteen months ago. Working at the club until she's discovered or some such nonsense. Lived in a room on the second floor with seven other girls. Her shift didn't begin until three, so the manager hadn't missed her. He was shocked. Admitted, with dismay, that the girls occasionally dated customers— strictly against club policy. LeClerc agreed with Schneider that one of your guys could have been hassling her, dragged her outside, knifed her and stuffed her body into the car without anyone seeing."

"Schneider suggested that? Who taught him how to inter-rogate?"

"The bartender admitted he talked with Kearney, but wouldn't swear to the kid's every movement. Recalled he left the bar at least once, for the men's room. A performer re-membered Antrim, spoke to him for a few minutes only."

Mick pressed closer to shield Moore from the flow of lem-mings moving into the courtroom. He inhaled light flowery perfume.

"LeClerc claims the girl was eighteen, has the passport to prove it. The coroner said fourteen, maybe fifteen. Five-foot-one, ninety-five pounds. No signs of rape. The knife landed in the lower abdomen, mesentery of the bowel. Upward thrust, like the killer caught her from behind. Or, she could have stabbed herself. Her prints were on the hilt, along with some as-yet-unidentified partials."

"Stabbed herself?"

"She was a couple of months pregnant."

Moore's eyes dimmed to sad. "Fifteen, pregnant, alone, living in a foreign country, dancing at a nightclub. She might have been desperate enough."

"Maybe. But it doesn't play."

He rested his forearm on the wall above her head. Close enough to lick her nose, or nibble on her earlobe. "The club's closed mornings, but there's a slew of employees milling around. Per Schneider's notes, she had a doctor's appoint-ment for 'some female problem.' No one admitted seeing the victim after she returned, though she'd been upstairs and changed clothes. So what happened? She comes back, is put-ting on her dancing shoes, has a sudden bout of remorse, stabs herself, runs outside and hides in the first vintage car she sees? To me that's about as likely as her being the own-er's legitimate niece."

"Where'd the knife come from?"

"Greek or Turkish, oldish, quality item. It just sort of showed up at the club. Manager used it as a letter opener for a while. Says it floated around. The girl could have picked it up, been carrying it for protection."

Moore thanked him. She eased sideways. "Enough questions there to deflect Lieutenant Schneider away from Val and Paulie."

"Don't count on it. I've watched Snide eat chicken wings. Bites hard, pulls off every morsel of flesh, sauce running down his chin. Sucks the bones until they're white before starting on the next one. He won't let go of your boys until he's bled them dry."

Bled dry. It wasn't a pretty phrase. The image was worse. He'd seen the photographs of the petite dancer with large eyes, skin turned gray from loss of blood, loss of life. Much preferable to watch Moore exit the courthouse, her white form dissolving into sunlight.

Nine

Edna peeked her head around the door. Half glasses with mother-of-pearl frames dangled on a gold chain around her neck. Her lipstick and nail polish were burgundy, one side of her blouse had pulled free of her waistband.

"Mr. Delacroix, do you have a minute to speak with Mrs. Dorothea Wetherly? She says it's about Rebecca Moore."

Normally, his secretary would have forced an unknown visitor to schedule an appointment for weeks down the road. Even if Jo wasn't terribly busy, Edna would have insisted that the decorum due a lawyer be observed. But Mrs. Wetherly had used the magic words. Edna knew how her boss felt about Rebecca. Undoubtedly most of Head Tide suspected how he felt about her, with the possible exception of Rebecca herself. Jo set down his pen.

"Show Mrs. Wetherly in, Edna. Thank you."

Dorothea Wetherly was a lady. Her periwinkle suit was couturier, well cut and expensive. Her leather pumps and purse had been recently purchased from the same designer.

Three strands of discreet pearls graced her neck. Similar pearls clustered on her ears just below a halo of white curls. Her gait was a tad unsteady, but she walked with her shoulders erect, without the assistance of the man behind her. Jo suspected that, like many of her breed, there was steel beneath the magnolia exterior. Resolve had etched creases around her mouth, a frown line between her eyes. There was a flinty directness in her gaze as she took the seat across from his desk and evaluated Joachim Delacroix.

"Are you a good lawyer, young man, or the only one around?"

Jo grinned at her opening gambit. "Both."

"Honest answer. I'm not sure you can help, but I'll pay you to listen. Have your girl give the bill to Talmadge."

Her associate stepped to the side of the desk. He handed Jo an embossed card with Mrs. Wetherly's name in script in the center. M. L. Talmadge's name appeared in the lower left-hand corner along with a phone number. Jo nodded at the slim man, then returned to Mrs. Wetherly.

"How may I help you?"

She sat back in the chair. "First, I shall tell you the story of my daughter and how it relates to Rebecca Moore. After that, we'll see if you can help."

Jo removed tortoiseshell glasses. "I must caution you that I represent Ms. Moore on several matters. My first responsibility is to protect her interests."

"Naturally. It is because of your relationship with Miss Moore that I'm here."

Dorothea Wetherly was used to having center stage. The type of poised matron who conducts business meetings for the DAR, or greets strangers in the receiving line at a diplomatic function. She would not suffer fools gladly, or with any other sentiment. She was a woman Jo could envision heeding Kipling's advice—meeting with triumph and disaster, and treating those two imposters just the same.

She told her story without emotion or sentimentality, though neither would have been out of place. She had married late in life to an art collector, Leon Wetherly. They had one child, a daughter. Because of her husband's business, and because she enjoyed it, the couple traveled together extensively. That left the girl to be raised largely by live-in governesses.

"I was not a good mother, Mr. Delacroix. I should have invested more time and interest in the girl." A fact, not an excuse.

"Does she have a name?" Jo asked, pen poised to jot it down.

Dorothea Wetherly blushed. "Of course, Nicole. Nicole Marie."

"You're estranged?"

"She's dead."

Given her undisciplined upbringing, Nicole Marie had been rebellious. At eighteen she'd left home for college. She'd never returned again for any length of time. She drifted in and out of schools for a couple of years, then landed at the University of Massachusetts. Five years later she'd earned enough credits to graduate. She talked about entering a masters program but dropped the idea in favor of finding herself. Instead, one summer in Provincetown, Massachusetts, she'd found Jamie.

"It was the only name I knew him by until years after her death. My fault, I could have known about him if I'd given her a chance."

"You didn't approve of him?"

"I never met the young man. He's dead as well."

Mrs. Wetherly stared out the window at the thread-leafed

maple shading the lawn. She refolded her hands in her lap. "In the autumn of 1967, Nicole came home for an impromptu visit. It was unfortunate timing. Leon and I were leaving that afternoon for a year-long buying trip—Europe, South America, India, the Orient. I was packing. I assumed Nicole had come to demand money. Or my help in getting out of another peccadillo. She was tense and disagreeable. I was short with her, preoccupied, annoyed at the intrusion. An argument erupted. It escalated before I could learn why she'd come. I ended it by telling her that I would make sure she had sufficient funds to survive my absence. We would talk when I returned."

Mrs. Wetherly brought her gaze back to meet Jo's. "I never saw my daughter again." One hand fluttered to her throat. "Talmadge, could you fetch me a glass of water?"

"Let me have Edna get that." Jo reached toward the intercom.

"No, please don't bother her. Talmadge."

Her assistant rose, nodded and exited the inner office. He closed the door softly behind him. A puff of air escaped from Mrs. Wetherly. It could have been a laugh.

"I should have outgrown caring about appearances by now, shouldn't I? Pointless, really. Talmadge knows more about my failings than I care to think about. I don't imagine any of it matters to him." She smiled. A dimple appeared in her left cheek, making her look twenty years younger. "Lawyer Delacroix, you are quite unnerving. You listen far too intently."

"I enjoy a good tale."

"So I would have guessed." Wetherly pointed toward the highest shelf of the bookcases. Instead of legal tomes, it held a collection of American Indian Pueblo Storytellers. Lively clay figurines, each the embodiment of centuries of universal, oft-told tales.

"I noticed Talmadge drooling over the storytellers. He's quite a fetishist. You should ask to see his collection some time."

"I might do that. Shall we continue before he returns?"

Ten

Rebecca didn't stop for lunch. Food wasn't important enough to eat if she wasn't hungry. She hadn't been since seeing the body. Besides, she had to get the brake shoes to Gus if she wanted them back tomorrow.

On the way, she phoned the shop.

Frank said no emergencies, only one message. "Hayes called. Said the Back Room had been located at 112 Hannin Place, SE. Manager's name was Henry Chandal. Only one el. Why you calling that reporter? You going to tell me what you're messing in that's none of your business?"

Rebecca hung up.

Past the next intersection, she pulled over to the side of the road. Hannin Place sounded familiar.

From behind the seat she fished out a bound street map of Maryland, DC and Virginia. She checked the index. Hannin Place stopped and started three times, which was not uncommon in older parts of the city. One spur was a few short blocks from the brake repair shop. It was possible she'd driven down it on her first frustrating attempt to locate the shop.

Gus, the brake doctor, operated out of an industrial park on the eastern fringes of DC. The rolling door to the repair shop was up when she arrived. She parked in one of his three spaces. Swinging her legs over the doorsill, she regretted being dressed as she was—in white, a tight skirt, with bare legs. At least they were tanned. The machinist who turned his head gave her a thumbs-up at the flash of thigh.

She pushed her sunglasses into her hair as she entered. The shop was noisy with the drone of grinding machines, filthy with the grit of shavings and brake dust. Dim light filtered down from the overhead fluorescent tubes. The men at the machines wore safety glasses and long sleeves. Despite the large rotating fans, it was as steamy as a Hollywood hell inside the metal building.

Rebecca plunked the brake shoes on the counter, careful not to lean against it. Gus handed her a paper towel to wipe her hands. He nodded over the din. He was expecting her. Of course the shoes would be ready. For a little extra—like a fifty percent rush charge. Expensive, but Gus was dependable.

He walked her out of the building. As she slid behind the steering wheel, Gus shut the car door. He leaned his belly against the side, listening to the rough idle. He asked if she ever tuned the thing. She asked if he'd heard of the cobbler's children. She was waiting for someone to do it for her.

He guffawed. She blipped the throttle.

"Gus, you ever know of a strip joint called the Back Room? Used to be on Hannin Place?"

"Sure." He spat beside the car. "Some of the fellas used to drop in there on paydays before the wife got her hands on their checks. Not me. My old lady'd perform elective surgery she catches me in a place like that. If we're going to waste money going out, she wants to be included."

Rebecca squelched the image of Gus sprinting around furniture to escape Lorena Bobbitt. She said she'd heard that the place had burned. Gus nodded. He'd heard that the fire was set. Maybe by the owner, imagine that? Gus figured it had to be a torch job. Someone reported it right away. Nobody hurt. Enough structural damage to level the joint. Had insurance claim written all over it.

"Only there wasn't one. The owner'd cancelled the insurance a couple of weeks before the blaze. Bad timing, or what?" Gus laughed, his belly shaking the car. "Then you know what he does? He brings in bulldozers, plows the place under. Plants a bunch of flowering trees. Makes a community playground. A little patch of green in a scummy neighborhood. Still looks pretty good—during the day. You should see it."

Rebecca thought she might take a look. Gus gave her directions to the section of Hannin Place where the strip joint had stood.

She asked Gus if he'd heard other rumors about the owner.

He rested a hairy arm along the windscreen, smiled like the Cheshire cat waiting for someone to come along and quiz him. He claimed the owner was almost a customer. Few months after the raid, he showed up with a shiny black Rolls-Royce. Hydraulic problems. Gus didn't mess with hydraulics.

"But, hey, I'm getting ahead of myself."

Rebecca wedged her foot against the accelerator to keep the car idling. She leaned back and willed her shoulders to relax. Gus had a captive audience. This could take a while.

Gus thought the guy's name was Domani. Foreigner. Had an eventful year, a few years back. He's away in the old country, flaunting his success in the U.S. of A. While he's gone, the manager held a private auction. He closed the club for the evening. If you'd been specially invited, you entered around the back. From what Gus heard, bodies were being passed around instead of them little canapés. The girls were wearing numbers and not much else. You saw something you liked, you bid for it, bought it, did what you wanted. Girls were getting half the dough, which was a sizable pay hike. Rest of the money went to the manager. What was his name?

"Henry Chandal?"

"Yeah. Hank. Reminded me of a hockey player. Stiff walk, missing a couple of teeth. Gossips said someone in the know must have tipped the cops. The place was busted in the early A.M."

The manager, girls and a handful of customers had been hauled in. Owner fired everyone in sight. Had a reputation as a prude about the girls doing anything more than flaunting it. Seemed kind of arbitrary to Gus. Rebecca agreed.

"Any idea where the manager lives now?"

Gus rubbed his nose with the side of his hand, smearing soot. "Doesn't. He's dead. Six months after the blaze, he gets flattened in a hit and run. Right near the park. Kind of queer, ain't it? And that's only half. One of the strippers used to work there was killed a couple of weeks before that, near a fancy hotel downtown. I seen it in the paper. Like I said, an eventful year for that place."

Rush-hour traffic was building when Rebecca accelerated onto Route 4, heading east. The sun was dropping behind her like a ball of fire, but she could still feel its heat on her neck and shoulders. She drove on autopilot, mulling over the snippets she'd picked up from Gus's ramblings.

The former club's former manager was a pig who sold his girls, apparently willingly, for profit. He was killed by a hit-and-run driver, coincidently near the razed site of the club. It sounded symbolic, suggestive, the sum impression being darker than the individual incidents. Like an urban legend that springs up when the neighborhood can't get a handle on what really happened. One Friday after work a group of machinists collaborate over a few beers, come up with some wild guesses, add in a lie or two, and the story sticks. More colorful than the truth.

Rebecca was more disturbed by the stripper who had died about the same time. Gus didn't know the details, only that she was found dead in an alley. Could have involved drugs or been the work of a mugger. He didn't think she was knifed. He thought it was a crying shame. She'd been a tall brunette, neat and hardworking. Supported her kid by dancing at the club. A step up from hooking, but not a big step. Gus often wondered what happened to the daughter.

Rebecca wondered if the *Post* had carried the story. Hayes could find out.

She also wondered if Dohlmani had been asked to account for his whereabouts the night the stripper was killed. Or the night his ex-manager was run over.

Eleven

According to Mick's mother, there was good in every situation. The good of spending a couple of weeks in court testifying was that you weren't assigned to breaking cases. Since you weren't on any roster, no one pestered you when you wandered around the precinct. Mick pawed through stacks of flyers discarded on the central briefing table without attracting comment.

All afternoon in court something had annoyed him like a mosquito buzzing in the dark. Something he said to Moore had triggered a memory. He stewed on it with half a mind through the boring testimony on the admissibility of wire taps.

As the gavel struck adjourning the session, the mosquito landed. It wasn't what he'd said, but Moore's recap. "Fifteen, pregnant, alone, living in a foreign country, dancing at a nightclub." He'd seen a similar string of words recently on an unidentified body report circulating the office. That was another good thing about court duty—he had more time to read the routine crap that came across his desk.

Mick found the faxed sheet in the overflowing to-be-filed bin. It had been sent over from Prince Georges County, dated

June 2. It described an unidentified female body: mid-teens, black hair, brown eyes, previously healthy, Middle Eastern descent, pregnant. A floater pulled from the Potomac, the body was bloated and picked half clean. A corroded necklace had been wedged between the vertebrae of her neck, presumably when someone broke it. Her neck, not the necklace.

Description didn't match any person reported missing in Maryland. No one had come forward to claim her. The MD police were circulating the flyer to neighboring locales. Mick stared at the notice without seeing the string of words. Instead he saw an itch waiting to be scratched. A blister like poison ivy, red and festering. His nails flexed, poised to gouge.

There was no overt indication that the floater had been a dancer at Gentlemen Only. Probably hadn't been. Undoubtedly there were lots of young, pregnant, Middle Eastern girls wandering the suburbs with no one watching over them. This one hadn't been stabbed. Her neck had been broken. Still, it was similar enough to get you thinking. Wouldn't hurt to call the Maryland police.

He rested one thigh on the desk and picked up the phone. The desk sergeant at the sheriff's station sounded almost pleased by his request. She agreed to fax over the file photos right away, though cautioned him that they wouldn't help much. Girl had been in the water for a while, crabs snacking on her like a buffet table. Hell of a way to go and much too young. Child deserved a name on a gravestone. She asked Mick to let her know if he made any progress. Mick promised he would.

If he was in on it.

If the floater turned out to be linked to the knifing victim, he would have to hand it over to Schneider or his compatriot in Maryland. Otherwise, the captain would accuse him of meddling—which he was. Offer to give him plenty of other cases in his own district, if he was so bored. Suggest, and not for the first time, that if he wanted to pursue Moore, he should do it on personal time.

The fax machine came alive. Mick strolled over to it. A black-and-white image rolled into view. Page one of three.

Was he interested in pursuing Moore, or wasn't he? That was the question. The answer slithered around like the planchette on a Ouija board. Never quite settled on either yes or no. Though seeing her again definitely tilted the board.

Mick picked up the fax sheets. They were warm from the machine, but the photos turned him cold. He was glad he'd been warned.

Page one was a close-up, head shot. From what was left of her face, Mick could imagine that the girl had been exotic. Large eyes, decent cheekbones. Eliminate the bloating and the full body shot on page two suggested a soft figure, baby fat that would have dissolved if she'd matured. If she hadn't been chewed up for fish food. Page three was a staged shot of a chunky necklace with dangling coins that had been removed from her neck and cleaned.

Mick studied each of the pages, folded them, and tucked them into his back pocket. He pulled out a toothpick and unwrapped it. He should track down Schneider and share this with him. Suggest that he might want to see if Gentlemen Only was missing another sweet young dancer. That was what a responsible officer, a team player, would do.

Mick sucked on the wooden stick.

The machine whirred again, spewed out another page. Bold handwriting slashed across the paper: HAGAN, CALL BACK NOW. It was followed by the Maryland phone number he had just dialed.

Curious, Mick punched in the number again. The duty officer answered and connected him to Sergeant Brian Llewellyn.

Mick had come across the name Brian Llewellyn when he'd rifled through Schneider's notes. As the Prince Georges County officer assigned to the case, Llewellyn seemed content to let Schneider run with it, even though the club was under his jurisdiction.

Apparently, the sergeant was less sanguine about Mick's interest in his floater.

"So tell me, DC cop, you know something I should know? You're the second badge waving a red flag at me today. Didn't your partner report in? You want to talk to me, say something smart."

Lacking anything like proof, Mick rambled on like an overeager rookie as he tried to make the similarities between the floater and the knifing victim sound like clues worth investigating. He ended by asking if Llewellyn had heard of another girl who might have gone missing from the club.

"Hagan, is it? Hagan, I've known Mr. Dohlmani ever since he opened the joint. Good businessman. Cooperative. Never any trouble, other than drunks messing it up in the parking lot. If he was missing a dancer, he would have come to me. Instead, you city slickers are annoying me like hornets from a fallen nest. First cop says there's a one-in-a-thousand chance that Dohlmani's dancer was killed in my county. Not to worry, he'll keep me posted. I can tend to my knitting.

"Now you insist, based on a hunch and a guess, that another dancer—a second little girl—came to a tragic end on my watch." He slammed something solid, like a drawer. "I suppose you and your partner will be taking care of that case as well? You'll let me know when I should wake up and pay attention?"

Mick leaned against the side of the desk. He understood the reasons for Llewellyn's attitude. Overworked, underappreciated, with a couple of city hotshots breathing down his neck, implying he wasn't on top of things. Mick knew he would be pissed under the circumstances, pissed enough to do something to take back control.

"So, Llewellyn, you get a chance to check out the club?"

Dead air. Llewellyn sighed.

"Yeah, I checked it out. Trailed in hours behind you boys. And found something you missed. Or didn't want to see. Fresh blood. Along the edge of the wall-to-wall in the hallway. Somebody'd been scrubbing at it with cleaner. Tossed the bloody rags in the trash. Overlooked what rolled underneath. I'm waiting for a DNA match to the girl's hair.

"So, listen good, Hagan. I don't care what county she died in. That girl returned to the club by taxi at eleven fourteen in time for lunch. An hour later she's bleeding to death. Barring proof to the contrary, I'm assuming she was knifed in my county, which makes this my case. Tell that to your partner."

After Llewellyn hung up, Mick sat on the desk, stewing.

There was a forty-minute window from the time the dancer was deposited at the club until Antrim and Kearney left with the Bentley. Plenty of time for one, or both of them, to have argued with her, killed her, and stuffed her into the car. That was not a happy thought.

On the other hand, if the blood was Aziz's, that confirmed the girl had been stabbed inside the club, which widened the field of suspects. Someone had scoured the stain. Someone who worked at the club knew she had been stabbed, yet hadn't told the police about it. Which looked rosier for Kearney and Antrim. They weren't likely to know where cleaning supplies were kept. Mick doubted Antrim knew what a mop looked like.

As for the floater, Llewellyn could be correct and she hadn't been a dancer at the club. The coincidence could be just that—a waste of time, which would only complicate the current investigation. Schneider would not thank Mick for bringing it up any more than Llewellyn had.

Mick pushed off from the desk.

On the other hand, he wasn't doing anything at the moment. No date tonight. He could nose around the club a little, see what panned out. If he left now, he'd be there for the tail end of happy hour. Chat up a waitress, see if she remembered another girl who was a couple of months late for her shift. He could save Schneider and Llewellyn the bother.

Mick ditched the toothpick and headed out of the building.

It wasn't that he didn't trust Schneider to handle it. He was sure the lieutenant would. If pushed. It was just that the man didn't like complications, particularly ones involving multiple jurisdictions.

Mick had crossed paths with Schneider a couple of times before. Most aggressively over the murder of a drug-dealing pimp who had plied his trade all over the city. At the time, Schneider had been in Vice, working out of PSA 209, within spitting distance of the hushed avenues circling the White House. Mick had labeled him a plodder. Nothing wrong with that, lots of room for solid, by-the-books investigating. But it didn't produce quick results. Or solve quirky crimes, where too many of the players skirted the edges and were real good at ducking out of sight.

Some months after the case, Schneider had been transferred from the high-visibility slot to Homicide in the Sixth. Homicide was considered a step up, and there were plenty of deaths to investigate in the southeast sector of the city, but no matter how fancy you wrapped it, the Sixth District was one step down and two steps away from the glamour of the high-dollar beats.

Since he'd switched precincts, Schneider'd become even more of a loner, saying he preferred to ride solo, holding the reins and loading the shotgun himself. Probably suited him fine that his partner, Stall, had caught a bullet in his leg last week and was chained to a desk. But it bothered Mick. He knew that the downside to working alone was you had half the needed manpower and no one looking over your shoulder.

That seemed to be Schneider's problem. According to his notes, Schneider had only interviewed three people at the club, none of the dancers. According to Llewellyn, Schneider had overlooked fresh blood on a carpet. Sloppy investigating? Or was Schneider so convinced that Kearney or Antrim was a killer that he was just going through the motions?

Twelve

Jo breathed in the soft darkness of the summer dusk. It reminded him of Jamaica, minus the heady smells and rhythmic pulsing of neighborhood parties. Tonight nature was providing the music. Basso frogs belched out sonorous notes on the banks of Ryder's Mill Road. Ubiquitous summer crickets gave a free concert on the lawn in front of Rebecca's home.

Jo left the sidewalk. He crossed through the grove, heading for the shop. A wind-felled walnut husk crunched beneath his foot. He skipped and punted it out of his way. For the occasion, he had rolled up the sleeves of his shirt, left the tie at the office. He carried a bottle of Michel Lynch's merlot in a brown bag. And two stemmed glasses.

Blindfold, he could have covered the quarter mile between his office and Vintage & Classics. Over the past months, Rebecca's business and her house next door had become more of a refuge than his own farm. Rebecca was a breath of fresh air in his stifling existence. Her unflinching handle on reality forced him to confront the way he was living. To reexamine a past that he had shelved higher than the

Storytellers in his office. He was about to ask her to take a hard look at her own.

Lights were on in the front office, but Jo circled around back. He assumed Rebecca would be in the car shop working on the P III since it was due out by the weekend. He pounded on the metal door. It still amused him that a sensuous, literate woman, a former investigative reporter, should choose to run a restoration shop. Then she opened the door. Clad neck to ankle in denim coveralls, a grease smudge on her cheek, screwdriver in her hand, was Rebecca Moore, auto mechanic. She looked disappointed. He sighed.

"I'm not your first choice?"

"Praying you were Frank. Come on in."

She tossed the screwdriver on the car lift and hopped up, letting her boots dangle. The cat was stretched out on the rail, his head resting against a tire. He meowed in welcome. Rebecca played with his tail.

"Paulie insisted on returning to the strip club tonight. I'd talked him out of it last night, but his nerves couldn't take it any longer. I forced Frank go along as his bodyguard. When you knocked, I hoped they'd reconsidered." She leaned back against the Phantom's running board. "Tell me some good news: Have the police released Val?"

Jo said no. He retaliated by asking if she'd heard anything. Rebecca sighed, explained about taking the brake shoes to DC and admitted she'd tracked down Hagan, badgered him into filling her in on the dead girl.

"He didn't paint a pretty picture, Jo. Nor was he encouraging about Lieutenant Schneider. The moron's convinced that Val and Paulie are the only possible suspects."

Jo set the paper bag on a workbench. "You know of others?"

Rebecca slid off the lift. She unzipped the coveralls, let them fall to the floor kicked them aside. From the pocket of her shorts she extracted a small notepad and flipped it open.

Paulie had given her the names of club employees who'd been present around the time the dancer was knifed. She pushed the pad toward Jo. He scanned through it. The owner, Sergio Dohlmani, topped the scribbled list, the man Val had heard but not seen. Next was the manager, Oswald LeClerc, followed by the bartender, janitor, a dozen dancers, performers and waitresses.

"Can anyone be eliminated?"

"Paulie claims everyone had opportunity. Everyone was alone for a few minutes, out of sight of the others. Lots of spontaneous milling around. You know, one minute a girl's doing warm-ups. Next minute she's tripping upstairs to change stockings or to look for sheet music. And too many entrances."

Rebecca pulled a folded sheet from another pocket and spread it on the workbench. Jo smoothed out the creases. On the back of a take-out menu, Paulie had sketched the club layout. It was a large rectangle. The foyer opened into the bar area, which flowed into the main dance hall, ending in a raised stage. He'd drawn in pillars, curved glass block walls, tall potted palms used to section the open space into intimate alcoves.

The functional areas were along the left side: coat check, then a short hallway with pay phones and janitor's closet at the end. After that, a long hallway ran parallel to the main room. Off it were the patrons' rest rooms, the lounge where the girls changed, a couple of offices. A stairway between the lounge and the offices gave access to the live-in girls' dormitory on the second floor.

There were two entrances linking the corridor and the entertainment area. One was at the end of the bar closest to the front door. The second one was in the main room. There were three emergency exits. Two from the main room and one next to the ladies' rest room going into the alley. That was the door Val had seen the janitor prop open. Presumably, the one through which the bleeding girl had fled.

"Neither Val nor Paulie heard any commotion near the exit?"

Rebecca shook her head. "Girls were chatting, bartender clanging bottles, janitor unboxing supplies, music level being adjusted. But there might not have been anything to hear. It's possible that the girl was stabbed upstairs, then tripped downstairs and out of the building."

Jo sighed. "With all those suspects, I almost don't blame Schneider for holding on to Val. Much simpler."

Jo collected the wine sack. He took Rebecca's hand and led her into the lunchroom. The cat joined them and sprawled on the table, washing his paws.

Rebecca sat on the far side of the table. Jo folded his glasses into his pocket, leaned against the counter. Holding the bottle of wine in one hand, corkscrew in the other, he told her about Mrs. Wetherly's visit to his office. About the elderly woman's contention that Rebecca was her granddaughter, the product of a union between Nicole Marie Wetherly and a young man named Jamie Roberts. He thought he presented it logically, without bias.

Rebecca regarded him as if he had sprouted snakes from his head like Medusa.

He jumped in before she could find her voice. "Mrs. Wetherly seems sincere, Rebecca."

"Sincerely crazy."

"Her story is plausible."

"Maybe, but she's mistaken. She has the wrong person. There's no question about my parentage. Robert and Pauline

Moore, 27 State Street, Boston, Massachusetts. My earliest memories are of them and that house."

Jo handed Rebecca a glass. "You were born in Boston?"

"Didn't you know that?"

She tasted the wine, then glared at it in mock horror, changed the subject. "What, no juice glasses?"

Jo had to smile. The night of Vera Stuck's murder, Rebecca had returned home from the fire to find her own place in shambles. He had revived her by forcing her to drink expensive bourbon from a juice glass. It was all he could find in the panic of the moment.

Despite Rebecca's light tone, he knew the episode haunted her. Her long lashes didn't hide the dark circles under her eyes. He touched her hand to bring her back to the present.

"Will you please just produce your birth certificate?"

"Why should I?"

Jo sympathized. It must seem unnecessary to Rebecca, but a simple piece of paper would pacify Mrs. Wetherly and put an end to the matter. Why wouldn't she cooperate?

Rebecca picked up the wine, regarded him over the rim. Then set down the glass and sighed.

"Will my passport suffice? It's in my desk. Who knows where my birth certificate is?"

"Your mother?"

"My parents are cruising the fjords of Norway. They won't be back until August seventh."

"Then call Mrs. Bellotti."

"No." Rebecca shoved back from the table. "Jo, think about what you're asking. You want me to question my birth, my roots, the very foundation of my existence. Why? Because a demented old lady's granddaughter was reported drowned thirty-five years ago, but the body was never found, and she thinks I resemble her? I have parents, Jo. Twin brothers and remnants of the requisite four grandparents. I'm not related to Dorothea Wetherly."

Jo set down his glass.

"Fine. Prove it. Call the housekeeper and get a copy of your birth certificate."

Thirteen

Mick exited Route 704 at Sheriff Road, headed east. He turned right at a sign for Gentlemen Only. Carved and gilded, low to the ground, the sign subtly proclaimed that customers entering here were men of taste, who knew where they were going in life.

There was a Prince Georges patrol car idling opposite the turnoff.

The setting sun bled between the trees, an occasional post lamp flickered on. The long winding drive opened out into a parking lot that would hold a hundred cars. About half that number were there. Mostly new, many expensive. Mick parked in the back row.

Weaving his way between the cars, he checked out the alley. Metal exit door was ajar. He estimated the spot where Kearney had parked the flatbed. Confirmed that the kid could have seen the alley from the driver's seat. If the girl had fled the building through the side alley, the first car she would have smacked into would have been the Bentley. Maybe the only car. A safe spot to hide in. Private spot to die.

A bouncer on steroids opened the front door for him. Inside, it was murky. Mick shoved his sunglasses into his shirt pocket. Decent crowd at the bar. Regulars who were more interested in booze and baseball scores than broads. Haircuts and pressed creases tagged some of them as military.

As he started forward, a swell appeared at his elbow. He was Mick's height with a trim build draped in a white dinner jacket. If it hadn't been for the David Niven mustache, he might have been good-looking. Women probably thought so even with the face fuzz. The bedroom eyes didn't hurt.

He welcomed Mick to the club, asked if it was his first time. He introduced himself as the owner, Sergio Dohlmani. Well-modulated voice, hint of an accent. Without quite grimacing at Mick's attire, he managed to convey his disapproval of the sartorial choices. Sartorial sounded so grand, but the Latin root meant "to patch." It fit. He had patched together an ensemble consisting of a woven checked shirt and black jeans. Clean, off-duty chic. Dohlmani relaxed when Mick said he'd sit at the bar, not infiltrate the high-class voyeurs in the main salon.

He took a stool near the end and ordered a Guinness from the bartender. Mick had checked out his story, knew Lambesco had done jail time. Visible proof was on his left hand—the tattoo of a viper encircled his wrist, its tongue flicking along the thumb. Appropriate symbol; Lambesco was as scrawny as a snake, tall, with a pronounced Adam's apple. Didn't look too venomous, but without a rattle, who could tell?

As he sipped his beer, Mick studied the framed glossy photos of movie stars covering the back wall. It was a double time warp. Photos from the 1930s displayed à la sixties, when contact with a celebrity meant you'd shaken their hand, not viewed a virtual picture of them on the Internet. Dohlmani reinforced the pre-WWII ambience, gliding back and forth, seating customers at tiny round tables. He held the chairs for the ladies, bent over their hands, nodded his approval at the gents.

Mick swigged the last inch of beer and signaled for another. He asked Lambesco if the owner was always hanging around.

Lambesco gave him the once-over, raised both wispy eyebrows. Mick reached for his ID. Lambesco shrugged. He'd figured Mick for a cop, would cooperate as long as it didn't cost him.

"Yeah. Mr. D's here noon to midnight every day except Fridays, when he leaves early. Sunday we're closed. He comes in and watches the accountant do the books."

"Conscientious kind of boss."

Mick asked if the girls liked working there. Lambesco said he'd have to ask the girls. Mick said he would, only the one he wanted to ask was dead.

Lambesco stiffened. "Look, I gave my statement to the other cops. Both of them."

Mick looked skeptical. "Hasn't got to me yet." He took a sip, licked off the foam. "You know the victim well?"

Lambesco's Adam's apple bobbed in his throat. Not well; same as the others. She was quieter than some. Nice kid. Maybe kind of jumpy lately. You know, all fluttery and big eyes.

"You know why?"

The bartender wagged his head. He turned as two guys picked up their drinks to head into the pole room. They were well-lubricated and ready to switch from home runs to home wreckers—equal long shots. He rang up their bill, gave them change, knocked a glass off the edge in the process. He muttered as he picked up the pieces.

Mick watched every move, feeling like a snake himself—a ten-foot boa constrictor paralyzing its prey with a stare. In college he'd seen one kill a white mouse from the psych lab without ever touching it. The little guy quivered inside the boa's coil until it had a heart attack. The snake just waited. Mick didn't want to wait. Time to ask the nagging question: whether another girl had gone missing some months earlier.

Lambesco pretended he didn't hear. He concentrated on wiping a martini glass, inspected it for water spots. Mick repeated the question. Lambesco mixed a Black Russian for the stiff at the far end.

Mick took the faxed sheets from his hip pocket, unfolded them. He shoved them across toward the bartender. They went over the edge, fluttered to the floor. He asked Lambesco to pick them up. When he set them on the bar, Mick grabbed his wrist, squeezed the viper. He pointed to the photo of the decomposed body.

"She ever work here?"

Lambesco looked against his will. He pulled away in horror. "Jesus Christ, if it was my mother I wouldn't know her."

"It's not your mother. She was a teenager, Middle Easterner. Just like the one from your club found knifed yesterday. This one was last seen wearing a bronze necklace—the one in this picture." Mick smoothed the third photo on the bar.

"Recognize it?"

That photo elicited a response, but not from Lambesco. A frizzy redhead in pink satin hot pants had sauntered to the bar to place an order. She leaned over to get a look at what was making the bartender blanch. Her eyes widened. She muttered "Shit," grabbed a tray from the bar and bolted before Mick could stop her.

He ordered Lambesco to look at the photos again. Before he could, a short fireplug in his late thirties with a gut and Buddy Holly glasses hoisted himself onto the next stool. He tapped the slick surface with a stubby finger. Lambesco got busy, fixing a gin and tonic: double gin, double limes, a whisper of tonic. The pudge slurped, then swiveled toward Mick.

"Ozzie LeClerc. I'm the manager here."

Mick congratulated him.

He meant to slide the photos toward LeClerc, go on the offensive before the manager could ask to see his identification. Quiz LeClerc about how many dancers he employed, how many waitresses, how many had gone missing recently, other than Shauna Aziz. Until he felt a fist punch his shoulder.

Mick slowly twirled the seat around, leaned back against the bar on his elbows. Schneider, bigger than the blue ox, blocked his view. The cop clenched his teeth, a glistening white slash between rouge-mottled jowls. He wasn't alone. A muscular black loitered one step back and off to the right. Former Marine, judging by the physique, haircut, and attitude. Even in civilian clothes he looked like a cop.

Mick nodded in greeting and took a guess. "Llewellyn?"

"Hagan?"

Mick couldn't deny it. "Is this where one of us asks what the other one's doing here?"

Llewellyn's eyes narrowed. "I know what you're doing—stirring up trouble. According to Lieutenant Schneider, you're a rogue cop from another district protecting the interests of known criminals. Mucking up my investigation with bullshit about a drowned Jane Doe." Llewellyn slapped his arm along the back of LeClerc's chair. "I'm here doing my job."

Schneider edged past Mick. He snatched up the faxed photos from the bar, crumpled them as he shuffled through them.

Mick set down his beer and regarded Llewellyn. "You found new evidence?"

"Don't quit, do you? Nothing new, just evidence we need to go over. Don't *we,* Mr. LeClerc? You've been keeping secrets." He clasped the manager's slumped shoulders and squeezed. "How about it, Ozzie? How 'bout we talk in your office?"

Mick watched the three men push through a beaded curtain. Pity that Llewellyn had moved the meeting. Mick would have loved to be in on the discussion. He could wait. Maybe they'd fill him in later.

Maybe.

He looked around for the waitress in hot pink. She was serving drinks to a table of jocks salivating over the pole dancers. The men were oblivious as she set down the drinks and walked off with their money. *Saps.* They were indeed slipping toward the smooth void of nothingness. Missing the best show in the house—watching her bend over the tables. The shiny pants rode up on her cheeks and her breasts strained the buttons. More provocative than the near-naked girls going through the motions.

Mick heard Schneider's heavy tread before his beefy hand slapped the fax photos of the floater down on the bar. Schneider hissed in his ear.

"Hate to admit it, Hagan, but you may be on to something. LeClerc recognized the necklace. Seen the performer called Juliette wearing it. She complained that it was stolen. Maybe by a dancer named—" He uncrumpled a sheet torn from a notepad. "—Karin Petra. Left in the spring for Baltimore. Or maybe not. Maybe she only got as far as the Potomac. Don't matter. The manager thinks he knows who gave it to the girls. Dandy who comes in alone once a week. The manager's looking through charge slips right now to see if he can come up with the name. You want to know who I think it is?"

Mick spun around. The chair back clipped Schneider's arm. He flinched, then laughed through stained teeth. His eyes became slits.

"No? Well, I'll tell you, Hagan. I think I got the wrong mechanic in jail. I'm betting that Antrim is the gift-giving kind. A wimp who can't satisfy a real woman, less threatened by juvie girls. The kind of pervert who snaps when a girl makes fun of him."

Schneider leaned against the bar, pointed his finger, gun style. "You may have solved two cases, Hagan, despite yourself. I should be grateful. Llewellyn is. He's giving you this."

Schneider shoved more photos at Mick—glossies of the floater, copies of those from the police folder.

Mick gripped them as he slid off the stool. He pulled out his wallet and tossed a twenty on the bar. Lambesco snatched it up, eager to make change and move him out.

Schneider wasn't through.

"Hey, don't go, Hagan. You'll miss all the fun. If it is Antrim, I get to haul him back in." He flung out his arm, pointing like the ghost of Christmas past. "The dope's in the front room right now, drooling over tender flesh."

Mick hesitated, then walked toward the main salon.

Antrim and Frank Lewes, the head mechanic at Vintage & Classics, were indeed sitting at a table near the front, unsuspecting as they nursed bottled beers. Schneider pressed against Mick's shoulder. Llewellyn flanked his other side. Against the wall, next to a potted palm, the white-suited Dohlmani watched their interaction. He bent a slight nod in their direction, a wry smile playing at the corner of his lips.

Fourteen

Rebecca disapproved of sleeping pills. They were a crutch for the needy. Lately, though, she clung to the Ambien her doctor had prescribed, downed a pill at bedtime when she was too exhausted to function. The pill delivered eight hours of oblivion from her dreams. She'd swallowed a pill at midnight, when she'd given up on hearing from Frank and Paulie.

Now, some maniac was out to spoil her drug-induced sleep.

By the time the banging registered, it was loud and frantic. Rebecca tied a thin cotton robe around her waist and stumbled downstairs. She flicked on a table lamp. She stared at the door for a second before pulling it open—aware that she was alone, remembering that evil things do happen late at night to the unsuspecting. Then she rationalized that if the person on the other side of the door meant her harm, he wasn't being subtle about it. She twisted the dead bolt and yanked the heavy door inward.

Frank Lewes nearly fell into the room.

"You trying to scare me, Reb? I feared you was dead in

your bed." Frank straightened, walked past her into the living room. He sank into the armchair by the fireplace.

Rebecca followed. She stood over him, reached out and touched his cheek, forcing him to face her. His left eye was swollen shut. There was a gash over it, dried blood in his eyebrow. Defiance flashed from his open eye. She lowered herself to the footstool, smoothing the robe over her legs.

"Should I see the other guy?"

Frank grunted.

She tapped his knee. "Where's Paulie? You were supposed to watch out for him."

"How you think I got the shiner? Paulie's unscratched. But he ain't happy."

"Where is he, Frank?"

"In jail. Again. Thanks to your buddy, Hagan. That cop's like our own personal—what do they call that big ugly bird?"

"Albatross?"

"That's the one. We see him and one of us ends up behind bars."

"Well, don't shoot him. Ancients believed it was fatal to kill one." Besides, she might want the honor for herself. Why was Hagan rearresting Paulie? That was absurd. He knew Paulie wouldn't hurt anyone. Frank mumbled that it might be worth defying the Fates to be rid of Hagan. He asked for a drink. Rebecca fetched him a beer.

After emptying half the can, Frank told her of the evening's misadventures. They had eaten at a truck stop on the way up, arriving at Gentlemen Only before eight. Place was filling up. First stage show wasn't until nine. A couple of girls were swaying around on them small platforms surrounding pillars. It wasn't a strip joint like Frank remembered from his youth. The kind horny teens drove thirty miles to in the outskirts of Waldorf. That place didn't have windows or much light or sweet young girls, with or without clothes.

"This place is tony. Pretty gals with good bodies dressed in enough clothes to fire the imagination. Still, what those gals were strutting isn't near as exciting as the P III's twelve-cylinder engine."

They'd nursed beers for a bit, just checking the place out. No one paid them any mind. Paulie was full of chatter. Going on about the costumes, shoes, dance routines. You'd think he was doing PR for the place. He assured Frank that they were all wearing costumes from movies or TV shows. Like that made it more presentable. A knock-kneed brunette, dressed as Tarzan's date, was putting on a private performance for a group of fleshy men in a curved booth at the back.

"Cheesecloth-like drapes everywhere, so you can only half see what's happening. Feels like you're a Peeping Tom." Frank shook his head as he set down the beer.

"Paulie spies the one he's sweet on coming through the curtain and I had to hold him in his seat. She's a pretty thing, Reb, but she don't look right to me. Too timid to be sashaying half naked above tables of leering old men. She takes one look at Paulie and it's like she don't know whether to run to him or out the back door. He's got it bad."

Rebecca groaned. "I need coffee."

Frank followed her down the hall and into the dark kitchen.

She flicked on the overhead lights, went for the coffeemaker. "You want ice for the swelling?"

"Nope." Frank reached into the refrigerator, emerged with another Miller. He held the can to his face and lounged against the kitchen counter. "Fun started when a stocky black guy and big cop swaggered into the room. Manager points them in our direction. Hagan's lagging two steps behind. The tall cop was sloppy, graying brown hair, bent nose, sour face. Licks his lips when he talks. He marches right over to Paulie. The brother tags along."

Frank pulled out a chair and sank into it.

"Paulie should of listened to you; being there was not a good idea. The cop takes ahold of Paulie to escort him out. Kid starts shaking his head. Mumbles about Serena. I try to calm him, but he bolts. Planning to go through that beaded curtain to find her. A bouncer type is coming through from the other side. He shoves Paulie. Paulie squirms to go around him. Guy swings and misses. I decide our boy needs help, fool that I am. I arrive as the sucker winds up for a good one. Paulie ducks. I didn't. Got me with his ring."

Rebecca wrapped both hands around an empty mug. "Okay, so the cops break up a bar fight. Why haul Paulie off to jail?"

Frank shrugged, popped the tab on the beer. "That's what's got me nervous. I figured it had to be about the murdered girl. Like the cops are pissed 'cause Paulie made bail. But the big guy's jawing about a second body what washed up a few months ago. Used to dance at the club as well. Credits Hagan with putting him on to it. Cop's in Paulie's face, screaming at him like he's some kind of Ted Bundy. Paulie pushes his glasses up on his nose, sniffs. Asks me, all polite, to please not call his mother."

Frank reached for her wrist.

"Reb, something's wrong. All glitter on the surface, but those gals are robots. Fear in their eyes. And most of them is way too young. If I was hot for Serena like Paulie, I'd want her out of there fast."

"She's probably fine, just high-strung. Who are we to judge? We know nothing about her situation."

The coffee finished dripping. Rebecca rose to pour a cup.

Frank leaned back, regarded her across the room. "We could know. They're advertising for a dancer."

Rebecca replaced the carafe. "And your point is?"

"You the best dancer in Blue Marsh County."

She shot him a look.

"You are. Win the locals' vote hands down every weekend you party at Tony's saloon. Besides that, you're a professional snoop."

"Retired."

"You go in there for a couple of nights, you'd know everything that's going on, solve the killing. Maybe two killings. Then both boys get handed 'get out of jail free' cards. Maybe you get your name in the press."

"Maybe I run my business right into the ground through neglect."

Frank winked. "Hell, we can run the place without you. Better still, you can work days at the shop, dance at night. You never sleep anyway. Might even pick up some tips. Or a new customer. There's a Shadow parked out back of the place. Damn cars always need work."

"You're out of your ever-loving mind, Frank."

"Could be. But think about it, okay? For Paulie."

Part Two

Damsels in Disguise

Fifteen

After Frank left, Rebecca crawled back to bed, planning to let the Ambien do its magic. She lay under the sheet, closed her eyes and tried to drift off.

No way. The drug was rendered ineffectual by her worries. And her building anger.

Val was still in jail, though he should be released in the next twenty-four hours. She would appeal to his parole officer. He might give him a break. Maybe house arrest with time out to work. She needed him at the shop. Juanita needed him at home. Val would survive.

She was not as sure about Paulie.

It appeared that the police had picked him up the second time based on new evidence. Frank had overheard a reference to a floater, possibly another dancer from the club.

Could Paulie have known her, been infatuated with her? By his own admission, he'd frequented the club for more than a year. Was he some kind of closet Casanova? Sweeping unsuspecting dancers off their feet, then killing them when they started to annoy him? Had he dispensed with the floater when he became smitten with Shauna? Then killed Shauna to free him up for a relationship with Serena?

Way too improbable.

Rebecca opened her eyes. Wispy patches of sky cut through the branches of the sycamore. They reminded her of the halo of white hair framing Mrs. Wetherly's face. Rebecca had promised Talmadge that she would call the old woman. More guilt to feed on, because she knew she wouldn't dial the number. She had enough problems to juggle.

She flipped over, buried her face in the pillow, returned to fretting about dead dancers.

Serena had told Paulie that other girls had died. Plural, more than just one, more than the floater. Who else? Why hadn't their deaths been reported to the police? How long had girls been disappearing and why didn't anyone care?

Rebecca rolled onto her back, stared at the ceiling, thought about who would want to kill young girls.

A sicko, but what kind?

A casual customer at the club craving to do more than look? An introvert who fantasizes about touching and ends up destroying? Or a coworker—a jealous performer, obsessive manager, janitor tired of being ignored by sweet young things? Or the owner? A prudish man who can't stand to be crossed. Who thinks nothing of exacting revenge on ingrates. Or, more probably, so controlling he orders a minion to handle it. As in the case of Henry Chandal, the manager of the Back Room. Had Dohlmani promised LeClerc that the manager's job would be his once Chandal was dead?

There was no question that the manager of the Back Room had been run over and a British car had been used to do it. According to Peter's police contact, a chunk of broken amber Lucite with the letters LUC had been found at the scene of the hit and run. Dohlmani owned a Silver Shadow, a tank of a car, capable of flattening a grown man without checking the paint. A car equipped with amber Lucas side lamps, for which only a handful of suppliers stocked replacements. With a few phone calls, she could track down both the dealer who had sold the lens and owner who had bought it.

Rebecca threw back the sheet and padded into the bathroom. Moe jumped down and followed.

Hagan had been at the club during Paulie's second arrest, so he knew what was going on. But she'd be damned if she would call him. He'd been there with Schneider. He had advance warning that Paulie was in trouble. He could have called her. He should have called her. Why hadn't he?

She scrubbed her teeth, spit, and dumped her toothbrush in the sink. Poured a glass of water for the cat and held it while he lapped.

Hell, the press never sleeps. Maybe Hayes could pry some details from the police.

By seven o'clock Rebecca was at the shop and wired on caffeine. She'd e-mailed Peter and fed Moe, gone through yesterday's mail. She paced in the back room, hunting for something mindless to do. She picked up the replacement horn button supplied by Powers Parts—correct button, new old stock, ready to install. It didn't need to be polished, but she did it anyway. Pressed the metal against the thick felt of the buffing wheel, watched as it brought out a mirror-bright finish. She stopped just shy of buffing through the chrome. Do that and she'd be back at square one. Original spares were getting harder to find.

She snapped off the buffer and gave in. She fished out the dog-eared card with all of Hagan's phone numbers. Her first call was to the precinct. He wasn't there. Then she tried Hagan's cell phone. No answer. She couldn't bring herself to dial his mother.

Rebecca pulled a crinkled map from the bottom drawer.

Following Paulie's directions, she located Gentlemen Only inches to the right of DC, north of Route 4. It looked to be a twenty-minute drive from Gus's brake shop.

She grabbed the company checkbook, tossed it and Hagan's card into her purse. The note she left for Frank and Billy Lee told them she was going to fetch the brake shoes. She would return after lunch.

Sixteen

Mick needed to be in court for the afternoon session but figured he could skip the financial testimony in the morning. He'd heard it before, followed the paper trail so many times he could have left the bread crumbs.

He filled a travel mug with coffee and drove over to the Sixth District. He'd woken with a hangover of guilt about landing Antrim back in jail. If he hadn't stirred the pot regarding the floater, Schneider wouldn't have discovered he had cause to rearrest Antrim. Who knew the mouse liked to give gaudy jewelry to dancers?

Schneider had taken Antrim into custody because the Maryland cop didn't have room. He was playing nursemaid to a flock of motorcyclists they'd hauled in for poaching crabs. Neither cop expected to hold on to Antrim for very long. Mick had called the precinct just before nine. He was a tad surprised to learn that the lad was still incarcerated. The old lady's legal team had had ten hours to spring her son.

In a cell, perched on the edge of the bunk, Antrim didn't look like a stalker or a killer, more like a tax accountant who forgot his April fifteenth filings. Tie was knotted, jacket unbuttoned, trousers smoothed, feet together, loafers shined. His right index finger pushed the bar of his glasses up the bridge of his nose.

He leapt up as Mick approached, leaned close to the bars, unsure where to put his hands without touching the steel. His voice cracked.

"Lieutenant Hagan, good of you to come. Is Rebecca angry with me? Have you seen Serena?"

Mick shook his head. "Have you called your mother?"

Antrim retreated to the bunk. Hands dangled between his legs. "No. And you'll find my reasons for not doing so offensive."

"You think I'm easily offended? That offends me." Mick rapped on a bar to get his attention. "Antrim, I'm on your side. Let me see if I can find an empty interview room and a cup of coffee."

Antrim's chin bobbed. "Kona, if you have it. Extra cream."

They were in interrogation room four again. Mick imagined he could smell Moore's scent, her energy lingering in the stale air, as if her compassion could overpower the stench of fear and the taint of lies heard in the dingy room.

Antrim sat, hiked his chair in to the table and reached for the cardboard cup of coffee. His face puckered at the first swig, but he got through it, becoming more talkative with each swallow.

He hadn't called his mother because he didn't want her lawyers looking too closely at his trips to the nightclub. Mother was dismayed at the sleazy nature of the establishment, which was understandable, but she could dismiss it as her boy being a boy. As long as she didn't look too closely.

"What would she see if she looked?" Mick leaned against the wall, wondered if he really wanted to know the answer.

Antrim shrugged. "Me, watching the dancing. Admiring the clothing."

Mick wanted to quip, *What clothing?* but bit it back. He waited for Antrim to go on.

The kid studied his coffee as if looking for bugs. "You see, I want to do it."

Do what? It, the infamous it of teenage confessions? The conversation was trying Mick's limited patience, reminding him why he'd never wanted kids. Communicating with them required too much work. He slipped into a chair beside Antrim and tried to look encouraging.

It paid off.

Antrim unfolded his hands and laid the confession out on the table, neatly folded like a fresh-washed towel. He wanted to be a dancer. Not a male dancer, a woman dancer. Or rather, a dancer dressed like a woman. It was the clothes. He didn't want to be a woman, exactly. He wanted to dress and move like one. Wear soft undergarments, high heels, flowing dresses. He turned to face Mick, man-to-man. Antrim wasn't blushing, which was impressive.

"It's not that uncommon, you know? There are lots of us who feel that way. There are clubs in most cities where men go and dress as they please. Many of them, us, are married. It's not a perversion."

Mick chewed on the inside of his cheek as he considered Antrim's pronouncement. On the scale of perversions cops were exposed to, Antrim's peculiarity was more humorous than heinous. Thinking about it, Mick could identify, on a certain level. During more than one amorous encounter— keenly aware of warm flesh through silk or satin—he'd wondered how it felt on the woman's end. Less adventuresome than Antrim, he'd never tried on lingerie to find out.

"That's why you go to the club? To watch women dance and wish it was you?"

"Sort of. Todd—I met him on the Internet—knew about the club. You have to admit, the girls wear wonderful costumes. The whole Hollywood theme allows for such personal variation: harem houris from Errol Flynn swashbucklers, Cyd Charisse gowns from Fred Astaire films, Scarlett and the belles from Tara, Indian maidens—"

"I've seen the pictures. Watching them is enough?"

At that, Antrim did blush. While his buddy Todd was auditioning at clubs that hired female impersonators, Antrim clung to the sidelines. He'd never had the nerve to do more. He couldn't. What would Mother say?

They had come full circle. Mick didn't see the problem. With some minor fibbing, Antrim could convince his mother that garden-variety male hormones induced him to hang out at strip joints. She didn't have to know that he was a fabric fancier.

There had to be more. Something else hidden in the closet.

Mick set down his coffee. Took one look at Antrim and knew he wouldn't have to ask. The kid was bursting to tell.

"Lieutenant Hagan—"

"Call me Mick. This is just between us boys."

"Thank you."

Antrim removed his glasses. He looked vulnerable as a newborn without them.

"Over the past year, I've made friends with several of the dancers. They like talking to me because I'm no threat to them. At least not much of one. They know about my interests. They don't make fun. They give me advice on where to shop locally for dresses that fit men, recommend flattering styles."

"They sent you to Naomi's?"

"Yes, Serena did. And Juliette—the tall singer who acts like a transvestite—she lets me use a locker at the club. That's where I keep my feminine attire."

Antrim looked up with pleading eyes. "To thank her, I gave her the necklace. It was perfect with her Cleopatra outfit. I'd bought the jewelry as part of a lot at auction." He crushed the cardboard cup. "The letter knife was in the same lot."

Mick whistled. "The knife? As in the knife found in the dancer's belly?"

Antrim nodded. Mick leaned into his face.

"You're saying that you can be tied to both the knife and the necklace found on the dead girl?"

Antrim's shoulders sagged. There was a receipt from the auction house for the items, it described them in detail. The receipt was in his locker at the club. He wrinkled his brow. "Unless Schneider, or the other policeman, has found it already. Do you know?"

Mick pushed back from the table. He wished Antrim hadn't told him. It placed him on the horns of a dilemma, which Mick figured must look something like the mythical Minotaur. He was a police officer, not a lawyer. Their conversation wasn't privileged. In fact, Mick was expected to divulge any information pertinent to an active investigation. He should call Schneider right now. Or Llewellyn. Ask if they'd searched through the girls' lockers and located the receipt.

Instead, he asked Antrim who else knew about the locker.

"Just Juliette and Serena. Juliette gave me a padlock for it after the necklace went missing. She was furious, claimed a jealous tart had run off and taken it with her. I gave the lock combination to Serena. She keeps some papers there. You may have the combination, if it would help."

Mick told him to wait on that. He tried to reassure Antrim that his secret was probably safe.

"LeClerc fingered you, not the girls. He remembered the necklace, but didn't mention the locker. He rendered a pretty good description of you, then came up with your name on a credit card receipt. You ever do something that would attract his attention?"

Antrim fiddled with his glasses, thought a minute, then shook his head. There was no reason LeClerc would know who he was. Unless one of the girls had reported him for being a pest.

Seventeen

Before Rebecca had exited the industrial park, her cell phone rang. She recognized Jo's mellow voice over the static. He had good news: Val was being released from police custody that morning. As long as she was in the District, could she pick him up?

Val was waiting on the curb outside the Sixth District. He shaded his eyes as he ogled a girl in red shorts and belly-baring tee. Cocky about his incarceration now that he was on the outside. Grinning, he settled into the passenger seat of the sports car. "Home, James."

"Not so fast. Did you see Paulie in there? He was rear-rested last night. They found him back at Gentlemen Only."

Val banged his head against the back of the seat. "Man, what was he thinking?"

"Perceptive question, coming from an ex-felon who saun-tered in there to consort with criminals."

"Hey."

"Hey what?"

"Nothing." Val sucked air through the gap in his teeth.

"What'd they think he did anyway?"

"That's what I intend to find out."

Hunting for Hagan was a frustrating waste of gas, which fueled Rebecca's anger. By the time she'd driven across town to the courthouse, *U.S. v. Alonso* had recessed for an early lunch. Standing on the marble steps, she'd called Hagan's precinct. She reached Officer Batisto again. He let drop the fact that Hagan planned to lunch with his mother at her house. She lived just over the Francis Scott Key Bridge in Arlington, a scant twenty-minute drive from the courthouse, in light traffic.

Traffic was never light downtown during a weekday. During the repeated stops for red lights and unexplained backups, Rebecca amused Val with Frank's suggestion that she go "undercover" at the club. Typical male, Val thought it was a fab idea. Promised he'd go along, sit at the bar to discourage balding leches.

"You step foot in that club again, you'll be doing two years in Hagerstown."

"Aw, who could blame me for wanting to protect you? You're like my mother." He chuckled. "And the sexiest woman I ever seen in steel-toed boots."

They made it to Kathleen Hagan's neighborhood in thirty-five minutes. Built in the forties, the single-family homes originally belonged to the upwardly mobile. Proximity to city, once desirable, became less so as the crime rate escalated. The lots had been divided. More houses had been squeezed in. Most of them belonged to blue-collar families or one-half of divorced households.

As was the case of Hagan's mother. Her second marriage, to Brian Semple, was shaky before his son committed suicide. Apparently, it hadn't survived the strain. According to the mailbox, Kathleen Hagan had resumed using her first husband's name.

The house was narrow, two stories, with a walk-in attic. Half the shutters had been removed for painting. They leaned against the foundation. A Ford station wagon with rust on the back quarter panels sat in the driveway. No Jeep.

Val squirmed sideways and regarded Rebecca as she parallel-parked on the street.

"What are we doing here, boss? Hounding Hagan is not a good idea."

No, it wasn't. Talking to him in person wasn't imperative. Much more sensible to keep trying his cell phone, once her anger cooled. If he was willing to answer her questions at all, he would do it over the phone.

But when Sal Batisto told her that Hagan was going to his mother's house, Rebecca accepted it as an omen. She had driven there to do something she should have done a year ago.

She told Val to wait in the car. He hitched himself up on the cowl behind the seats. She could feel him watching as she walked up the concrete path, skirting a gallon can of True Spruce left on the walkway, a one-inch brush balanced on the lid.

Rebecca knocked on the frame of the screen door.

The woman who opened it held a threaded needle in one hand, an Indian headdress in the other. She wore a powder-blue linen blouse and Capri pants. Both eyebrows were raised and arched. Then she smiled.

Rebecca rocked back. The woman was unquestionably Mick's mother. A few inches shorter and very feminine, but a product of the same genes. Her almost-black hair was shot with gray. Pulled back into a clip at the nape of her neck, it revealed high cheekbones, clear skin and intense blue eyes under thick black lashes. Eyes that appraised Rebecca with amused interest. Kathleen Hagan lodged the needle in a turned-back cuff before unlatching the door.

"Rebecca Moore. Please come in. It's time we talked." She

held the door wide and squinted in Val's direction. "Is your friend too shy to join us?"

Rebecca shook her head and waved Val over.

The conversation was not what Rebecca had imagined in too many predawn hours. Kathleen Hagan was completely at ease. She listened quietly to Rebecca's remorse over not having faced her sooner after David's death. It had been too much of a shock. She was too much of a coward. She'd tried to escape the horror by fleeing her job and DC. The excuses tumbled out. Kathleen Hagan nodded as if she'd heard the story already and found it understandable. Perhaps she had; perhaps she did.

She rose from the tweed armchair and joined Rebecca on the matching sofa. Val slipped around the corner, into the kitchen, ostensibly to get a glass of water. Outside, a jay complained from a low tree branch.

Kathleen held Rebecca by her shoulders.

"I'm glad you've got it off your chest. Like I tell Michael, no one could have stopped his stepbrother from taking his own life, if that was what he set out to do. His father admitted David was self-destructive even as a child. It was meant to be. Forgive yourself and go on."

Kathleen pulled her into a gentle embrace, smelling of lavender. With her cheek pressed against Rebecca's, she whispered loud enough for Val to hear: "However, if you get Michael killed, I will not forgive you. Him, either."

She sat back. "Now, why did you decide to come see me today?"

Rebecca confessed she was hoping to find Mick, hoping he had information about a case involving her employees. The sergeant at his precinct had directed her to Kathleen's home.

"Michael's running an errand for me. I've a new hobby—making costumes for the youth theater group. Some fabric

I'd ordered had come in at a shop on G Street. Can you wait for him?"

Rebecca checked her watch. She needed to return to the shop. Thom Carroll would be calling at two about the P III. If the brake shoes were reinstalled on the car, there would be progress to report. She rose to go.

Val lolled in the doorway to the kitchen. He called out for her to wait. His eyes were full of mischief.

"Reb, you ought to see what Mrs. Hagan has in the kitchen. You really should."

Kathleen crossed to Val, curious as to what he held out of sight.

"Ah, you're admiring Salome? I'm quite proud of that. Pity the show's been postponed until November. Lead broke her leg in three places, skateboarding. They've switched to *Peter Pan*."

Kathleen held out her hand to Val. With a flourish, she displayed a costume suspended from a padded hanger. It shimmered in the light. Panels of aqua chiffon flowed from a satin hip band. There was a matching bra with a gold-toned snake clasp between the breasts and a haik of the thinnest gauze to cover hair and shoulders.

"It's not Salome, of course, it's the other one I can never pronounce. The storyteller in *Arabian Nights*."

Val fingered the floating fabric. "It'd be perfect, Reb."

Kathleen looked pleased. "You have a need for it?"

"Yeah, she's going to dance at—ah, be in a dance contest."

"Wonderful. I wouldn't need it back until the fall. Oh, and I have the proper wig. And jewelry. Let me get it." Kathleen was halfway up the stairs. "The outfit's a size four. If it doesn't fit, I can alter it."

Rebecca struggled to ease the filmy costume behind the seat next to the brake shoes. She didn't want to mangle it in front of the seamstress. She wanted to use it to throttle Val. She restrained herself, since a potential witness was waving at her. Still, if Val didn't stop giggling, she would wind it around his childish throat.

Rebecca could accept that Sergeant Batisto's directing her to Kathleen's house was an omen, but she refused to see the scrap of aqua chiffon as a symbol. No way was the harem outfit the Fates' invitation to dance at a strip club. No way. That was simply too deus ex machina for a jaded reporter to swallow.

She slapped on her sunglasses and started the car. Ignoring Val's grin, she pulled away from the curb. Making the turn at the end of the block, she spotted a Jeep Cherokee pull in to claim the vacated parking spot. It was Hagan. She had escaped just in time. Or maybe he had. If she confronted him now, it wouldn't be pretty.

Eighteen

"Hon, I told the guy I know nothing about you." Flo laid down a plastic-covered menu. "Other than you drink too much coffee. And you'll eat anything, long as it ain't hiding under gravy."

Rebecca held out her mug.

"Mousy hair, mustache, suit?"

Flo nodded as she poured. Rebecca grimaced. "M. L. Talmadge. Personal assistant to a new customer. Highly paid busybody."

"Well, he won't get nothing out of me, don't care how much he's paying."

That said, the self-proclaimed town gossip and owner of Flo's Café waddled away between tables.

Rebecca blew on the coffee. What did Flo really know about her worth revealing? Plenty, but it was all old news. Still, if Talmadge was grilling the locals, he'd collect a few tales to amuse Mrs. Wetherly, which might help. If the old lady believed them, she'd drop the nonsense about the two of them being related: who'd want a severely damaged branch on their family's tree?

Mention of Talmadge reminded her that she hadn't called for a copy of her birth certificate. She hadn't done it because she didn't want to. Why should she have to prove who she was to a stranger? She felt foolish even asking. Of course, her parents' housekeeper would know where it was. There wasn't anything in the house on State Street that Mrs. Bellotti couldn't find.

"Did you lose this?"

Rebecca looked up. Her lawyer, trim in his chestnut suit and crimson striped tie, was twirling an ankle bracelet alive with dangling gold disks. She grabbed for it, missed.

"It must have fallen out of the car. Long story."

"Do tell. I'm intrigued."

Jo dropped the bracelet in the ashtray between them. He lowered himself onto a red vinyl seat. He waved at Flo. She waved back. Their shorthand for *I'll have the special . . . Okay.*

"I'm late because I was on the phone with your friend, Hagan. He was anxious to know if I'd spoken to you in the past several hours."

"To which you answered no. Any news about Paulie?"

Jo nodded. "Some. The body of a woman was found north of Bryan Point two months ago by fishermen. It had snagged on the splintered wreckage of a rotting ship. She ended up in the Prince Georges County morgue. The coroner estimates she'd been in the water for close to a week before she surfaced. He placed her death around the end of May."

Jo pried napkins from the dispenser. "She was another teenager of Middle Eastern descent, four months pregnant. When Hagan read the police report, the similarity leapt out at him. He alerted an officer from Prince Georges County who initially refused to consider that their deaths were connected. Rebecca, Hagan was hoping that such a connection would point away from your employees."

"Instead, he provided more nails for their coffins."

Jo didn't disagree. He spread two napkins in his lap, placed another two to the left of his fork while he told her that a necklace found on the floater was the link to Paulie. He admitted buying it and giving it to a dancer.

"So? Paulie gives away more gifts than Santa Claus. To us, to customers, to anyone he thinks will enjoy a trinket. He's compulsive about it. Too thoughtful. That doesn't mean he was involved with the dead girl. Either dead girl. Or had reasons to kill them."

Rebecca pushed back from the table, sloshing her coffee. "Jo, this is driving me crazy. Last week I thought Paulie was a stay-at-home-and-serve-tea-to-mother's-bridge-club kind of son. Now the police suspect him of stalking and killing young dancers. That's ludicrous. I mean, have you ever seen Paulie with a girl?"

Jo dabbed at her spilled coffee. "I guess I assumed Paulie was gay. But I never really thought about it. Paulie is so totally Paulie."

"Exactly. Totally incapable of harming anyone."

"Uh-huh. Ain't we heard that before?" Flo dropped a thick white plate before Rebecca. "Chicken salad on wheat toast. Low country crab cakes, potato salad, grits and my extra-flaky biscuits for the growing boy."

Flo returned to her grill.

Rebecca ignored her sandwich. She retrieved the ankle bracelet from the ashtray and turned it over in her hand, as if searching the coins for secret runes. Finding none, she let go of the bracelet.

"Jo, I have to do something."

"Eat."

"I won't fit into the costume if I do."

Jo halted the fork midway to his mouth. "That wisp of

cloth spilling over the shelf in your car? Are you about to spoil my appetite?"

Rebecca shrugged. "They're advertising for a dancer at Gentlemen Only, which is understandable considering the recent fatalities. I've decided to apply."

Jo choked on a lump of crabmeat. He reached for a water glass. Rebecca slid one closer.

"Paulie's friend Serena is scared to death. She told him that Shauna Aziz wasn't the first; other girls have died. Now a second dead girl has surfaced. What if an employee at the club, or a customer, is systematically killing girls? Someone has to find out what's going on before another girl dies. Before Paulie is railroaded for the murders. I don't think I could stand the guilt if I do nothing."

She reached over and touched Jo's arm. "I have to try to help. The club is out of Hagan's jurisdiction. Schneider is a slug. And the cop from Prince Georges doesn't sound like a ball of fire."

Jo flipped his fork onto the plate. "Has it occurred to you that it might be dangerous?"

"It won't be. I won't be hired, or kept on. Look at me, I'm not exotic dancer material. Jo, I won't be there long enough to get in trouble, but I might be able to meet some of the girls, learn something. Just nose around a bit."

Jo pushed his plate away.

"Which will get you into trouble."

"I thought you had faith in my investigative abilities?"

"That was before I'd witnessed their disastrous consequences firsthand."

Nineteen

Disastrous consequences be damned. Jo was being sanctimonious. Her entanglement with a deranged killer had not been her fault. Despite her recent track record, she knew how to investigate and how to do it discreetly. Hell, she'd won awards for her investigative reporting.

Rebecca stopped at the shop. Frank was installing the second set of brake shoes. Billy Lee and Val were finishing up the first. They would adjust the brakes and road-test the car before closing up. They didn't need her. They barely knew when she left.

At the house, Rebecca fed Moe. She pulled out a black trash bag and punched the coat hanger through the bottom seam. She'd feel less foolish dragging around a harem costume if it was hidden from sight.

From the outside, Gentlemen Only looked decent, like a well-run operation. The lot was paved, the parking spaces freshly lined. Fruit trees and maple saplings dotted the perimeter of the lot. Music pulsed through outdoor speakers. A bouncer in white shirt, vest and black trousers stood near the door, smoking. The building was a neat single story in front with a high rounded auditorium, resembling a large Quonset hut, added at the back. Both sides of the front door were edged with mulched flower beds alive with Stella d'Ora lilies. Pleasant, though Rebecca doubted that most of the customers noticed.

From Paulie and Frank, she knew what to expect inside. Except they forgot to mention the smell. Make that smells. Perspiration, cigars, cheap liquor, cheaper perfumes and the odor of body fluids she didn't want to identify. They hung like smoke in the stale, chilled air, a pungent ozone soup.

She paused just inside the door while her eyes adjusted to the half-light. A janitor next to the pay phones steadied his mop and stared at her. When she asked where she could find the manager, he pointed to a stocky man in drooping jeans and a too-tight polo shirt. He was half listening to a pair of bar-hugging salesman commiserate about cold calls. The place wasn't hopping yet.

Rebecca took a deep breath and sashayed across the room. The floor, sticky like a movie theater's, tried to suck the toe-pinching heels from her feet.

The manager slid off his stool when she tapped his arm. He gave his name without raising his eyes from her chest. To be charitable, Oswald LeClerc was short as a fifth grader. Probably strained his neck looking up all the time. And very nearsighted, if the Coke-bottle glasses were a valid indicator. Rebecca took a step back, in case he was dependent on braille.

"You brought a costume?" A dimple dented his cheek, only the right side, like only one side of his face got the joke.

Rebecca wiggled the coat hanger. "Is that a problem?"

"Nah, just uncommon. But then, you look like an uncommon kind of dancer. How'd you hear we're hiring?"

"From a regular. Guy knows I'm looking for a night job."

LeClerc nodded. Like he understood how even an educated broad could be in need of extra cash, or a change of scenery, or friskier playmates.

Rebecca was ready with a story—ex-husband was a louse, slow on alimony, kid to feed and clothe, company's downsizing. If pushed, she'd add hints of cancer and chemotherapy to explain away the wig Kathleen Hagan had loaned her. It was realistic: dark brown, loose flowing ringlets halfway down her back. Perfect for the costume. But a nightclub manager would have seen too many wigs not to spot one.

"Lose the sunglasses, turn around."

There was a snideness in his tone that made it an order, not a request. LeClerc winked at the bar patrons. Big man giving them a free show.

Rebecca felt heat flush her face. She bit her bottom lip, which could have looked coy. It wasn't. It was necessary to keep from telling the short stuff to go to hell and how he could get there. She blew out a breath and smiled at the businessmen. Well, she was here to perform, wasn't she?

She flung the bagged costume over her shoulder, upper arm squeezing her right breast, pushing it above the neckline of her knit top. She curved her left hand over her hip bone, thumb pulling at the low waistband of her skirt, fingers aimed at her crotch. She pirouetted slowly, tensing her glutes, first one cheek, then the other, then the first one again. Full front, she posed in third position, chest at attention. With her left hand, she slid the dark glasses down her nose, peering over the top like a practiced coquette. Her eyes were trashed out with eye shadow, liner and mascara. Already deep-set, they looked enormous and knowing. She hoped. She folded the sunglasses and tucked a bow into the cleavage of her top.

The balding salesman applauded. She blew him a kiss.

LeClerc sneered. He'd seen it before, done better. No doubt, but probably not by an auto mechanic. He got right in her face, lower lip jutting. "Thanks, love, but no thanks. You're not what we need here. We have—"

He sputtered to a stop. He straightened to at least five-six, squinted at someone in the distance.

Rebecca finished his sentence to herself—*an attitude problem; your club has a personnel problem.* But the manager's immediate problem was out of sight behind her. Staying in character, Rebecca moistened her upper lip with a lazy tongue and let her head drift in the direction of LeClerc's gaze.

The man standing in the archway was gorgeous.

Mid-forties, six feet tall. He was lithe and muscular at the same time, like the statues the Romans left scattered along the Mediterranean coast. Tanned swarthy skin, black hair brushed back from a high forehead and cat-shaped, heavy-lidded, hazel eyes. Hint of a mustache. He wore a dress shirt the color of butter, which fit him like it had been smeared on with a knife. Same could be said for the black trousers. He held a riding crop. His gaze floated from the manager up to Rebecca. Full lips smiled over impossibly white teeth.

LeClerc slithered around Rebecca like an animal afraid of the light and trotted over to the Roman warrior. LeClerc spoke with his hands. The man tapped the crop against his leg, his gaze fixed on Rebecca. He seemed to like what he saw.

She maintained eye contact until she felt flesh press against her thigh. She recoiled from a sibilant voice so close to her ear that she could feel spit, the warmth of breath. The voice hissed, "That be the boss. Mr. Sergio Dohlmani himself."

Rebecca turned her face fractionally and bumped noses with a statuesque woman with flawless mocha skin and eyes made up for the stage. The actress fluttered false eyelashes as she stroked Rebecca's hand holding the trash-cum-garment bag.

"What do we have in here? Do show Juliette. Do. Pretty please."

Rebecca laughed at the childlike entreaty. She twisted around to lean against the bar where she could watch LeClerc interact with his boss. She shinnied the trash bag up and off the harem costume. Then twirled it so it flickered in the lights spotting the bar.

Juliette squealed, stamped her size ten sequined heels in delight. "Oooh, gorgeous. May I? May I touch?"

Assuming she meant the skirt, Rebecca nodded. The performer hummed as she rubbed the fabric on her face.

"What you fellows think? This be my color?"

The drinkers murmured encouragement. Juliette pranced and cooed until LeClerc made his way back to the bar. He bellied her aside as if he didn't see her, which would have been impossible. In heels, Juliette was six inches taller than the manager. She was gowned, neck to ankle, in gold lamé, with a spangled turban thrown in for good measure. She let go of the chiffon, slid onto a stool against the wall and pouted.

LeClerc showed her his back.

"Mr. Dohlmani says we don't have time for auditions today, love, but he likes your style. If you want, you can wait tables for a couple of nights, get the feel of the place. It works out, he'll see you dance on the weekend."

It pained LeClerc to be overruled.

Rebecca was delighted. She was in. Slinging drinks would be a lot less embarrassing than dancing. She cocked her head and smiled at Sergio Dohlmani. He bowed slightly, then strolled from the building.

LeClerc yanked on her arm. He pointed to the bartender setting a glass in front of him.

"This is Vince. You do what he says. Shift starts at six. Julie, fix her up."

Twenty

Frustration. Mick couldn't recall the derivation of the word. Something about being rendered useless. Which summed up the way he felt. The trial was stalling. Too much compelling evidence for the jury to absorb. Too many lousy rulings by Justice Thomas. Too many high-powered lawyers casting innuendos about the police, throwing pearls before swine. Whatever that meant.

And Alonso, playacting. Sitting hunched over between his lawyers: a pitiful, hardworking stiff mystified by the proceedings. Same blank look as was on his mother's face when Mick asked why Moore had paid her a visit. Took her a full minute to remember that Moore supposedly was looking for him.

The thought of those two women swapping gossip made Mick's skin crawl. What could his mother and Moore have to discuss except Kathleen Hagan's boys? Scintillating topics. Stepson, David Semple, Moore's lover who committed suicide after she betrayed him. And her natural son, the one and only Michael Hagan, Moore's nemesis who, unable to believe her innocent, nearly got her killed.

Mick started the Jeep. He paid the parking attendant and

inched forward into the street. The light was red, which gave him time to decide. He could turn right and call it day. Maybe go back to his mother's, finish painting the shutters.

Or he could turn left, work his way to 295 south, take the beltway north, exit at Route 4. Be in Head Tide in time to take Moore to dinner. Crab soup and fried oysters at the Marina. Watch the hazy ball of sun dip into the water. Walk along the shore. Maybe stop in and chat with Sheriff Zimmer. See if the Blue Marsh County deputy's job was still open. On days like this giving out speeding tickets in the country had nostalgic appeal.

Before Mick could find a coin to flip, the light went green. He turned left. Why not? How much worse could one day get?

As if in response, his cell phone rang.

It was Sal. The captain wanted to see him pronto—as in now.

Mick had driven back to the precinct and visited with the captain. It had not been pleasant.

Dexter had slammed the door and remained standing while he reamed Mick a new one. Seemed officers he didn't know, from departments he'd never worked with, had taken turns badgering him. The complaints concerned Lieutenant Michael Hagan's interference in their cases. Schneider from the Sixth ranted that Hagan was trying to muddy the waters in the case of a dead dancer. Claimed he was doing it to protect Rebecca Moore's ex-cons. A guy named Llewellyn from over in Prince Georges County fumed that Hagan was investigating a floater death that happened in Maryland.

What the hell was Hagan doing?

At that precise moment, Mick had been struggling to keep his temper. He had no defense. He was meddling in other cops' cases. That didn't mean he liked being chewed out for it.

* * *

Screw the captain.

Mick had somewhere to go, someone more important to think about. He rattled coat hangers, looking for his tan slacks. He topped them with a silk tee, black linen blazer. Very *GQ*, if he said so himself.

At the wine store on the corner he picked up a bottle of Australian Shiraz and a chilled fumé blanc from the refrigerator case. Cashier slipped it into an insulated pack to keep it cool and added $4.99 to the total. Hagan, last of the big spenders.

He drove out of the city, filled up with gas just past Andrews Air Force Base. Turned up the radio and let the SUV do the driving. Forty minutes later he was in Blue Marsh County. The traffic had dried to a trickle. The sun was losing some of its heat. He cut back on the air-conditioning and rolled down his window.

The muscles in his neck were starting to unknot. His mood was improving. He'd made the right decision. Tonight would be good. He'd put off seeing Moore for too long. They had unfinished business he couldn't work out alone. First, he'd have to convince her that he hadn't meant to get Antrim rearrested. That had been a fluke. After she accepted his apology for the fiasco, they could move on to more personal issues.

As Mick sped past the town sign for Head Tide he let out a sigh. It was like a mini-homecoming. He'd kind of missed the place. He wondered if Flo's Café still packed in the lunch crowd. If Henry had found a fresher source for doughnuts. If Lu Chan had a boarder staying in the room over the restaurant. Wondered if he'd be welcomed at Vintage & Classics.

He parked on the tarmac in front of the car shop. It was close to six o'clock. Lewes's Toyota was rusting under the tree. No sign of Moore's car, but it could be parked at the house. She probably left it there and walked to work to exercise the cat.

He checked his smile in the rearview mirror and exited the

car. No need to lock it. Peaceable kind of town—if you discounted the recent murders.

He was back out front in under a minute, slamming the door behind him.

Moore wasn't at the shop. Lewes was there alone and not pleased to see him. But Lewes was remorseful enough to confess that he knew where his boss had gone and why. He felt to blame for what might be a mighty foolish move. It had seemed like a good idea the other night after a few beers.

Mick started the Jeep. He slammed the steering wheel with his palm. *Damn.* He couldn't believe it. Yes, he could. He didn't blame Lewes. Moore could get into trouble without half trying. In this case, she'd strayed from town to do it. And taken his mother's damn costume with her.

He drove south on Main Street, past the narrow storefronts, the Chinese restaurant, and around the bend where the stately old houses began. He scraped the tire against the curb in front of Delacroix's law office. No lines on the road marking spaces, no meters, no other cars.

Probably no lawyer.

Mick pounded on the door anyway.

Delacroix answered before Mick had fully vented his frustrations. He dropped his fists to his sides. The attorney looked surprised. Pen in his hand, sleeves rolled up, there was a slightly rumpled after-hours aura about him. Once he focused on Mick, he came alert. His face clouded.

"Everyone all right?"

"Not me." Mick barged past him into the waiting room. "Do you have a clue where your client is?"

"Given your agitation, I assume you mean Rebecca? I do have others."

"Why bother? She can keep you busy 24/7."

Mick ripped off his jacket and tossed it toward the sofa. It landed, slithered to the floor.

Delacroix picked it up. He slipped it onto a hanger, hung it on the hook of an old-fashioned coat tree. Stalling. "I'm almost afraid to ask: What has she done?"

"You don't know? Well, let me tell you."

Mick plopped into the leather side chair. He struggled to control his voice as he explained that, according to Lewes, Moore had driven to Gentlemen Only and applied for a job as a dancer. Lewes wanted to pretend that she was moonlighting for a few extra bucks. Gotten tired of working on old cars and decided to take up a more feminine occupation.

But to Mick the timing was a mite suspicious. Knowing her background as a reporter, it could appear that she was attempting to go undercover—to get inside, to investigate an establishment where a murder, or two, may have occurred. Where there might be a serial murderer looking for his next victim. Someone nosy like Moore, whom he could butcher and stuff into that sports car of hers, leave her to rot. Such interference in a police investigation could be construed as obstruction.

Delacroix leaned back against his secretary's desk. "Asking questions isn't against any law that I know of."

"Try telling that to Captain Dexter. There are two jurisdictions already nosing around the place. They're not amused at *my* innocent questions. Imagine how they'll react to an amateur inside stirring up trouble."

Delacroix sighed, pushed off and paced to the window.

Mick bristled. "You knew about her scheme?"

"Rebecca mentioned it this afternoon. Foolishly, I thought I'd convinced her to wait."

"You are a fool."

"Granted." The lawyer crossed the room, reached behind the door for his jacket. "If you plan to race up there and confront her, I'm coming with you."

"Correct, you are. I'll drive you to the club. Then you'll go inside and drag her out. Screaming and shouting if you have to. Then I will explain—in words of one syllable—why she's never going in there again, and you will escort her back to Head Tide."

"It sounds like a plan." He snapped off the desk lamp.

Mick crossed to yank his coat from the hanger. "Think you can handle it? If not I'll take her into protective custody."

The lawyer frowned. "You think she's in danger?"

"From me, if she enters that club again."

Twenty-one

Rebecca followed Juliette down the ill-lit corridor. It was like being on the prow of a sailing ship. The wings of her gown fluttered, molten gold flowed over anyone in her path.

One victim was a delicate girl who turned out to be Paulie's friend, Serena. Rebecca got only a glimpse of the woman-child as Juliette tossed out an introduction without slowing. The girl hugged the wall, smiled with her mouth, forced her eyes to make contact. When they did, they clung to Rebecca like the only log in a stormy sea.

Juliette stopped halfway down the hall. A metallic paper star hung crookedly on a door that opened into the communal dressing room. She ushered Rebecca inside. "Voilà. This be where we do our magic transformations. Green room of another color."

The room was tangerine. It smelled of air-conditioned dampness. Two banks of makeup tables sat back-to-back in the center. Metal lockers lined the left wall. A couple of mismatched armchairs from the Salvation Army hunkered near the outside windows. A waitress with a flame-red perm sat smoking in one of them, wiggling her toes. Her I've-seen-it-all stare was run-down as the heels of her shoes.

Juliette wiggled fingers in the waitress's direction. "That's Lucy. She's a sourpuss."

"Madam Sourpuss, to you, Big J." Lucy spoke around the cigarette. "Fresh blood?"

Juliette turned to Rebecca. "What's your name, hon? I should have asked."

Rebecca should have been prepared. Assuming the ladies' monikers were stage names, she uttered the one that Kathleen tagged on the costume. "Salome."

Lucy snorted. "Ain't had one of them before."

"You ain't seen no costume like the one she's toting neither. Sal, you take any locker that's empty. Martine's is cool. She's not coming back. You want to lock it, you bring your own. You want to hold on to that sexy outfit, I'll put it in mine for the time being. Quality stuff disappears quicker than foam on beer. I gets you a working outfit. How you feel about being a Gypsy? Be right with the hair."

Juliette sailed from the room.

Lucy put out the cigarette in a Coke can. She sashayed over to the makeup table. She was clad from cleavage to crotch in electric pink satin: an open-neck shirt and matching hot pants. On her left breast, *Lucy* had been embroidered inside a purple heart. She retied a small white apron. It reached just below the shorts, tickling her thighs. She bore an uncanny resemblance to Lucille Ball.

Rebecca draped the trash bag over a chair and hung her purse in a locker. She could feel Lucy watching her from under her inch-long eyelashes.

"Something wrong?"

Lucy shrugged. "Ain't none of my business why someone like you'd want to work here. Bigger question's why that prick Ozzie hired you?"

"He didn't want to. It was the owner's idea."

Lucy picked at her curls with neon nails. "Sounds right. Oz likes 'em young. Brings them in from Baltimore. Dohlmani thinks he's class. Both those jokers are fools."

With that comment, Lucy admired her bottom in the three-way mirror and sauntered from the room.

Rebecca sank onto a stool at the make-up tables and muttered at her reflection. "In the room the women come and go, talking of Maybelline, not Michelangelo."

She was glad for the breathing space, for time to reconsider what she was doing there. The women who worked here were pros. They'd soon know she wasn't. Already Lucy suspected that she wasn't quite kosher. Would they be inclined to talk to her if she leveled with them? Didn't seem likely, not if they wanted to keep their jobs. And a regular paycheck had to be the place's main attraction.

Frank had deduced that there were three levels of female drones. First were the headliners, like Juliette, who did routines on the main stage. They rated photographs dusted with glitter, pinned on a board near the entrance. The second tier worked the poles as erotic dancers or filled in as chorus for stage acts. The live-ins were in this group. Last were the cocktail waitresses, wiggling their bottoms and walking their feet off for tips. All positions required suggestive costumes and high heels.

Rebecca subscribed to the theory that most clothes were essentially costumes. Uniforms to designate professions; designer suits to convey status; gang colors to show affiliation. And G-strings and pasties to titillate men's libidos. Titillation was what these girls were paid for. They weren't paid to get killed.

The door to the dressing room popped open. Juliette entered carrying a bundle of clothing over her arm. Rebecca heard whispers and the tap of high heels in the hallway as the resident dancers descended to begin the night's entertainment. Juliette laid the outfit on a chair, claiming it was Esmeralda from that hunchback movie.

"Mr. D is crazy for old movies and old televison shows, long as they was seen in black and white. A black-and-white kind of guy. You get changed, I'll introduce you around. I'll be out front."

Rebecca finished lacing the black bodice over her ribs. She plucked at the full cotton sleeves to make them poof and looked in the mirrors. *Not bad.* She tossed her head. The gold hoop earrings and long tresses danced. If she squinted, she kind of looked like the Gypsy from Hugo's novel. Thanks to the bustier and the ruby satin skirt, she looked almost voluptuous. Certainly made a change from coveralls and padded socks.

She joined Juliette at the bar.

Vince Lambesco wiped his hands on a rag and extended long, limp fingers in greeting. He said the costume suited her. Rebecca thanked him as she hitched up onto a bar stool. He said she could have all the sodas she wanted. No alcohol during hours. He'd fix her something after closing if she was so inclined. She'd get a dinner break about three hours into her shift. Work out the timing with the other waitresses. Most of them were pretty cooperative. He set a ginger ale in front of her.

Rebecca nodded. "That's good to hear. I imagine you get a lot of turnover."

He swished a glass in soapy water, set it to dry. "Not as much as you might think. Except with the young ones. They come and go."

"Why is that?"

Rebecca sipped at the soda. The bartender turned away. She hoped she hadn't spooked him.

Lambesco scratched under his chin, both sides of his Adam's apple. Shrugged.

"Lots of reasons. Most are only here until they get discovered by an agent or a sugar daddy. Or till they get so homesick their folks start to look good. Lots of dreams. Most of which ain't real."

Juliette leaned over Rebecca's shoulder, plucked an olive from the tray of garnishes. "What about Martine? She made good. Got some rich guy to marry her. Probably living the high life."

"Yeah? You get an invite to the wedding?"

Juliette crowed. "You just jealous 'cause you were sweet on her."

The bartender scowled. "Martine was a trusting kind of kid. I just hope she made the right decision."

"Unlike Karin. That gal sure must have ticked someone off big-time. With her ways, it could have been most anyone, for 'most any reason."

Lambesco told Juliette to can it. It had no effect. She reached for another olive. It was obvious she loved to gossip. She had a new audience and saw no reason to stop. In short order Juliette filled Rebecca in on Karin Petra's body being found floating in the river and on the knifing death of Shauna Aziz.

"Only thing they had in common is they was both knocked-up, according to the police. We never knew. Shauna was timid and obedient. Karin was a brazen man-ip-u-lator." Juliette shook her turbaned head. "You knows the type. Always acting smug. Pretends like she knows dirt about you. Squabbled a lot with the Oz. You too, Vince. Didn't you go ten rounds with her? What was it you argued about?"

Lambesco turned his skinny back. He lined up the house brand bottles. The arm with a snake tattoo slithered upward as he started straightening the high-priced ones.

Juliette winked at Rebecca, raised her voice. "Must have been a week or so before she quit? You gotta remember, Vince. I sure do."

Vince swung around. He leaned across the bar close enough to rip the olive from her lips. "That bitch thought she knew something LeClerc didn't. She was wrong. I told him about the jail time up front. Figured it was his business. Not hers. Not yours." Juliette sank back on the stool. He shooed at her to go away. "Now why don't you shut your trap before you frighten the new girl."

Juliette huffed. "Good to be warned, else she could end up like Karin—food for fishes."

"Salome's not like Karin. She'll be fine."

Juliette slid off the stool. "Not young like her? That what you mean, Vince? 'Round here it don't pay to be young."

It was a good exit line. Juliette left it dangling as she swished away.

Lambesco handed Rebecca a round plastic tray, order pad, and twenty ones to make change with. He told her to pay no attention to Juliette. She had a good heart but was way too nosy. His cheeks were flushed.

Rebecca sagged against the bar. "It's sad, though, both young girls being pregnant when they died."

The bartender agreed.

"Sad. And queer. The live-ins ain't permitted to date. So how'd it happen?"

Twenty-two

Jo was reluctant to get out of the Jeep. He abhorred strip joints, dance halls, gentlemen's clubs—whatever you wanted to call them. Even as a teenager he had found places that pandered to men's prurient impulses to be degrading. Not so much to the women who flaunted their bodies, more to the men who allowed them to do it. To the women it was a job, steady work that took little talent. There was the allure of power attached to it. To the men watching, it should have been demeaning, proof that they had no self-control, no respect for themselves or womankind. Jo knew he was unrealistically old-fashioned.

He turned in his seat to face Hagan. "Other than your foul humor, is there a reason why you're not coming in?"

Hagan removed a toothpick. "Don't want to alarm the management with another visit. What's the matter, lawyer, can't you handle Moore by yourself?"

Rather than respond, Jo opened the car door and got out.

Hagan called after him. "Try to act like a customer. And don't take all night."

"You don't have to wait. I'll ride home with Rebecca."

"Oh, but I want to wait. I have a few words for the lady, which I will deliver in person."

Jo slammed the car door.

The club wasn't as déclassé as Jo expected. Still, the artificial lighting couldn't hide the cheap paneling in the bar area or the industrial carpeting soiled with spilled drinks, cigarette burns and detritus tracked in from back alleys.

Jo hesitated just inside the door. There were too many unknowns.

Had Rebecca actually been hired as a dancer? Would she be assigned to a pole? Or would she be waiting in the wings, the dressing room, until her number? How could he contact her? He assumed she was too bright to use her own name. Would any of the other dancers know whom he was talking about? How much time would Hagan allow him before barging in with guns blazing? How would he feel if he had to watch Rebecca perform in front of him? Jo loosened his tie.

How long could he imitate a statue blocking the doorway before the middle-aged Latin lover in the white tuxedo asked him to take a seat or leave?

Jo walked a few yards into the bar area and selected a small table that afforded a view of the semiprivate pole dancing and a glimpse of the main stage beyond.

The walls and ceilings were hung with billowing fabrics: sheers in hot dessert colors and rich dark paisleys creating nooks of intimacy. Seductive lighting, designed to make everyone look healthier, a little less creased and ragged. The music, presently a bad rendition of a song made popular by Barry Manilow, came through an expensive sound system with decent clarity. Where he was sitting, the volume was low enough to allow table conversations. The padded seat was more comfortable than he expected. But why not? They wanted the patrons to linger. And drink.

Drink—that sounded like a very good idea.

Jo looked around for a waitress. A shapely woman in a peasant garb stood at the bar balancing a tray, talking to the bartender. She was shod in heels with ribbons wound around her ankles. Smooth white skin showed above the off-the-shoulder blouse. She was gently bouncing in time with the music. Her skirt swayed. Long dark tresses fell to the middle of her back. She looked clean.

Jo signaled to the bartender, who sent the woman over.

He chided himself for noticing, but her walk was seductive, shoulders back, hips swinging, face obscured in a cloud of dark ringlets. He didn't want her to speak, afraid her diction would shatter the illusion her costume created. He averted his eyes, studied the exotic drinks and light snack card propped next to the ashtray. Maybe he'd order something to eat. He was unexpectedly hungry.

The woman stopped near his elbow.

"Shit."

The expletive startled Jo. He expected coarse grammar, but not swearing.

He looked up. *Shit, indeed.*

The waitress was Rebecca. Amazement gave way to relief. He beamed at her and sent a mental thanks to the gods who had arranged it. "Rebec—"

"What can I bring you?"

Her voice was harsh. She was sucking on a mint, something he'd never seen her do. Nor had he ever seen her with that much makeup. *Could he be mistaken?* Then he laughed. Only Rebecca could stare you down the way this waitress did. He ordered the first thing on the menu.

"How about a Singapore Sling?" It sounded intriguing. Through clenched teeth he said, "Hagan's waiting outside for you."

"You're kidding?"

Jo put down the menu. "About the Sling or about Hagan?"

"The drink. You'll be under the table before you finish it."

"Then you'll have to leave with me quickly."

"No way."

She pirouetted and recrossed to the bar. When she returned, it was with an enormous pink-and-gold beverage, decorated with fruit and a paper umbrella. She set it down on a small paper coaster embossed with the name of the club. "Twelve-fifty."

"Now you're kidding."

"Nope. Twelve-fifty. What are you doing here?"

Jo fished fifteen dollars from his wallet. "I told you. Hagan's outside threatening to jail you if you don't leave here this minute. My assignment is to drag you out. Keep the change."

"I'm not going yet. I want to talk with the live-in girls. Half of them are scared to death."

"So am I. For you."

"Juliette assures me I'm too old to get in trouble."

"Unlike the dead girls?"

"Exactly. I've got to go. LeClerc's watching. Don't turn. He's the pudgy manager in the purple shirt. Drink up."

Ninety minutes later Jo was outside choking down the muggy night air. He buttoned his jacket and nodded to the bouncer. He crossed the parking lot with great dignity.

Or so he thought.

He wasn't drunk. Not really. But he was reeling. It had all happened too fast. Or maybe it hadn't. He wasn't certain.

In order to converse with Rebecca, he first had ordered nachos—disgusting, limp and made with Cheez Whiz—then a second Sling. It slid down as smoothly as the first. Which proved to be a problem. Rather, it proved to be responsible for the problems that followed.

Problem number one: He was paying too much attention to Rebecca. Watching her too closely as she carried drinks to other patrons. She was so easy to watch. She moved much more fluidly than when dressed in coveralls. She seemed to be keeping beat with some primitive rhythm. She should dress like that all the time. Bare shoulders, flowing skirts. Maybe not at the shop, but definitely in his office. And at home. If he could be with her at home. He'd like that. Then he could stop worrying about her.

He did worry about her. Too much of the time.

Rebecca was unaware of her impact on people. Blinder than the proverbial bat in a cave. She focused so much energy observing others, she didn't seem to see herself in the picture. Absent, like a vampire's reflection in a mirror. Or just to the left of the frame, a camera hidden out of sight.

She was so unconcerned with herself, she didn't comprehend that others weren't always indifferent. That others might be jealous of her. Or threatened by her presence. Or want something from her.

Like everyone in that seedy place.

Jo didn't like the way the patrons ogled her. Or when the bartender patted her hand. Or the envy evident as the other girls watched her work. He especially didn't like the way the manager followed her movements. Any one of them could be a murderer.

That train of thought led to problem number two.

When Rebecca had disappeared behind a beaded curtain, LeClerc dropped off his stool and followed close behind.

Jo panicked. He did what any honorable man would do. He staggered after her. He was barely through the beads when she headed back. Relieved, he started to call her name, unaware that LeClerc was watching from the end of the hallway.

Startled, she swore at Jo. Insisted she was not his "niece," kicked him in the shin. He sputtered.

She whispered, "Kiss me, hard."

Which gave rise to problem number three. Made mellow by the rum, he didn't hesitate. Rebecca struggled, he clung tighter. She struggled more. He wrapped his arms around her, pulled her close, felt her warmth. He was thoroughly enjoying the encounter until the manager grabbed his elbow and spun him away from Rebecca.

Released, Rebecca wiped the back of her hand across her mouth and ran from the hallway.

Which left him to deal with Oswald LeClerc. The offensive shrimp raised up on his toes and hissed at Jo's chin. He threatened to call the police. Jo encouraged him to do so. He was not afraid of the police. As a lawyer, he knew his rights.

LeClerc settled for evicting him, yelling after him to call a cab, or walk to wherever the hell he came from.

Good idea. He would rather walk back to Head Tide than face Hagan with his failure.

"And don't ever come back," the odious troll shouted after him.

"Avec plaisir." Jo bowed and walked into the night.

Twenty-three

Shoot. Jo hadn't been kidding.

Rebecca spotted Hagan's Jeep lurking at the side of the road just south of the drive to the club. She didn't stop or look in its direction. She might get lucky and slip by him.

Then again . . .

She wasn't surprised when the Jeep pulled out and followed. Hagan sat on her bumper and flashed his headlights. She considered trying to outrun him. But on a straight stretch of road the Jeep's six cylinders would outpower the sports car. Probably flatten it when he caught up. Both the MG and her.

At the first wide spot, Rebecca pulled the car onto the shoulder and waited.

Hagan stopped behind her. Jo exited the passenger side and approached. Without speaking, he reached in and pulled the door cord. He held out a hand to help her from the car. They walked in silence to Hagan's vehicle. Jo held the door as she slipped in the front.

"Hagan, meet Salome."

Jo sounded exhausted and looked sullen. Hagan looked

sullen and angry. Rebecca was working on anger herself. Since no one seemed inclined to talk, she did.

"Is this a conspiracy to blow my cover?"

Hagan erupted. "Your cover? You shouldn't have a cover. What the hell do you think you're doing? Aren't two dead girls enough to convince you that someone in there could be dangerous?"

Rebecca twisted around to Jo. "Has he been going on like this all night?"

"More or less. He has a point, Rebecca. Please promise to keep clear of that place."

She turned back to Hagan. "Do you have proof that someone working at the club murdered those girls? It's just as likely to be a customer who befriends a dancer, seduces her, then kills her. Someone who may be working other clubs as well. You were the one who complained that Schneider has been dragging his heels. Maybe I can learn something that will hurry him along."

Hagan drummed his fingers on the steering wheel. He might have been counting to ten. Finally he asked if she had in fact learned anything.

Rebecca waffled. She had sizzle but not much steak. She fed them Martine, a third live-in who had left in the past seven months. The rumor was that she'd gone off to marry her beau. No one had heard from her since.

Jo mumbled from the back seat, "Martine sounds French, not Middle Eastern."

"Maybe, but her father was Lebanese. She had his dark coloring."

Jo sank back against the seat. Rebecca continued.

Among possible male suspects, all the customers looked disreputable. Ditto for the employees. The bartender had been sweet on Martine and antagonistic toward Karin. Either emotion, if warped, could drive a man to kill. He claimed he'd known Shauna only in passing.

Then there was LeClerc, who was in charge of the dancers. He was a scrapper and volatile. He routinely argued with Karin, and probably everyone else. He could have flown off the handle upon learning that one of his girls was pregnant. Killed her in a rage. Or out of fear that Dohlmani would blame him, fire him, or do worse.

Dohlmani by contrast was said to be rigidly controlled. Very religious.

Jo perked up, leaned forward. "Is he so repressed he would be capable of dispensing with the girls once they've been defiled?"

"You're thinking of honor killings?"

"Zealots frighten me, Rebecca. They can justify the most outrageous atrocities. The girls were both Middle Eastern. Let's assume that Mr. Dohlmani paid to bring them to this country, or at least promised their families that he would watch over them. He might have become outraged when they disobeyed him. As they obviously did."

Rebecca pulled at a fake curl. "He could be that self-righteous, Jo, but he's a businessman. Not the kind who'd risk getting a spot on his shirt. I can picture him ordering LeClerc to do it. As long as it didn't give the manager power over Dohlmani. Dohlmani wouldn't tolerate that, he's definitely an alpha dog."

Hagan smacked the dash. Jo jumped. Rebecca cringed.

He snapped on the overhead light. "That's it? You're risking your life for a few vague impressions? A smattering of 'what ifs' and a handful of 'maybes.' I'm talking reality here."

He lunged past her to pull a manila envelope from the glove box. He tossed it into her lap. He stank of wine.

Rebecca pried up the clasp, opened the flap and slid the photographs onto her lap. In the course of investigations, she had seen hundreds of similar pictures. Impersonal, black-and-white or colored shots of untimely deaths or disasters. This stack was mainly photocopies. She wondered if Schneider had given them to Hagan or if he'd helped himself.

The first set was of Shauna, the girl Rebecca had been forced to look at in the Bentley. They showed her stretched out on a morgue table. Firm smooth flesh rendered gray by death. Her eyes were as open and as questioning as Rebecca recalled. Had she seen the knife coming and accepted her fate? Or, as Hagan suggested, had she thrust it in herself? How much neater it would be if there were no serial stalker, just miserable lonely girls, unable to face life.

A second mangled set of pictures showed a girl scarcely identifiable as a once living being. Half of her flesh had been torn from the bones by sea predators. What remained was bloated. Sinew and bits of muscle still clung to her thighs and ribs. One eye socket was picked clean, the other covered with a limp lid hinged at the outer corner. Incongruously, a thick chain with medallions encircled the bones of her neck. The necklace they claimed Paulie had given to one of the dancers.

Rebecca shuffled quickly to get through the sheets, anxious to finish.

She wished she hadn't bothered.

The bottom photograph made her flesh go cold. It wasn't a police shot. It was a faded Polaroid, out of focus, presumably taken by the fisherman. The girl's body bobbed faceup, light flesh against the dark water. Bumped against a splintered wooden stake jutting into the air. One arm floated out to sea, legs languishing just below the surface. Her hair drifted across the whiteness of her bones like seaweed, obscuring her face.

A single strand had slithered into the void of her open mouth.

Rebecca gasped. The photographs slipped to the floor.

Hagan snarled in triumph. He reached across her lap to retrieve the pictures. He jammed them back into the glove box and started the Jeep. The lecture was clearly over. If the photos hadn't convinced Rebecca, he wasn't going to try.

He ordered them from the car. Rebecca balked.

"Five years ago a stripper from Dohlmani's first club was throttled to death and dumped in an alley behind some posh hotel downtown in DC."

"So?"

"You could check it out. Maybe there's a connection. Maybe there have been others in the intervening years."

"Maybe pigs have wings." He snapped off the overhead light. "This is not my case, remember? Out."

Twenty-four

"Yeah, I heard you." How could Mick not hear? Schneider was yelling into the receiver. "The D.A.'s indicting Antrim for killing Shauna Aziz." It was too early in the day for shouting, but Schneider kept bellowing.

"Correcto. I got opportunity—he was there when she was stabbed. I got means—he bought the freakin' knife for the dancers, left the receipt right there at the club. And I got him tied to the floater."

Schneider was gleeful.

He and Llewellyn had gone to the club after closing to do a more thorough search. They were going to make the manager open the girls' lockers, just for a look-see. One of the performers had tipped them, thought they'd be interested.

"But guess what? Little Serena's in the room spinning the dial on a brand new padlock. Blushes, admits the locker doesn't belong to her, it belongs to Antrim. She wanted her diary, which she kept there. Rest of the locker was chock full of women's clothing—his—disgusting.

"What's not disgusting is a receipt for the necklace worn by the floater *and* the knife that killed Aziz, *and* a bracelet he was probably saving for the next victim. Freedman's Auctions, dated in April, paid sixty-five dollars for the junk." Schneider chuckled. "Surprised the fairy hadn't told you about the locker. Or had he?"

Mick rooted in a desk drawer for a toothpick. "You got motive?"

"You mean like—what's Mommy going say if sonny-boy comes home with a knocked-up foreign tramp on his arm? Think the rich biddy would welcome her to the family? Or be a tad disappointed? And let's not discuss his hobby of dressing in women's underwear. Christ, Hagan, he was stupid enough to drag the body off premises in a car worth a zillion bucks."

"You haven't got him tied to the floater. Other than the necklace you've got nothing. Antrim doesn't own a boat, gets seasick in a bathtub. He lives near the Chesapeake Bay. How'd he dump the body in the Potomac?"

Mick sucked in a breath, blew it out. "Look, Schneider, Coast Guard's willing to work with us. Help us approximate where and when Petra's body went in the water, using currents and such. How can it hurt to talk to them, or to the guys who pulled her out? You afraid we'll blow holes in your pet theory? Hell, with my help we may discover enough evidence to hang Antrim for both murders."

Mick could almost hear the wheels grinding in Schneider's head. Curiosity alone would motivate most detectives to spend an hour with the fishermen who found the dancer. Get a little fresh air, drool over a few boats at trendy marinas. Maybe find the key to explain the deaths. When Schneider's wheels stopped turning, Mick gave up.

"I'm going, Schneider—with or without you. Your call."

* * *

The prosecution had rested in the Alonso trial. Defense would begin on Monday. Mick had the day off from court to get back in the captain's good graces. So what was he doing? Chasing after hunches on a cold case that belonged to the Maryland police, and messing with another case he'd been warned to stay away from. About normal for him.

Schneider met Mick at the Second's headquarters. He wanted to drive, which was fine by Mick. Gave him a chance to loll in the bouncing Buick and study his companion during the trek to the Coast Guard station. Schneider tried to hide his annoyance at being dragged along on what he considered a wild goose chase. Couldn't do it. Kept muttering that the only reason he agreed to go was to cover his butt. Afraid that if Mick uncovered anything incriminating, he would bury it.

Mick let the accusation pass. He leaned against the car door. He was ninety percent sure Antrim had had nothing to do with either girl's death, but he had been fooled before by less complex customers than P. Antrim III. The boy had some strange habits, plus enough family money to buy a chain of silence. For Moore's sake, Mick hoped the kid was as harmless as he came across. But Anthony Perkins had showed the world in *Psycho* that not every lad who lives at home and dotes on Mom can be trusted.

Still, Antrim was hardly the only shady character in the script. Mick pried a mint from his pocket, offered one to Schneider. "You read the fax I sent over on the bartender?"

Schneider shifted his hands on the wheel. "So what? Lambesco did two years for assaulting a minor? Sister of a rival gang member, out to dis her brother by sleeping with the enemy. He claims the girl came on to him. He didn't know she was underage. Says she was a pro, just not getting paid for it."

"He might still like them young. Club provides plenty of temptation."

Schneider grunted, stared at the road like a blind man in a snow storm.

Mick cracked the mint. Chomped. Swallowed. "Or how about the manager? I hear he can't control his temper. Takes his frustrations out on weak girls who won't fight back."

No comment from Schneider.

Mick angled to watch him. "Then there's Dohlmani. He thinks girls should be pure as snow or not exist at all. You think about checking out their alibis, Snide?"

Schneider hit the brakes. He yanked the wheel and swerved the barge into the breakdown lane. Before the heavy car stopped rocking, he lunged at Mick. Red-faced, he screamed at him to lay off. He knew how to conduct an investigation. The coroner, his captain, the D.A. and Llewellyn all agreed. There was plenty of evidence to arraign the fruitcake. He had a solid case. If Hagan had a problem with that, too bad.

"You're a freakin' loose cannon, Hagan. And a major pain in the ass."

Mick couldn't argue with him, so he didn't try. He promised to confine his comments to flotsam and jetsam.

Schneider banged the steering wheel. "You're also fucking perverted."

With that, Mick did object. Or would have, but Schneider continued spewing.

"I asked around about you. Any cop defends ex-cons smells fishy to me. Then the stench gets worse. I hear you're chasing after the snatch that murdered your brother, for Christ's sake. You got no family feeling? She can't be that good a fuck. I thought my ex was screwed up, preferring to sleep with her freaking Shar-Pei."

Mick felt his face flame, fists curl into claws. He leaned across the seat into Schneider. Ached to pummel him, to defend his feelings for Moore—messed up as they were. Not that they were any of Schneider's business. Schneider was sneering. One eye ticked. Mick watched it jump, counted five pulses. He slammed his head back against the seat. He let his breath out in a steady stream. Even if he thought the moron could understand the dynamics, he wasn't sure he could explain them. *Let it go.*

He cocked his head at Schneider. "Shar-Pei, huh? What, you don't have enough wrinkles on your bod to satisfy your old lady? Or is she hot for Asians?"

Schneider spat.

Mick pulled out his cell phone. "Start driving, Snide, or I'm calling a cab."

As they neared the Coast Guard station, Mick unfolded a chart of the Potomac. He had no trouble locating the three pilings and visible shipwreck where Karin Petra's body had been found. The fisherman had drifted too close to shore and snagged a line. Trying to free it, they damn near ran over the body.

Schneider wrestled the Buick into the lot. The station was plunked on the very edge of the river. Wind had picked up, sky clouded over. Gray waves were topped with whipped foam. A rescue boat was on the ramp, winched to a foot above sea level, ready to be launched. Five cars huddled against the shrubs lining the front of the low building.

Inside it was muggy and stale. Like the air-conditioning couldn't ever dry out the humidity from the water. Knowlton, the officer Mick had spoken with, greeted them across the high barrier. He let go of Mick's hand and produced a chart similar to the one Mick carried. As he spread it out, he used an orange soft-leaded pencil to draw arrows showing the direction of the currents.

"Got thinking about what you said. Assuming the girl was already dead, whoever dumped her would have done it midriver, in the channel. She surfaced the end of May. They're guessing she went in five days to a week before she was found. River would have been cool near the bottom. It would have taken several days for the gases in her body to warm, expand and bring her up.

"No storm action recorded for the last two weeks of the month. Channel's deep off Bryan Point, thirty feet or so depending on tide action. Little lady could have bumped along underwater for a quarter mile or so before surfacing. Might have drifted another eighth of a mile on the surface before being snagged. Or she could have caught right away. Lots of ifs."

Knowlton returned to the chart. He drew dots to represent marinas. All were north of where Petra's body was found.

"Anyone who boats on the river knows which way the water flows. You'd want the body to get as far away from your home slip as possible to avoid any connection. These are the harbors I'd try first."

Mick thanked him. Schneider snorted, slapped his meaty hand down on the chart.

"How's your math, Hagan? Try multiplying the number of marinas by about two hundred resident craft each. Add in your sightseeing day-trippers coming in off the Chesapeake or trolling downriver. Think it's worth it? Pissing off hundreds of write-your-congressmen rich bastards? For what—a dead hooker?"

* * *

They were back in Schneider's car. Mick folded the chart with the list of marinas on top, concentrating on the best place to start. Schneider was against starting at all. He howled about the amount of work. He refused to waste time looking for a craft that two months before *might* have shown signs of a struggle. There was nothing civilized about their debate. It was loud and heated, closer to the Old French derivation of the term *de batter*—beat again and again and again.

Schneider's cell phone interrupted the argument.

He grunted into the handset. He was as charming and monosyllabic as he had been for most of the drive. He nodded once. Listened. Then two red patches rouged his cheeks like an out-of-season Santa. He hissed into the receiver.

"I said okay." He hung up.

Mick asked, "Everybody happy?"

"Fuck you, Hagan. We're going back."

Schneider aimed the car north toward DC. He slapped a blue light on the roof, continued ranting while he scared honest citizens off the highway.

"Give it up, Hagan. If anyone had seen a body being loaded in a boat or dumped overboard, they would have reported it before now. Most likely, the slut went on board willingly. Maybe expecting a hot date before things turned nasty. Most likely she provoked it."

Mick concurred, which shut Schneider up, caused him to raise an eyebrow. Mick ignored him and watched the foggy road.

"My guess is they were at sea when the argument started. Guy loses control, his temper flares and he snaps her neck. She falls overboard where it happens. It might have been an accident. Only he's too much of a coward to report it. He wipes down the deck, sails back to harbor and keeps his fingers crossed. With luck, when or if she surfaces, she'll be too far gone to ID."

Mick leaned forward, swiped at the moisture sweating on the windshield.

"In short, if it hadn't been for my meddling, no one would have connected her to the club."

Twenty-five

"You're calling to warn me?"

Rebecca braced the phone under her chin as she lowered the left side of the bonnet. She secured the chrome latches. The P III was fully tested, brakes working. The guys were psyched. The transporter was due in an hour. Once she got her lawyer off the phone—if she got him off the phone in time—they'd celebrate.

Jo was sounding petulant and slower than usual. He'd already apologized twice for his behavior the previous night. Blamed it on the club's ambience. All those forties' movie posters had made him feel like a celluloid hero. Instead, he'd looked like a fool.

So had she. She couldn't believe she'd let the photo of the floater spook her in front of Hagan. She'd spent most of the morning fuming over his patronizing attitude. And struggling not to dwell on the images of the dead girls, which was like pretending the thorn jammed under your fingernail wasn't throbbing.

She switched the phone to her other ear. "Hold on a minute, Jo."

Rebecca gave Frank the thumbs-up. She watched along one side, Billy Lee guided on the other. Frank backed the P III out of the garage and into position for loading. Then she returned to her lawyer's most immediate concern.

"What or whom are you warning me against?"

"This morning, against Mrs. Wetherly and her minion. They just stormed out of my office en route to visit the sheriff. She called him yesterday about the proper legal instrument needed to obtain a sample of your DNA. He suggested arresting you until you complied. He mumbled something about nosebleeds being common in jail cells. I assume he was joking."

Rebecca cursed. "I know, I forgot to get my birth certificate. I'll phone Mrs. Bellotti, I promise. As soon as the P III is out of here."

"Too little, too late, Rebecca. Mrs. Wetherly has convinced herself that documents can be forged. A blood match cannot. She wants her pound of flesh, so to speak."

"And you're sharpening the knife for her?"

"I advised her against forcing you. She didn't listen. Won't you at least meet with her, be polite, hear her out?"

"I don't have time."

"Meet with me, then, on your lunch break. I'll give you the condensed version. Fifteen minutes tops."

Still in coveralls and boots, Rebecca left the shop, strode past her home on the hill and down Ryder's Mill Road. A favorite necking spot, the dirt road dead-ended at the abandoned mill for which it was named. When the underground stream had shriveled to the width of a brook, the mill wheel stopped turning and the mill shut down. In rainy spells, or during high spring tides, seawater seeped into the riverbed and rejuvenated the stream for a few days. The past winter had been damp. Despite the summer heat, the water was deep enough to float the marsh grasses.

Jo was sitting on a felled block from the old retaining wall, sipping bottled water. On the ground at his feet was a length of partially carved wood and a smattering of fresh shavings. Jo's jackknife balanced, point first, in the earth.

Rebecca plopped down beside him and began unlacing her boots.

"You have ten minutes."

Jo wedged the plastic bottle between his knees, slapped the sports top closed.

"Very well. Let me bring you up-to-date on Mrs. Wetherly's tale." He clasped his fingers and squinted as he gazed at the brook.

"Mrs. Wetherly last saw her daughter thirty-five years ago. They quarreled just as she was leaving on a year-long buying trip with her husband. When she returned, she attempted to contact the young woman. The phone number she had was no longer in service. Letters came back unopened. She hired a private eye. It took him six months to track down Nicole and Jamie, the man she was living with. They were summering in Maine. The detective prevailed upon Nicole to call her mother. Mrs. Wetherly got more than she expected. Nicole announced that she had an infant daughter."

"Me?"

"Perhaps. Mrs. Wetherly admits she had mixed feelings. She was disappointed in Nicole's promiscuity, but delighted to realize that she had a grandchild. She handled the situation poorly. She demanded that Nicole bring the baby to her. Nicole refused. Dorothea dispatched lawyers to bully the girl. Nicole appeared to acquiesce: she would come home *if* her mother let them sail in the Friendship Regatta first. Jamie, the father, was an amateur boat racer."

Rebecca pulled off her socks, stuffed one in each boot. She stood, rolled up the legs of her coveralls to mid-calf.

"Let me guess, instead of entering the race, Nicole and Jamie sailed off into the sunset with the baby?"

"Close. Jamie entered the race with Nicole and the infant stowed belowdecks."

Rebecca waded into the stream. The water flowed around her ankles. "What happened?"

"At the farthest turn, they deviated from the race course, sailed south from Friendship. They reached the coast north of Bay Point, Maine, just before dawn. A severe squall kicked up that morning—black fog and high winds as they approached the mouth of the Kennebec River. Rescuers assumed that they used Sequin Light as a marker and turned inland to find shelter between the islands.

"Instead of keeping to the channel, they hugged the eastern coastline, not realizing that it was tidal and at low ebb. The boat split apart on the shoals. The shattered hull was found lodged on rocks twenty yards from land. Wreckage washed up—is it upstream or downstream? I never know which when the tide runs counter to the flow of the river. Farther inland, anyway. Sections of the mast, bits of sail, one life jacket."

Rebecca faced Jo. "The bodies weren't recovered?"

"The parents' were found."

"But not the baby girl."

She hugged her arms tight against her chest. "What does Mrs. Wetherly really hope to achieve, Jo? Why is she doing this to me?"

He set the water bottle aside. "She wants what most humans want: a living legacy. Her genes passed on to future generations."

Rebecca's voice was stretched thin. "It's more than that, isn't it?"

He slipped out of his loafers, peeled off his socks, held them dangling. "I imagine so. I would guess she wants what you, or I, would give a king's ransom for—the chance to rewrite the past. At least one episode of it. Take a hauntingly familiar tale and change the dark ending. Make it come out the way we want it. Make it something we can live with."

He stood. He had trouble smiling. "Inattentive mothers aren't the only ones who want second chances."

Inattentive mothers. Rebecca closed her eyes. She was sure Jo had used the term intentionally. More subtle chiding her about her distant relationship with her own distant mother. A woman so smitten with her sons, she forgot she had a daughter. The dominant family personality. The person Rebecca spoke about least.

She turned her back on Jo and splashed to the middle of the stream. She spied a small flat rock, plucked it from the clear water, held it dripping at her side.

"Do you swim, Jo?"

He sloshed through the water, closing the distance between them. "Of course. If you're raised on an island, you had better. You don't?"

Rebecca pitched the rock, skimming it over the surface. "One, two, three, four, five." She shrugged. "Nope. I can't stand the seaweed."

"Rivers don't have seaweed, Rebecca."

"All right, then, marsh grass. The way water moves. The murky depths. The enveloping cold. Knee deep is okay. But don't make me jump in. The last time I did was after watching a murderer fry. I haven't slept since."

Twenty-six

By the time Mick reached Head Tide it was close to noon. Once he crossed the town line, he picked up his cell phone. He tried Moore first. She wasn't at the shop. Frank Lewes didn't know, or wasn't saying, when she'd be back. Delacroix's secretary was more helpful. She volunteered that the lawyer and Moore were having a picnic by the stream on Ryder's Mill. Lovely day to be out-of-doors. Mick agreed.

He postponed interrupting them by going to visit Zimmer.

When Mick pushed his way into the station, the sheriff of Blue Marsh County grinned like he'd won tickets to the Super Bowl. Mick hadn't seen Brad Zimmer in a couple of months but they averaged a call a week. Zimmer seemed to think Mick was a sophisticated police resource he could tap at whim. Mick didn't mind; in a way, he was flattered.

The sheriff pumped Mick's hand, dragged him into his office, pushed him into a chair. Then handed him an application to fill out. There hadn't been any murders since Hagan left town, so he hadn't bothered to fill the deputy's job. Hagan could have it tomorrow.

Mick was touched by the offer. He promised to consider it.

But confessed that he'd come to discuss an active case. Take advantage of another officer's experience.

Zimmer straightened his tie and grinned.

"Before we get down to business, boy, you hear about Moore? Some daft old lady wants to be related to her so bad she's trying to get a court order for a DNA match. She is one glutton for punishment. Maybe you could warn her off?"

Mick chortled along with the sheriff, although he could imagine being related to Moore, just not by blood. Wouldn't be dull. He reached across the desk for a sheet of paper, borrowed a pencil from a cup of sharpened number twos. He drew three columns, then penned in headings:

Shauna Aziz—knifed   Karin Petra—throttled   Martine Bufa—?

Mick dropped the pencil. He told Zimmer that the first two were official homicides. The third girl had vanished eight, ten months before. Supposedly moved in with a guy. Not a word from her since.

"You're thinking she's dead as well, but don't know for sure? You've got two different modus operandi already. You like two killers, or three?"

Mick held up a finger while he jotted down notes in each column. Then he sat back. Three killers seemed like a bit much. He admitted he was guessing, but his favorite scenario had Bufa being throttled and disposed of in the Potomac, just like Petra. Only more effectively, so her body had never surfaced.

Zimmer grunted. "Okay, two killers, then. Or one killer with a changeable style?"

"I'm thinking one consistent killer. *If* we accept Aziz's death as accidental, or a spur-of-the-moment suicide."

"You don't like the knifing as a murder?"

Mick rolled the pencil back and forth on the surface of the

desk. He told Zimmer that the coroner could sleep well with a ruling of either suicide or accidental death. Fingerprints said the girl's hand had gripped the knife when it sank into her flesh. Angle of the wound was consistent with self-infliction.

"You think our perp was pressuring her? So she foils his plans for a midnight boat ride by killing herself first? Or, they struggle, he tries to stop her but the knife goes in anyway? Doesn't make him much less guilty in my book." The sheriff slid the pencil from underneath Mick's fingers. He started tapping the eraser end on the desk.

"Three dead girls. At least two of them pregnant. Part of a group of seven living together. The girls weren't supposed to date, but obviously were. If they were going out on the sly, the others would have known. Somebody would have ratted, 'cause teens don't keep quiet about that kind of thing. Sooner or later the management would have found out."

He pointed the pencil at Mick. "You know what that means?"

Mick nodded. "We have two possible scenarios. One of the managers could be servicing the girls himself. Or he's selling the girls for fun and profit."

Zimmer pitched the pencil at the wall.

"Well, that makes me mad. Selling a little girl for sex, raking in the dough, when he should be watching over her. Then she gets pregnant, or becomes a problem, so she's killed and another one is supplied in her place? You think that Martine was the first, or the first one who got to be a liability?

Mick parked the Jeep on Main Street and walked down to Ryder's Mill. He felt better after discussing the case with Zimmer, but not about the news he'd come to deliver to Moore. The bucolic scene in the glade made it seem even worse.

Sun filtered down through the trees and danced on the surface of the shallow stream. Moore sat on the ground wiping her feet with thick socks. Delacroix was in shirtsleeves, perched on an upended chunk of concrete, whittling a piece of drift wood. Blond shavings stuck to the tops of his bare feet. Remnants of lunch were piled by a fallen tree. Looming in the background was the dilapidated ruin of a stone mill. Birds chattered on the bank. One took off as Mick approached.

Moore turned, cocked her head, startled by his presence. Her look said, "What are you doing here?" It was a fair question. She wasn't going to like the answer.

He stood over Moore, shielding her from the sun so she didn't have to squint. He told them that Antrim was going to be arraigned on Monday for the murder of Shauna Aziz.

Their reactions were pretty much what he'd expected: outrage and denial. The lawyer recovered first. He looked a little green around the gills, but he was thinking clearly. He listed the evidence, stressed that it was all circumstantial. And insufficient for charges.

Mick agreed that it might be circumstantial, but there was more of it than there had been the day before. He explained that Schneider had uncovered a receipt for the necklace found on the floater, and the knife that had killed Shauna. The receipt was made out to Antrim, kept in his locker at the club.

Antrim claimed the knife had been lifted months before; he didn't remember exactly when. Anyone at the club could have taken it. He didn't get a padlock until after the necklace went missing. None of which mattered to Schneider. For him, the receipt was enough to link Antrim to both dead girls.

Moore fumbled with the lacings on her boots. Mick spoke

over her head to Delacroix. "A waitress recognized the necklace. Said a performer called Juliette had thrown a hissy fit when it was stolen. Carried on as if the ugly thing was diamonds, or real gold. Moaned that the guy what gave it to her was going to be mighty pissed."

Moore looked up. "Paulie doesn't get pissed. And Juliette moans and coos about everything. And what do you mean, 'his locker'? Why would Paulie have a locker at the club?"

"Ask him. All I know is the D.A. figures there's enough for an indictment, if they can introduce the evidence from the floater case."

Delacroix folded a jackknife into his pants pockets. He thanked Mick for coming to tell them in person. He was so damn gracious that Mick didn't blurt out that Antrim would need a more experienced attorney. Didn't have to, as it turned out. Delacroix said he would contact some lawyer in the District.

"Hope that's not Mrs. Antrim's law firm. The fool kid doesn't want his mother's henchmen involved. If I were him, I'd go for the best she can afford."

"So would I." Delacroix rammed the wood figure into his pocket. "However, in deference to Paulson's wishes, I have made arrangements with a colleague." He slipped on his jacket, told Moore he'd be in touch, and scrambled up the bank to the road.

Mick offered Moore a hand up.

She accepted, but stepped back once on her feet. Her eyes were blanched to sea foam, made iridescent by the sun. She leveled them at him. "Why are you being so coy about Paulie and the club? If he told you about the locker, it can't be that much of a secret. What are you keeping from me? Why can't you be straight with me?"

Mick opened his mouth to argue, then shut it. He jammed his hands in his pockets.

"Everyone's entitled to a private life, Moore, even your employees. If Antrim wants you to know his secrets, he'll have to tell you."

Twenty-seven

Thom Carroll and two of his twelve-year-old triplets arrived at three-thirty. Despite their assistance, the Phantom III was loaded into his trailer without mishap.

Rebecca and the guys waved as it disappeared from sight. She let out a sigh of relief. She told Frank, Val and Billy Lee to take the rest of the afternoon off. They deserved it. She was going to check with Delacroix for news about Paulie.

She phoned Jo from the house. He'd reached his law school friend, Lea Johansson. She was already at the jail interviewing her client. Paulie had relented and called his mother. He'd assured her that his reincarceration was nothing to worry about. It was a mistake, typical police incompetency. He preferred to handle it himself with his own lawyer. So far, the matriarch was letting her only son amuse himself in a jail cell.

Jo had not asked Paulie why he had a locker at the club. He wasn't sure he wanted to know.

Rebecca sympathized, though she was irked that Hagan had refused to explain. And hurt that Paulie would again confide in the detective instead of one of his friends at the shop.

She stripped off her coveralls and socks and dumped them in the laundry room. The phone rang before she'd turned on the shower. Still in her underwear, she grabbed it off the dresser. She plopped onto the bed, folded her legs in a modified Lotus position and answered it.

Hayes squealed in the receiver, "I'm on deadline, grab a pencil."

"Go ahead."

"Precious little on your club manager. LeClerc's a Canadian citizen, works here on a visa. Goes back once a year to visit a crippled brother in Montreal. Dohlmani has employed him for about ten years. Began as a gofer at the Back Room. Was assistant manager when the club was raided. Apparently he convinced Mr. D that he had nothing to do with the after-hours body sale, so Dohlmani kept him on.

"Promoted him to manager of the new club when it opened. No police record, other than two speeding tickets. Both southbound on the Baltimore-Washington Expressway, couple months apart. Goes to Baltimore regularly for supplies. Or maybe to get new girls. My sources tell me there are a couple of well-known 'talent' agencies."

"Could be." Rebecca leaned back against the pillow, stretched her legs. "But that's not where the newest girl came from—I got hired yesterday."

Peter tittered with glee. He asked typical reporter's questions about what she hoped to uncover and would she share what she found out. Even if it turned out to be a jealous-boyfriend-kills-girl saga, Peter might be able to exploit the international aspect.

When he grilled her about days and hours she'd be dancing, Rebecca confessed that so far she was just waiting tables. She might be promoted by the weekend, which reminded her she needed a phone number from the newspaper files. Patty Jenks was a stripper turned dance instructor. Rebecca had met her doing a story several years before. With luck she'd still be teaching girls to strut their stuff.

Peter promised to look it up when he got a second.

"As for Dohlmani, I came across a follow-up piece Sydney did on him. The man has a ninety-eight-foot yacht, the *Floating D*. Lucky stiff. Throws a party once a month, year-round. Invites movers and shakers and a handful of good customers from the club. Scatters a few dancers around for decoration. The main activity is gambling. He has a gaming license and a staff of pros doing the dealing. Blackjack, roulette, that kind of thing. Attendees are encouraged to lose with good grace. The proceeds go to Children's National Medical Center. Beaucoup de money changes hands. Lots of visibility. A good time for a good cause, which explains how Dohlmani got such damn good press when the second club opened."

"Dohlmani's looking holier and holier. This boat stay docked or does it actually sail?"

"It cruises the Potomac from about nine P.M. to two A.M. Picks up at a half dozen places on both sides of the river."

Rebecca sat up. "It crosses deep water?"

"Meanders back and forth."

Before Peter could ask why, Rebecca blurted out that a second dancer had been found floating in the Potomac. Her neck had been broken before she was dumped.

"Dumped? Like from a passing vessel?"

"Very possibly."

Peter whistled. "Sounds like the *Floating D* could be a high-stakes boat ride. Want my advice? Stay on dry land."

"Believe me, Hayes, I try to."

Twenty-eight

Mick cursed and turned up the radio. He was stuck behind a plodding horse trailer. Nowhere to pass. He might as well relax. He went over his conversation with Zimmer. Tried to put a face on the neck of a wealthy pervert who liked to deflower young foreign girls. It was less painful than thinking about Moore. That tooth was hurting again and he couldn't stop wiggling it.

Moore hadn't exactly been angry at him; more like irritated. As she strode away from the stream, he'd asked if she was returning to the club that night. That made her turn. Eyes defiant, she'd said yes. He didn't try to talk her out of it. He knew she was pigheaded. In truth, it was a tendency he admired. It was one of the attributes that had made her so good at investigating. And one of the things that had nearly gotten her killed.

He followed her to the street. At his car, he stopped to pull a small brown shopping bag from the back seat. It was emblazoned with NAOMI written in purple marker and dusted with glitter.

"Antrim asked if you'd give these to Serena."

She glanced in the bag. "The infamous red shoes."

"The catalyst. If Antrim hadn't wanted to impress the dancer, the Bentley wouldn't have been on Fifty-sixth Street. It might have made it back to Head Tide before the body was discovered. This could have been Zimmer's case. I wouldn't be standing here."

"You think he could solve the case without your help?"

"He might have had my help. He says the deputy's job is still open."

Moore hadn't asked if he was planning to apply.

Mick had watched as she crossed the road, cut through the trees toward the shop. Easy, smooth stride. Suggestive in pants, sensuous in a skirt. He was relieved she was only waiting tables. But he couldn't help it—he wondered what she'd look like in a G-string. Wondered if he'd want to find out in public. Even if he could step foot in the club without losing his job, would he want to see her perform, live and on stage?

He was flabbergasted she would do it voluntarily for an assignment of her own making. The dead girls weren't given a choice about baring their bodies in public. Probably not in private, either. Moore could choose. She could stay home, play with nothing more dangerous than a screwdriver or an air rachet.

Mick settled in the car, tried to relax his shoulders. He'd been trained at the Academy to never get ahead of the facts. But his Gaelic heritage taunted him to go on, to weave an intricate tale from the slenderest of threads. The trick was not to get tangled in your own yarn.

First, he tossed out Zimmer's argument that a club employee was having sex with the girls. Too close to home. Too much to lose.

Sure, Lambesco had a record for messing with a minor, but if he was caught, he'd be out of a job and back in jail. If

LeClerc was diddling his dancers, he risked Dohlmani's wrath. Besides, LeClerc impressed Mick as inherently lazy. He would have used a condom, if only so he wouldn't have to deal with a pregnancy causing downtime, or costing him the price of an abortion.

And Dohlmani, if he were the sperm donor, would have handled it better. The suave owner was arrogant enough to sample his own merchandise, and maybe twisted enough to think it was noblesse oblige. But he seemed too slick to be sloppy. He wouldn't have let the girls get pregnant. Or let one be killed at the club. For that matter, he would have made sure Petra never surfaced if he dropped her in the river. There would have been no whispers to tarnish Dohlmani's reputation.

Mick rolled down the window, inhaled, tried to catch the scent of new-mowed grass. Nothing but diesel fuel. He closed the window. On WBIG, Aretha was wailing for a little respect. He lowered the volume.

An outsider, then. Someone with a penchant for pure, un-sullied teenagers. Why virgins—so he wouldn't have to use a condom? Lot of guys didn't like the pesky things, but there were other solutions. Like putting the girl on birth control. Unless he liked playing Russian roulette with a loaded sperm. Liked the idea of spreading his seed, but found the re-sulting misshapen vessels unappealing.

Unappealing enough to kill them and the impending off-spring?

Of course, the pervert who was screwing them didn't have to be the killer. He could have sent them back to the club for LeClerc or Dohlmani to deal with. Calmly requested a fresher model. Moved on, never questioned what happened to the rejects.

Or he could have hired outside talent to dispense with the mothers-to-be. Told the club that the girls had left town.

So many choices.

Whatever the game, the guy had to have money. Underage goods would command top dollar, and whoever got rid of them would demand a megapile more.

Mick wanted to believe that there was only one villain lurking in this cesspool. It seemed likely from a timing standpoint. Bufa had gone off to get married about eight months ago. Petra had started dating shortly thereafter. Several months later she left to dance at a club in Baltimore, only ended up in the Potomac. She was pulled out but went unidentified for a couple of months. During which time the unlucky Aziz began dating. It sure sounded like the same guy, with the same thirst, going back to the same well.

Mick cranked up the air-conditioning as he killed the music.

Merging onto the beltway, he toyed with the idea of sneaking into the club to check out the clientele. See if any one of the customers jumped up and screamed, "I did it." Keep an eye on Moore, who would resent his hovering. Both activities would be futile and undoubtedly get back to the captain.

Besides, what would it gain? The man he'd been molding in his imagination wasn't the type to frequent a nightclub. He wouldn't chance having his perversions revealed to those around him. Mick could almost see him standing in the shadows of his room, manicured fingers pulling on heavy drapes as he called the club for a delivery. Lisping into the phone, "Surprise me. Send whichever girl you think I'll savor."

Mick exited the beltway, merged with the traffic heading north on 295. It was heavy going out of the city for the weekend, lighter heading in. He twisted the visor to block the sun.

Maybe it was the money.

Or the lack of sexual protection.

Or the international makeup of the girls at the club. Or the fact that both Dohlmani and LeClerc were from outside the country. Or the direction he was traveling. Whatever. The predator's face was beginning to look foreign—as in DC's inner elite, foreign dignitaries and politicos shielded from prying eyes behind the sedate facades of the embassies. Men of privilege who lived coddled existences. Men of power with diplomatic immunity who were used to having their whims satisfied.

Hearing about the cases for the first time, Zimmer had fretted over earlier killings that might have escaped official notice. In a society of serial killers, it seemed all too possible. If the deaths had involved embassy personnel they would have been covered up quietly. They'd be hard to uncover. But if the diplomat, or whoever, had been in the District for any length of time, there was a slim chance he was known to the police. Transgressions might have surfaced from his younger days when he was less controlled, had less to lose. His name could have been noted in the margin whether or not charges were filed.

It might be worth checking with Vice, see if the crimes rang any bells. It wouldn't take long if Wang was on duty. Sounded a whole lot more productive than painting Mom's shutters while fantasizing about Moore in pasties.

Twenty-nine

Rebecca waited tables in Boothbay Harbor, Maine, the summer she turned eighteen. It was her first job, her first delicious few months living on her own, free of her parents and the confines of Boston. She'd landed the job at Brown Brothers Wharf on Memorial Day weekend, mostly by being there and willing to start work that day. She stayed the summer despite her parent's objections to the menial work, the distance from home, and her roommate from Albany, New York. Her mother would have loathed the shared attic room in Lydia Pinkham's boardinghouse, if she'd ever visited. To Rebecca, the crowded space perched above the harbor town was just the right size to test her untrained wings.

Brown's Wharf was a tourist restaurant, built out over the water, where customers selected their personal crustacean from a bubbling tank on their way in to be seated. For boiled, the waitresses dumped the lobster into a numbered mesh bag and handed it to the cook. For baked-stuffed, the waitresses had to prep them, live.

By the end of the summer Rebecca could split a lobster open—stab the point into the thorax, pierce the brain, smack the blade through the belly to the tail, gut it and crack the claws, all in under five seconds. And keep her apron clean—a point of hygiene, or you stank of lobster entrails all shift. Baked-stuffed lobster was not something she ever ordered when dining out.

This stint was way sexier than Brown Brothers.

Primping in the girls' lounge, Rebecca realized she was pumped. For the first time in months, she felt like her former self, confident and purposeful. Which was ironic, since in the wig and Gypsy costume, she looked, walked and talked like someone she'd never met. She floated through the lounge, a sexy enigma in ankle-strapped pumps. She was Salome, a modern Mata Hari. Rebecca added another layer of "Carmine Divine."

It was only her second night but she had the routine down cold. Waiting tables took less than half a brain. Unlike at the shop, she had no job-related worries other than giving the correct change. The club's cash flow wasn't her concern. Argumentative customers were turned over to the night bouncer. Spilled drinks were mopped up by the gloomy custodian. Costumes were provided by the management. Makeup tips came free from Juliette. Bottom pinchers were easily discouraged—most of the time.

She found working at the club liberating. She doubted the live-in dancers did.

Their setup reminded her of the workers in turn-of-the-century factory towns. All their physical needs were taken care of: They each had a bed upstairs, they were fed, given work clothes, received medical care when needed. In return, they were expected to dance.

What they didn't have was freedom. Most of their pay went to cover daily expenses. The pittance that was left was either sent back to their family or "banked" for them by LeClerc. They barely spoke English. Vince made phone calls for them from the bar. The girls didn't know how to drive, and wouldn't have had access to a car if they did. Someone had to pick them up if they were allowed to go out. In short, they were innocents in a strange land, dependent upon management.

They should have been protected.

Rebecca flounced her way to the bar. Juliette and LeClerc were squabbling over her early number. When the phone under the bar rang, Juliette pushed Vince aside and leaned over to get it. LeClerc yanked the receiver away from her. He mumbled something into the mouthpiece, listened, nodded once and hung up. Tongue wetting his lips, he dropped down from the bar stool and swaggered into the main room.

Juliette crowed, held out her hand palm up to Lambesco and exchanged slaps.

Rebecca settled on the end stool. "What's got you so tickled?"

"Mr. Manager. Somebody's pulling his strings. Most every Friday he gets a mystery call makes him sweat."

"An illicit affair?"

"Go on girl, who'd have him?"

For the next hour Rebecca half listened to the mindless table chatter as her Salome persona moved between the patrons, delivering drinks and fried cheese sticks. At each table, she checked out the customers. If the killer was among them, he blended. As well he might. She imagined him as a loner. Or someone who would lag behind after his drinking pals left. Someone who never took his eyes from the girls, placid on the surface, sipping steadily without haste.

Or she could be totally off base.

No one even came close to that description. Other than LeClerc. His myopic eyes were glued to the dancers. Mostly he glared, annoyed by a girl smiling too much at an interested customer, or not smiling enough at the nerd checking his watch.

Juliette and Lucy were the only women not intimidated by LeClerc. Both women were in the dancers' lounge when Rebecca took her first break. Lucy was contracting cancer near the open window. Juliette was stooped over, hunting for something in a locker. Not in her locker. In Rebecca's locker.

Rebecca stopped just inside the door. "Lose something, Julie?"

The performer straightened, banged her head on the shelf. She repositioned her turban. "I was hoping you had a safety pin. My strap come loose."

Lucy snorted. "That's what happens when you start to sag."

Juliette snapped, "You ain't long behind, sister."

Lucy winked at Rebecca. "Guess now you see the honest-to-God, real reason you need a padlock. Don't you, Sal?"

Thirty

Mick took Route 395 to Arlington, 110 north, then crossed into the District on the Francis Scott Key Bridge. Up Wisconsin to the Second's headquarters on Idaho. He parked, strode inside, breezed through security and was seated beside Sergeant M. Wang's desk in under ten minutes.

The Vice sector was enveloped in the end-of-the-week hiatus. Those who pretended to have lives had left for family dinners or movie dates. Those on duty were resting up before the crazies of the night were dragged through the door. Sergeant Wang was in the men's room.

From the hallway, Wang saw he had company and scurried back to his desk. He was short, potbellied, smiling. He looked too unlined to have been a cop for more than a dozen years—seven in Domestic Violence, six in Vice. But Mick knew that Wang was no innocent. He was simply a genius at compartmentalizing. He put his emotions in the drawer when he pulled out graph paper and started charting data. Retrieved them only when it was safe to feel again.

Wang cocked his head and listened to Mick's supposition

that over the past twelve months several now dead dancers had been hired out to provide sex to the same man. Someone with money and a particular taste for young flesh. Mick described the victims, their deaths and the guesses he could make about their lives.

Wang bowed once, raised his head. He fired off a dozen questions. Was the man a sadist? Sodomizer? Were the girls beaten? Did he favor group orgies? Did he give them gifts? Force drugs on them? How often did he see the girls? Did he keep them overnight? How did they arrive, leave? How much money changed hands?

Mick gave the answers he had.

Wang scribbled notes with his nose close to the faint blue lines. He drew arrows, stars, connecting lines, crossed-through words. Nodded a lot. Chattered to himself when Mick couldn't answer.

Then Wang straightened, squared the paper on his desk. He asked Mick why he came to him.

"There are wealthy men with pubescent tastes in every quarter of every city. Every neighborhood of the suburbs. Every state in America. The world."

Mick thought for a minute. He decided against mentioning Moore's alleged stripper murder from five years back. If the killing had taken place at a posh city hotel, chances were good that the Second caught the case. If so, Wang would remember it. If there was a connection, he would make it.

Mick shrugged. "This feels vaguely foreign to me. Foreign like 'diplomatic immunity.' Like some arrogant SOB pissing in the neighbor's pool knowing he's not going to have to clean it up. Insouciant carelessness, if you know what I mean."

Wang nodded, that he did.

He held up one finger and swiveled to face the computer

screen. He hit a bunch of keys, then turned back.

"As I suspected, nothing."

"Nothing?"

"If there was something, it would mean I have misremembered. Come, I will buy us a cup of the least worst, affordable tea on the block."

Wang led Mick out of the building and down a hundred yards. They stepped into an almost empty coffee shop. Wang ordered hot tea. Mick had his cold with chemical lemon.

Wang stirred the steaming brown liquid with a bent spoon.

"About four, maybe five years ago a striking Hispanic woman—I recall her name was Sanchez—went to the police in her neighborhood with a complaint. She reported that a pervert was stalking her fourteen-year-old daughter. The first time, the man had followed them half a Saturday as they did errands. Then he'd approached the older woman. He waved a wad of money, tried to buy the girl. Ms. Sanchez had been horrified, screamed no, grabbed the girl and raced for home.

"Two weeks later she saw him again. Again he watched them as they shopped for produce in the market. He did not speak to them, but she was unnerved enough to report him to the police. She had no name, just a description: average height, pale eyes, very fair, spoke with an accent."

Wang reeled out the story much like Delacroix. They were both born storytellers. They knew how to keep you hooked. Mick finished his drink. Screwed the cap back on.

Wang blew on his tea, sipped, then continued.

A few weeks later Sanchez noticed that her daughter was acting moodier than normal, more scared than sullen. She cajoled, eventually got the girl to open up. The teen claimed that some man—a different man—had approached her. He was nice, like an uncle, didn't want anything. Brought her little gifts, lipsticks, that sort of thing. Made her feel grown-up.

One day he took her for a ride. They went to a fancy hotel with trees growing inside and men in maroon uniforms with gold trim. There he handed her off to the same white man who had tried earlier to buy her."

"White as in Caucasian or as in albino?"

Wang slurped. "Don't know, but if you make me guess, I would say Scandinavian white-blond, based on the mother's description. I never saw the man. It wasn't my case. Though this time she brought it to our station house. We were closest to the hotel."

"Someone followed up?"

"Not then. Too little to go on. And Ms. Sanchez was a stripper. Low credibility."

"But she came back?"

Wang nodded. He'd met her on the next occasion. She had been frazzled, but triumphant. Speed talking, eager to explain. She'd tried to keep her daughter under lock and key. Difficult, because she worked nights. Occasionally, she would come home to find the girl missing and feared that the man had taken her again. The girl always said no, but her mother did not believe her.

One night Sanchez pretended to go to work, called in sick, then hid out in the neighborhood. She saw a stranger go around to the back of her house and come out dragging the girl. He drove to the Park Hyatt, stashed the car in the garage and took the girl in. By the time Sanchez had made her way inside the building, she was too late to follow them upstairs.

She waited, first in the lobby, then outside. She saw the man go and return several hours later. She thought of tailing him and confronting the white man, rescuing her daughter. Prudently, she realized that it would be too dangerous. Better to follow when he returned the girl home, make sure she was safe.

"She got his license number. She had only seen him from a distance at night, but she wrote down everything she could remember of his physical appearance. She came to us, to make us do something at last."

"Did you?"

Wang raised his shoulders fractionally. "The case was passed up to a senior man."

"You remember who?"

"Not his name. I was new to Vice. He left a short time later. The detective tried to track down the license, but she must have got the numbers wrong. He went to the hotel. No one remembered the man with the girl, or any guest who fit the white man's description."

"So, that was it?" Mick tipped back in his chair.

Wang turned his hands palms up on the table, like he was he was waiting for rain, or the other shoe to fall.

Mick bobbed his head. "Okay, I'll bite. How is it you remember this case so well?"

Wang drained the last drop from his tea. Turned the cup over in the saucer. "The next day Ms. Sanchez was found dead in an alley not far from here. Her neck had been broken."

"The man in the suit realized he'd been tailed and cleaned up behind himself?"

Wang nodded. "Very thoroughly."

He dropped the other shoe.

"But that is not all. Some weeks later Ms. Sanchez's first complaint against the white man was forwarded to us from another district; they heard we had closed the case. I wished to add it to the record. I couldn't. The file folder was missing. The case record also had vanished from the computer."

Wang rose to go. His mouth was a hard line of distaste, as if the tea had been bitter.

"You understand, Lieutenant Hagan, files are often misplaced. There had been an epidemic of computer crashes. It happens. There were no further complaints of similar abductions in our district. So no one worried much."

Wang pushed through the door. "After all, Sanchez was merely a stripper."

Thirty-one

At nine-thirty the pole dancers took their first break while Juliette performed on stage. She was draped in scarlet lamé, turban, and more rhinestones than Liberace. Winston, the ebony piano player, was decked out in white tie and tails, a study in contrast. They were doing something by Gershwin. Rebecca could pick out the almost familiar tune, but not the words. From the way the audience tittered, the lyrics had been altered to suit Juliette's ribald style.

Rebecca rested her tray on the bar. She smiled at Serena as the girls filed past en route to the lounge for their break. Serena flashed her a look of puppy dog adoration, skirted the end stool to avoid contact with LeClerc. He scowled, his cheeks flushed from too much liquor. He tapped the bar beside his highball glass for a refill. Vince turned to pour the drink, nine-tenths gin. LeClerc snatched it up, pushed back from the bar and disappeared behind the beaded curtain. *Trouble looking for a place to happen.*

Rebecca was six paces behind. When the manager stopped outside the lounge, she slipped into the ladies' room, leaving the light off and her fingers holding the door ajar.

LeClerc opened the dressing room door, motioned to someone inside. Serena emerged. She hesitated partway into the hall. LeClerc pulled her toward him and shut the door behind her. He backed her against the wall. He leaned into her, one hand on her shoulder, the other holding his gin against her face.

Serena hung her head. Trapped. *"Pinned and wriggling on the wall,"* like J. Alfred.

LeClerc's nose was pressed against Serena's forehead, his voice muffled. Whatever he was saying was not news the tiny dancer wanted to hear. She wagged her head from side to side until the motion gave her courage. She raised her face to LeClerc and pushed at his chest, shouted, "No" loud enough for Rebecca to hear.

Rebecca also heard the smack as LeClerc backhanded the girl across her face.

Serena's head jerked, banged the wall. Blood pumped from her nose, splattered down the skimpy satin top that barely constrained her breasts. She didn't utter a sound. Or raise her hand to stop the blood or protect herself.

Her lack of response incited LeClerc. He smashed the highball against the doorframe, splashing gin on the wall as the glass shattered.

He thrust its ragged edge against Serena's cheek, an inch below her eye.

Rebecca burst from the bathroom, slamming the door into the wall. Prayed it would vibrate the bar glasses and send Vince scurrying to investigate. She waved at the girl frozen just yards down the hall.

"Hey, Serena, you were super out there tonight. Really hot. Liked the last number."

Rebecca closed in on them quickly.

"Didn't she look swell, Ozzie?"

She reached out to pat his shoulder, leaned between them to make eye contact with the girl.

LeClerc snarled. He twisted in Rebecca's direction, swung his fist before she could react.

Serena shrieked.

Rebecca jerked back. The jagged glass caught the side of her neck, slicing skin. A burning, then a flood of warmth as blood coursed down her throat. She swore at LeClerc and grabbed at the wound. Deep red oozed between her fingers.

With LeClerc's attention diverted, Serena yanked open the dressing room door and scuttled inside.

LeClerc spit in Rebecca's face. He pushed her, palm thumping against her sternum.

"Get the fuck out of here. It doesn't concern you, you nosy bitch."

With the second slam, Rebecca stumbled backward, tripping over her own feet. She would have gone down on her tail but unseen hands caught her from behind.

"Is there a problem, Mr. LeClerc?"

The voice was like whipped cream melting on warm gingerbread.

It had to belong to Sergio Dohlmani. Only a man who looked the way he did could have a voice like that. Or inspire the fear on LeClerc's pudgy face, now drained of its color.

LeClerc dropped the rest of the broken glass on the carpeting. He busied himself tucking in his shirttails. "Nothing to worry about. Salome, here, thinks she can take a drink break any time it suits her."

Dohlmani kicked at the slivers stuck in the nylon fibers as he walked closer.

"You were explaining differently when the cocktail spilled?" He peeled Rebecca's fingers away from her neck, fingered the blood, frowned at LeClerc. "We will speak of this later. Resume your duties."

LeClerc's nod was curt. He swaggered past them, returned to the bar.

Dohlmani held Rebecca's faux hair away from her neck as he applied a handkerchief to stanch the bleeding. "Come. I have seen *A Farewell to Arms* twenty-nine times. I know how to bandage."

He slid his hand to her elbow and led her toward his private office at the end of the hall. As they passed the dressing room, Rebecca noticed the door was not quite latched.

Dohlmani's office was of modest size, but opulent and as well turned out as the man himself. At the far end, closed draperies of mocha satin hung to the floor in sensuous folds. The walls were papered in a matching shade with a small gilded pattern that shimmered in the gentle light from the wall sconces. The rug was an Oriental from some very old tribe, judging by the muted shades and the thread count.

His desk was also antique: a massive double kneehole in mahogany. It had three drawers and a cabinet on each side, polished brass hardware. It was surprisingly egalitarian for a man who seemed to have cast himself for the role of benign despot.

Dohlmani seated Rebecca in the visitor's chair and went to fetch antiseptic from the adjoining washroom. He opened and closed cabinets as he searched.

"You say LeClerc was attempting to force the girl to drink?"

"That's what it looked like. Before the glass shattered."

"Yet he implied that the liquor was yours. No? Well then, perhaps he was taking a glass away from Serena? Some of the younger girls drink, thinking it will enhance their performance."

Dohlmani was obviously siding with his manager. There was nothing to be gained by annoying him, so Rebecca conceded that it was possible. She had been several yards away from the confrontation. Perhaps she did not see it clearly.

Dohlmani nodded. He set his supplies on the desk and turned on a lamp, directing its glow on her face. It reminded her of a unshaven cop grilling the suspect in a forties' detective flick. Probably where Dohlmani had seen the move before. Even in here there were souvenirs of the bygone era. A dozen black-and-white glossies of film stars hung on the side wall. She recognized a young Burt Lancaster.

Dohlmani stood behind her to gather the wig's tresses away from her neck. He deftly twisted the hair and pinned it up with a hair clip he must have found in the bathroom. His fingers traced the pulse in her throat before he examined the wound. His touch was light, his skin warm and smooth. Rebecca's grandmother had always claimed that one could tell a lady by her hands. Few ladies Rebecca knew had hands like Dohlmani's.

He remained just outside her peripheral vision as he dabbed at the cut with hydrogen peroxide. Rebecca winced. She imagined him gloating as he applied more.

"As you no doubt realize, the girls are Mr. LeClerc's responsibility."

"Does he hire them as well?"

"Some. The others are girls from my native country. Girls who feel deprived in their own land and wish to taste life in America. They are soft, silly things. Few have endured the void that true hardship gnaws in your belly. I want little to do with them. It is up to LeClerc to discipline them if it is necessary. I believe he has complained that Serena is high-strung. Not always obedient." Dohlmani emitted a gentle laugh. "So few women are."

He pivoted around to face her, leaned close. She could smell cologne. His eyes sparkled. "Are you, Salome—obedient?"

When she opened her mouth to respond, he swooped. His lips pressed against hers. Warm and moist with just enough pressure to linger on the skin, to make a woman crave more.

Then he was gone.

Behind her again, he smoothed a dab of ointment over the cut. He reached for the box of bandages and extracted two butterfly strips, snugged them over the cut to draw the edges together. He added a gauze pad, held it in place with multiple strips of white tape. Obviously, he'd patched up employees' wounds before. Or the film version of Hemingway's classic was a better teaching aid than she would have guessed.

Dohlmani sat on the edge of the desk and admired his handiwork. "I do not think you'll need stitches. Though perhaps you will want a doctor to examine it."

"It feels fine. Sure you weren't trained in medicine?"

"Sadly, I am self-taught. As a child, I was ambitious and so learned much on the streets. Rudimentary medicine. The laws of business. How to appreciate a woman."

He reached forward, took her face in both hands.

Rebecca's pulse quickened. She feared—maybe she hoped—he was going to kiss her again. How would Salome respond? The man was her boss, maybe a killer, definitely dangerous.

He didn't kiss her, he sighed. His palms were moist against her skin. His index fingers stroked her cheekbones.

"Though my clientele enjoy watching youthful dancers, I prefer women who have experienced something of life: the joys, pain, and disappointments. Your eyes say you have seen much, more than you would be willing to discuss. Am I right?"

Too right.

Rebecca pushed back on the heavy upholstered chair. She needed breathing space. He was intriguing, but he was crowding her, with his body and his words. She didn't like where the conversation was going.

Dohlmani noted her discomfort, shrugged one shoulder and acquiesced. He removed his hands and sat back. Then nodded, affirming a decision.

"Yes. I would like to see you dance. It is time. Tomorrow night. Rejoice, Salome. You have been chosen to dance for me."

Thirty-two

"Dohlmani didn't see the manager smack the girl and go after you?" Hagan's voice on the phone sounded tense.

Rebecca hunkered down in the dark in the MG. She pulled off her left shoe, gently fingered her toes.

"Who knows what he saw. I'm just glad he came around the corner when he did. LeClerc has a hair trigger. Dohlmani patched me up, then announced that I'm to dance tomorrow. Lucky me."

Hagan sputtered, bit back whatever he was going to say, then started again.

"Moore, that guy can't be as unsullied as he comes across. Has it occurred to you that his disdain for young dancers is an act? Why does he hire so many?"

"Ozzie hires them because they're good for business. Customers like them young and tender."

She unwound the straps from the second shoe and eased it off. She was getting a blister. In a contortionist's move she bent her leg over the stick shift to massage the arch of her right foot.

"Hagan, why are you calling me at one-fifteen in the morning?"

"I wanted to hear about your day, dear."

He sounded exactly like Desi Arnez talking to Lucy. Or maybe after working two shifts at the club, Rebecca had film stars on the brain.

Hagan cleared his throat, returned to his normal voice. "Moore, can't I convince you to stay away from the club? Let the police handle it."

"Believe me, if the police weren't incompetent, I wouldn't be—"

She started at the sound of footsteps clomping on the tarmac.

She sat up, clutched the phone to her chest. Two rows over Lambesco opened the door to a Taurus, got in, started the car. When he noticed Rebecca, he tooted the horn. Waved as he pulled out. Only a handful of cars remained. The club was dark except for the hallway leading to the offices.

Hagan hissed in the phone. "Moore, where the hell are you?"

"Parked outside the club."

"Get out of there. Now."

"I'd be long gone if you hadn't called."

"Now. Or I'll come and get you."

"Really? And do what?"

She grinned. She was alone, cocooned in a sports car, clad in a wig and a revealing costume only minimally stained with blood. She'd just spent six hours serving fruity drinks to fantasizing customers, stealing cherries and stale peanuts for dinner. Her feet ached, her neck throbbed and her head was light. The drive back to Head Tide seemed beyond her. Was Hagan about to make her a better offer?

He took his time. When he spoke his voice was husky. "Depends on—"

"Sssh."

She cut him off as a car sped into the parking lot of the closed club. She ducked, headlight beams swept over the MG. She popped back up in time to see the car slither down the alley alongside the building, triggering an overhead security light. It blinked on, revealing a limousine: black and three doors long with tinted windows.

The side exit door of the club swung open. Two figures emerged.

In the yellow glow, Rebecca could make out LeClerc gripping the arm of a top-heavy Hispanic dancer called Sandi—spelled with an *i* dotted with a heart. The girl had changed into stretch slacks, a clingy striped top and lots of gold chains. Even at a distance she wobbled as if drunk. LeClerc opened the back door and eased the girl inside. The front window slid down.

"Moore, talk to me." Hagan's annoyance cut through the dark.

"You talk to me." Rebecca banged her knee on the dash as she slithered lower. "What's going on here? The club's closed. Why is the manager sneaking a young woman out the back door into a limousine?"

"What's happening, Moore?"

"Aren't you listening? A late model stretch Lincoln just pulled in. I can't see who's inside, other than Sandi, one of the dancers. Wait a minute. Ozzie's getting agitated."

"The manager?"

"Arms waving, he's halfway in the car. Paunch biting into the window glass. Bet he's red in the face and hissing spit."

"Moore, you're making me nervous. Stay out of sight until the limo and manager leave. Any chance your car's on a rise? Can you coast out of there?"

"Hold on. It's backing into the light. Grab a pencil. DC plates: 1Q8 999. Got it?"

Mick grunted. "Once the limo's out of sight, you bolt. Stay on the phone until you're clear of the place."

Rebecca slid the stick shift into neutral. She depressed the button on the emergency brake with her thumb and lowered the handle. The car remained at rest.

The limo's taillights disappeared down the drive.

She checked out the building. LeClerc had retreated inside. She waited for the security light to blink off, for the shadows to blend to black.

When all looked quiet, she counted to one hundred, slowly. She set the cell phone on the passenger seat and got out of the car. With the door open and her hands on the windshield support, she rocked the car, then shoved it forward. It started to drift. She kept it moving until it picked up speed, then hopped into the driver's seat, aimed for the exit.

She retrieved the phone. "Still there, Hagan?"

"Stuck to you like gum on your shoe. You're moving?"

"Almost home free. Time for some power."

Rebecca turned the key. The sports car's engine fired to life, then sputtered and stopped.

"You ever tune that thing?" He was getting testy.

Rebecca cranked it again. It caught. She kept it going with a generous application of gas. She steered for the entrance road. Midway along the drive, she pulled the switch to bring on the headlamps. She eased the car through the curves, ignored the stop sign and swung onto the highway. She gunned the engine, upshifting into second, then third.

She ripped the wig from her head, reveling in the feel of air flowing over her scalp.

"We're under way and glad of it."

She accelerated until the engine roared, pulled the shifter back into fourth.

Then blinked.

"Oh, shit."

Rebecca stood on the brakes, eased off, double-clutched, slammed the shift lever down into second.

The car broke loose.

She yanked the steering wheel with both hands to counter the skid. The rear end fishtailed in the sand. The MG swerved across the shoulder, tottered, righted, slid back onto the road. The tires squealed, gripped, and left dual strips of rubber on the pavement.

The car quivered to a stop.

The engine sputtered and died, more with a whimper than a bang.

Rebecca's right leg wobbled on the brake pedal. Her hands, slick with sweat, slid off the wheel.

But she didn't run over the girl.

Part Three

Grand Prix Finale

Thirty-three

Five A.M. is an acceptable wake-up time only if four o'clock was the alternative. When the ringing woke her, Rebecca glared at the alarm clock. It wasn't the culprit. She slammed the off button anyway and pulled the sheet over her head.

The ringing continued. She'd been in bed a mere hour and a half. No one could possibly want to talk to her. No one could be cruel enough to wake her.

Except Hagan. He might be justified.

When she'd slammed on the brakes to avoid hitting Serena, the cell phone had fallen under the pedals. Their call had been disconnected and she'd forgotten about it.

It took her five minutes to cajole a white-faced Serena into the car. It took another ten minutes of sobs and murmurings in Arabic or Lebanese or whatever before Rebecca knew what was wrong. She would be soiled, Serena moaned, end up dead like the others. She had to run away. Salome was her only hope; she must protect her. Please.

Rebecca had patted the girl on her shoulder, tying to decide what to do with her at one-thirty in the morning, before she remembered the disconnected Hagan.

She'd redialed his number. He'd been so frantic he forgot to yell at her. He gave her directions to his condo on Avon Lane NW. He would be waiting.

Twenty-five minutes later Rebecca had hustled the scared girl into Hagan's apartment. Thirty minutes after that, she left, drifted home as foggy as the thin mist wafting across the deserted roads.

Now, Rebecca silenced the phone by answering it.

The caller was male, but it wasn't Hagan, it was worse— Thom Carroll, owner of the P III that had left the shop yesterday. He was calling from the grounds of the Washington Vintage Grand Prix. The car wouldn't start.

Impossible.

He handed the phone to the transport driver. Rebecca walked him through the starting procedure.

"Switch on the ignition, there should be a red light on the dash. Make sure the hand throttle lever is set to the closed position, at the bottom. Move the thumb lever on the dashboard to the 'START' position, it will open the throttle the correct amount. Don't step on the gas pedal. Count to twenty. Now, push the starter button on the dash. No, you don't need a key."

Rebecca strained to hear the sound of the engine firing. Nothing. The voice playing with the controls whined. The owner urged him to make another try. She yelled in the phone, cautioned him to wait. Allow the parts to resettle before trying again. She wouldn't be responsible if the amateurs damaged the pinion or flywheel teeth.

"Is the fuel pump clicking?"

She didn't wait for the "Say what?" She told him to put Mr. Carroll on. She directed the owner to open the right-side bonnet and listen for the pump. It should be suctioning fuel. It wasn't. It could be something simple like a bad fuse or loose connection. More likely the unit decided to fail at the worst possible moment. All British parts adhered to Murphy's Law of going bad when they could do the most damage to your reputation.

Rebecca had no choice. She promised Thom Carroll she would load tools into the car and bring a spare SU pump. She'd be there in under two hours.

The temporary race grounds set up in Rock Creek Park were due to open to the public at seven o'clock. At 6:56, Rebecca pulled into the East Gate checkpoint marked for show registrants only. A volunteer guard in an orange vest was turning away an overbearing family, condemning them to general parking. Rebecca swerved around the minivan, gunned the MG. She flicked a wave through the open top, trusting the guard to assume she was a late entry for British Car Day, though the sports car would barely pass the fifty-fifty rule— looks good when seen from fifty feet, going fifty miles per hour.

At the first placard proclaiming BRITISH CARS she slowed and turned left. She followed signs emblazoned with the Union Jack uphill through rows of Triumphs, Healeys, Mini Coopers and an occasional Morgan. Lower down the slope were sections for foreign makes: Italian, featuring Fiat and Alfa Romeo; German, mainly Porsches, Opels, and Volkswagens; then a smattering of French Peugeots and Renaults. In the distance basked the good old American muscle cars— Detroit iron on steroids, dwarfing their European counterparts, blinding them with an excess of chrome.

The section reserved for Rolls-Royce and Bentley motor cars fit their status. It was on the summit under a cluster of spreading maples. The cars circled the trees like Conestoga wagons fending off Indians. They faced outward, aristocratic grilles looking down on the spectators. In shade and semi-seclusion, their owners could enjoy tailgate libations among their own kind.

Thom Carroll wasn't enjoying his Bloody Mary.

He paced at the edge of the cars, fixated on his watch. He spotted Rebecca as she slowed to avoid hitting a youngster in jeopardy of losing his baggy shorts. Carroll was in her car before it stopped rolling. Without speaking, he pointed toward an enclosed transporter that was painted teal to match the Phantom. The driver was sitting in the cab, feet dangling out the door, sipping coffee from an insulated cup. He nodded but stayed put. He wasn't getting involved.

Rebecca shut down the car and slipped out. Thom Carroll's face colored as he struggled from the sports car. Not a good sign. She could feel an "eversensor failure" building.

As mythical as the phoenix, the eversensor is a part that doesn't exist but every mechanic knows about. It's mentioned in lots of customer complaints, like, "Ever since you worked on the engine the paint's been falling off." Or, "Ever since you rotated the tires, it's been using more oil." Not logical, but considering human nature, and the size of the average repair or restoration bill, it's understandable to blame the last mechanic who touched your precious car for anything new that goes wrong.

Rebecca pretended to listen to Carroll's explanation of the no start. When he paused for breath she asked if the detailer had taken a pressure washer to the engine compartment. Air drying could have corroded contacts. *No, nothing like that.* Just some detail spray and soft, nonlinting rags. The triplets knew to be gentle when polishing bits in the engine compartment.

Carrying a flashlight and her kit, Rebecca walked up the tailgate into the transporter. She opened the right side bonnet and looked around. All good on top. She removed the screw-in contacts from each end of the fuel pumps and smiled. Using tweezers she extracted one fuse from each side. With a paper towel, she wiped down the fuses and contacts to remove the puddled detail spray from the end caps. Then, she reassembled the pumps and relatched the bonnet.

She squeezed farther in on the driver's side, reached into the car, adjusted the throttle lever, heard the sound of fuel pumps ticking. She waited for them to stop and hit the starter button. The car sprang to life. Twelve cylinders, all smooth as silk. Roaring like a beast in a cave.

Carroll looked up at her, opened and closed his mouth a few times. With a face only slightly less colorful than the liquid in the cut-glass tumbler, he apologized for dragging her to the Grand Prix so early. He insisted that she join them for strawberry blintzes and champagne.

Rebecca accepted. To earn her breakfast, she got into the car, let it warm up, then backed it out of the enclosed trailer, down the ramp onto the grass. Watched with envy by the cognoscenti and the uninitiated alike, she circled the rise to find the Carrolls' appointed parking spot. She backed the car into the gap between a 25/30 with heavy carriage work and a Corniche with its top looking as if it had never been creased in the down position. Given the olive drab paint, she was surprised the vanity plate wasn't "Cornichon."

There was one empty space on the far side of the drophead.

Gawkers started gathering before Rebecca could alight from the car. Who could blame them? The P III was a knockout. The car's paint scheme when it arrived in the U.S. decades ago had been deep turquoise with black fenders and lipstick-red upholstery. Perched on the cowl in front of the windscreen had been a sapphire the size of a doughnut to designate the maharaja's status.

Recently repainted, the exterior had been toned down to teal; the interior done in claret leather. Both colors were more in keeping with the occasionally overcast weather of the East Coast of North America, less reminiscent of the scorching suns of India. The sapphire jewel remained. With the top down and the boot lid laden with crystal, the P III epitomized the good life.

Mrs. Carroll had coordinated her attire to match the car: a Laura Ashley flowered skirt, maroon and teal ribbons on a straw picture hat. She'd also made the blintzes. They were as smooth as the strawberries were luscious. The coffee she tipped from an etched silver pot was full-bodied enough to start Rebecca's brain functioning.

When it kicked in, Rebecca remembered Frank. She should let him know where she was.

She packed up her tools, excused herself and walked back to the MG. She punched Frank's home number into the cell phone, waited ten rings. When he didn't answer, she dialed the shop to leave a message. He answered on the second ring. She should have guessed he'd be there, even on his first Saturday off in a month. She gave him the lowdown on the P III no start. Frank's initial concern turned to disgust when he heard what had gone wrong.

"Can't fix ugly, and can't do nothing about operator error. Cars would run a lot better if the owners stopped mucking with them."

"No argument from me."

"Well maybe I got one with you. Albers faxed you six invoices from 1999 listing the same part they supplied for different cars. How come? What do you care about replacement lenses for Shadow sidelights? When did we ever work on a Shadow?"

"Great. Make me a list of the chassis numbers, will you?"

"Sure thing. And if you want them, I'll hand them over when you pick me up at the shop. If you're going to that club tonight, I'm going with you."

Frank's tone wasn't open to discussion. She said fine, she'd be there late afternoon. In the meantime, would Frank feed Moe? She had a few errands to run in the District. He agreed, if she met him no later than four o'clock.

The low battery light on her phone was flashing as Rebecca hung up. She leaned against the car door. She was touched that Frank cared enough to drag himself to the nightclub again, but she was uncomfortable about his witnessing her on stage. She was pretty sure Frank would not approve of her dance debut. Of course, if she didn't get help in the form of lessons, there wasn't going to be a debut.

She pocketed the cell phone and walked back up the rise. The last display car was maneuvering into the space next to the Corniche. It was a Shadow II, black from the tip of its exhaust to the shaded windscreen. Its vanity plate read GENTS.

Oh, hell. What were the odds that a man like Sergio Dohlmani, who ran a shady nightclub, also aspired to hobnob with the idle rich? Almost a given. What was the point of owning a Rolls-Royce if it wasn't an entrée into the circle of the elite? Once there, though, the competition was pretty stiff. In the enthusiasts' pecking order, Shadows were mired in the nouveau entry class.

Rebecca bid a fleeting good-bye to Thom Carroll and turned to make a dash for her car.

Dohlmani was out of his and strolling down the hill to photograph the array of cars posed beneath the trees. Framing his shot, he blocked her escape route.

Minus the long, curly wig and fully clothed, she should be invisible to Dohlmani. Even if he recognized her out of context, would it matter? Surely dancers were allowed to have other interests in life, why not vintage cars? Still, she was reluctant to have him think of her as other than a nightclub bimbo.

She changed direction, hurried along to join a throng of spectators in bright Izod shirts and pressed shorts. With her nearly shaved head, black jeans and blacker denim shirt, she stood out like a bruised thumb. She let the camera-toting, kids-clutching gaggle sweep her along toward the pit area. It would be busy, crammed with spectators ogling the cars being prepped for the qualifying runs. An ideal place to get lost.

They paused at the crosswalk as an Elva cruised by. Rebecca glanced over her shoulder. Dohlmani was listening to the owner of the 25/30, nodding while he snapped a picture. He shifted the lens south. She jerked her head around. From where she stood, it appeared that Dohlmani's camera was trained on her back.

She trudged up the slope into the shaded pit area. Trailers, transporters, campers and an occasional tent huddled under the foliage. Men strutted in single-piece race suits. Mechanics with wrenches stuck in their back pockets tinkered under hoods. Trophy wives, girlfriends or models hired by sponsors drank their beverage of choice and looked either bored or perky depending on their function.

Rebecca peeled away from the group to admire a Lotus 7, circa 1960. It was dark green, low-slung and unattended, its engine exposed. Standing at the nose, she could see newcomers ascend to the pit area.

Within minutes Dohlmani strolled into view. Two men flanked him. The gorilla in ill-fitting clothes was either his bodyguard or a stand-in from central casting. The other man was lithe, young and dark, wearing wraparound sunglasses. His chin was weaker than Dohlmani's, but he resembled him enough to be from the same gene pool. Dohlmani gestured gracefully toward an Allard on the opposite side of the dirt road. They walked toward it. Rebecca leaned farther into the Lotus's engine compartment.

"Jacob send you to sabotage it?"

Rebecca jerked upright. She spun to face the unexpected voice.

With carrot-red hair, freckles and an impish grin, the man looked more amused than accusatory. And very cool. Race suit rolled down to his waist, balaclava bunched at his throat and helmet under his arm.

He laughed as he leered. "On closer inspection, lass, you look more like a would-be driver, not a wrench turner come to ruin my day."

He proffered his helmet. "Let's see how you fit."

Rebecca clutched the helmet with its lime green and deep blue stripes like a child would a teddy, undecided of its purpose but not about to relinquish it. Until she heard Dohlmani ask the Allard owner which engine was in the car.

She swung the helmet up and onto her head, flipped down the full-face visor. As it settled, the padded edging caught on the gauze bandage and ripped it half off her neck.

The driver yanked the bandage off the rest of the way.

"Nasty cut. I've antibiotic cream if you fancy some. I'll fetch it after. Now in you go."

Rebecca could feel Dohlmani's eyes on her. Or perhaps on the wound he'd bandaged so adeptly the night before. Had he overheard the reference to her cut, witnessed his handiwork undone? She fought the urge to run. It would make her attendance at the car show seem suspicious, not coincidental.

The friendly race driver held her arm while she braced herself on the roll bar and stepped over the scooped-out threshold. She lowered herself onto the driver's side of the flat bench seat. Smaller than the MG, the Lotus could have held two in a pinch, but it had been stripped for racing. Her companion was a tubular roll bar welded to another one spanning the back. The passenger's side windscreen had been removed and an additional side mirror added. The brushed aluminum body tapered and dipped near the nose. Bicycle fenders curved over narrow tires, leaving the wheel struts exposed to the elements.

Rebecca gripped the steering wheel, played it back and forth, depressed the foot pedals, imagined she could hear the roar of the engine. Speed, the lure of it, was something she understood better than lusting after luxury status symbols.

The driver tapped on her helmet. "Kind of a rush, isn't it? I'm Ian, by the way."

Instead of a hand, he offered her the harness that came over both shoulders and snapped in to the strap between her legs and the lap belt. After she fastened them, Ian flipped up her visor. He leaned close and licked the tip of her nose.

"So, tell me, lass. Who am I saving you from? The dark-eyed Lothario—is he your husband, your lover, or your drug connection?"

Thirty-four

Mick snarled to the answering machine.

"You better be hightailing it over here, Moore. I've got things to do that don't include babysitting a quivering stripper."

He clicked off the cell phone. It was nowhere near as satisfying as slamming down a receiver. Not for the first time Mick bemoaned what was being lost in the mad shuffle toward progress. More and more ways to communicate instantly, less and less satisfying communication going on.

In the kitchen he drained the dregs of the coffeepot into the sink. Stared at the wall phone, willing it to ring. Like most appliances, it refused to cooperate.

He had to get moving. He'd frittered away yesterday on leads that went nowhere. Today, he had to convince the captain to let him back into the loop. That would be best accomplished face-to-face, but he couldn't leave the girl alone. Judging from the condition she was in last night, she'd freak.

Mick strode down the hallway. He paused outside the door to the guest room, leaned against heavy molding with so many coats of paint it had lost all detail. He wished he were walking in to wake Moore, not the girl. More truthfully, he wished he'd rolled over this morning to wake Moore. He'd admitted that to himself the moment she walked in. Barefoot, dressed in a ridiculous Gypsy costume, mascara smeared under her eyes and her hair matted from too many hours under a wig. One good look and he'd wanted to push Serena out into the hallway, wrap his arms around Moore and carry her into his bed. He was through blaming her for David's death as a means of punishing himself. It was time to move on.

She'd moved, all right, but without him. She couldn't get out the place fast enough. Dumped the girl like an abandoned pup on the doorstep and beat feet. Some malarkey about a Phantom and a vintage race. Barely a look around. No curiosity about how he lived. If Serena hadn't been blubbering, Moore wouldn't have stayed ten minutes. She'd lingered just inside the door long enough for the girl to give her version of her dead friend's last day.

Aziz, afraid she was pregnant, had confided in Serena and borrowed money for a taxi ride to the clinic. Serena didn't see her return, but Aziz's purse was upstairs in the room they shared. When Serena couldn't find her friend, she'd gone to LeClerc. The manager had snapped at her, claimed to know nothing. Serena was positive that if Shauna had learned she was pregnant, she would have gone to someone powerful for help. To Mr. LeClerc, or Mr. Dohlmani, or the father of the child. She was very religious. She would have wanted to do the right thing.

Mick had asked if the right thing could have been to end her own life.

Serena's eyes grew moist, she pulled at her finger. Finally she nodded.

"If Shauna's plea for assistance were rejected, she might have killed herself, unable to bear the shame. It is possible. She was a good girl."

Moore had listened as still as a lamppost, biting at her

lower lips, biting back tears. She thanked Mick for taking care of Serena, then was out the door.

The first time Mick had walked into Moore's house, it was in shambles, ripped apart by a maniac hunting for incriminating evidence. Moore had been huddled against the sofa in the arms of her lawyer. It was not a pretty sight. Still, Mick drank it in: the high ceilings and wide multipaned windows that made the house seem light even though the sun was barely up. Floor-to-ceiling bookcases, tapestry reading chair, glass-fronted corner cupboard in the dining room, square white kitchen looking onto flower beds and fields of hay in the distance. He hadn't seen upstairs.

Moore, by contrast, breezed in and out of his place. No glance around, no grimace at the apple green and puce walls, no raised eyebrow at the clutter. *Unbelievable.* Everyone raised eyebrows walking into his condo, if only at the cockatiel spouting fortune cookie Zen from his cage in the corner. An okay conversationalist if you were in the mood.

The condo wasn't Mick's; it belonged to his cousin. He was keeping it warm for a couple of years while cuz was in Tibet trying to find herself, or the Dali Lama, whichever one she stumbled across first. His nearly certifiable cousin, Emily, who collected anything that depicted an animal, vegetable or mineral. Like primitive Oaxacan carvings with detachable tails; a slab of stone from Pompeii embedded with the fossil of an herb, probably marijuana; a tourist headdress made of gull feathers and periwinkle shells; a Mardi Gras mask of a lion with real fur mane. Nature stuff. Cuz wasn't real big on people. She was the walking definition of a true homophobe: disdainful of all homo sapiens.

Privacy was why she'd moved into an end unit facing a cul de sac with little foot traffic. It was fine by Mick. He liked the quiet and the location on the fringes of Georgetown, in a relatively crime-free neighborhood with a whole lot more class than he could ever afford.

No one in the family talked about how Emily had made her money—enough to "retire" in her thirties and wander the world—least of all Mick. He was afraid that if he asked her, she'd tell him the truth. Then he'd have to arrest her and give up the place.

Mick knocked on the guest room door and pushed it open. Serena was lying on her side facing the wall, covers half off, slim body lost in the borrowed plaid shirt. Even in the harsh morning sunlight, the skin on her cheek was as unlined as a babe's. Which is what she almost was, but wouldn't be much longer if someone didn't get her out of that place.

He called her name. Her dark eyelashes flickered at the intrusion.

"Rise and shine, sleeping beauty. If you're coming with me, you've got five minutes."

"Salome?"

"Who? Oh, right, her. Among the missing. I wouldn't wait around if I were you. Come with me, or you're on your own."

The girl bolted from bed.

Mick loaned Serena a pair of Emily's shorts and a mocha T-shirt with an orangutan and the saying "Fashion can be bought. Style you must possess." As they say, the shirt fit. Even dressed like an everyday teen, the girl got an uncomfortable number of stares as she trailed Mick through the precinct. He got the leers. A gazelle following a wildebeest.

Mick deposited her with Sal for safekeeping. "Get her a doughnut. I've got to see the captain." He turned to leave.

"Not so fast, Mick, somebody's looking for you." Sal wagged pink memo sheets in his direction.

"Tell me Moore called."

"Nope. Reporter named Hayes. And before you barge in

on the captain, I should warn you a couple of grim-faced boys in suits just left."

The captain stood staring out the window. He was holding a Schimmelpenninck cigar. More like a cigarillo. Skinny like a long brown pencil. An appropriate accessory for a Cuban gangster in the twenties maybe, but incongruous balanced between Dexter's fleshy lips or clamped between his stubby pink fingers. Dexter used it to gesture Mick into the room.

"Glad you stopped in. Saved me hunting. Close the door."

The captain sat, chewed on the end of the unlit cigar. As he removed the cigar, he ran his tongue over his lips in case he missed some nicotine spit. He placed the cigar lovingly on a wooden tray designed to hold pens. He pressed his hands together, sighed.

He'd just had a cozy chat with a couple of Feds. They were surprisingly forthcoming. And insistent. No one, from any branch of the police, was to nose around Gentlemen Only until further notice. There was an operation in place scheduled to go down tonight and they didn't want the perps spooked. Interference would not be tolerated. Somehow they'd heard Hagan was the interfering type.

Mick sat in the visitor's chair, fished for a toothpick. "These Feds give you specifics about their raid?"

Dexter grunted. "Only clarified what you'd already guessed. Someone at the club is providing female companionship after hours for a fee. And not paying taxes on the income. Go figure. They're using underage girls, who don't speak English. Jail bait entering the country through Canada. Girls are given clean identification when they cross the border, which says they are U.S. citizens and eighteen. Plus, a bus ticket south to Baltimore and a couple of hundred dollars cash. Welcome to the promised land."

"Who's running it?"

"That's where the boys started hemming and hawing. The

only name they could or would give out was LeClerc. The manager handles the young lovelies once they arrive in this country. His brother in Montreal trolls for them on the Internet. Feds say there's a middleman who sets up the dates and handles the finances. The operation's not flashy enough to attract much official attention from the outside. If it wasn't for homeland security and the crackdown on foreigners slipping across our borders, they wouldn't care. Nice, huh? A bunch more girls could have died before red flags started popping up."

The Feds suspected that LeClerc was running the show behind Dohlmani's back, all cash lining his pockets and those of his accomplice. But the big pieces were missing. Like who received the money and where did it go? Who's the john, how much immunity does he have? After three months of monitoring the phones they should have figured it out.

"Reason they're giving Dohlmani a pass is he don't work Friday nights, takes off around five. Phone calls come on most Fridays after he's left. LeClerc grabs the phone. An unidentified patron asks if so-and-so is dancing. LeClerc usually says yes. Later on he tells so-and-so that she's got a date. Get ready."

Mick leaned back, stretched out his legs, grinned at Dexter. "Then the unknown pervert sends a limo to pick up the girl after closing."

"You've heard this before?"

"It's what I came to tell you. You need me on this, Dexter. I've got contacts." He coiled forward. "Moore stumbled on the limo pickup last night after closing. Got the plate number. The limo company's legit and the late-night run to the club is a regular thing. Some unidentified guy calls and sets it up. Cash arrives by courier. A tad unusual, but they're getting paid promptly so the limo company has no reason to complain. Serena confirmed it. She saw Petra leave in the car more than once."

Sitting in his kitchen, sipping warm milk with honey, Serena had told Mick about the mysterious boyfriend, an important man, too important to ever come to the club. One girl would be sent to him when he requested. The same girl would go every time. Until she left. The chosen one was not allowed to speak of him, of what he looked like, of what he did. Karin had disobeyed. She had flaunted the gifts he gave her. Bragged about how much she excited him. Not Martine or Shauna. They cried in the night.

Dexter squeezed his eyes into slits. "Moore saw the limo at the club? What the hell was she doing there after hours?" He grabbed up the cigar. "And this Serena, she's one of the dancers, right? Where'd she tell you this, Hagan? Honest to God, if you went to the club after I ordered you—"

Mick pushed away from the desk and stood in one motion. He mumbled through how the girl had been running away. Moore had rescued her, drove her to spend the night in his condo. He admitted that he'd brought her along to the precinct for safekeeping.

Dexter snapped the cigar in two; a chunk flipped across the room.

"Merciful mother of God, Hagan. The Feds assume Serena is hanging around at the club per usual. She's critical to their operation. She was supposed to go meet the john last night, only Ozzie substituted another girl. You're saying that's because she'd run away. From today's phone traffic, the guy don't want to wait a week. He's pressuring LeClerc to break the pattern, supply Serena tonight. He's demanding that LeClerc escort her himself.

"Hagan, how could you screw this up? It's not even your case. The Feds are chomping, they're in position to take down LeClerc, the go-between and the guy doing the girls. If it goes wrong, they'll harass me from now until retirement. That dancer has to go to the club tonight. She's the key. She's the only one the pervert's willing to pay for. Plus, she's the only one with proof of her real age."

Thirty-five

Rebecca told Ian she was a classic car mechanic trying to elude a customer who owned a Shadow. She'd refused to work on his car; the owner was annoyed. A tiny fib. Ian pretended to buy it. He fed her enough blarney to boost her ego while he tested her mechanical knowledge on the Lotus. The way his eyes twinkled said he was more impressed than he'd expected to be.

Dohlmani had wandered to the far end of the pit lane. He was huddled in an animated discussion with the owner of an Alfa. The car was belching expensive fumes as a crewman fiddled with a carb. Dohlmani's bodyguard posed nearby, rolling his shoulders, looking bored when he wasn't checking out babes lounging on the sidelines.

Opportune time to leave.

Ian urged her to stay and meet Peyton Madison, the owner of the Lotus. He also owned an Arrows, which Ian would drive in the warm-up festivities at the F1 race in Indianapolis in September. Maybe. Ian groaned repeatedly that the car was a piece of shit mechanically but Madison wouldn't listen.

Ian grinned as he took back his helmet. Rebecca could be the answer to his prayers. A sweet thing who could smile her way under the hood, ply her wrench with those delicate wrists and tune it up right in no time.

"Madison's free with his money if not his praise. Could be good for us both, lass."

"Does the job include tickets to the race?"

"Invites to all the festivities and the perks—parties, top-shelf booze, gambling and me."

Rebecca said she'd think about it. He said he'd call.

She did consider it on the half-mile walk from the pit area back to the British car field. Fantasizing about working an F1 race was far less stressful than fretting over dead teenagers or worrying about baring her flesh at the nightclub in a few hours.

She slipped into the MG, tossed Ian's business card into the glove box and exchanged it for the cell phone, which was dead, as she expected. No matter. It was just after ten, she had plenty of time to find a pay phone. Dance lesson first, then she'd pick up Serena. She shouldn't have dumped the girl on Hagan, then fled like a thief. She hadn't known what else to do. Serena whimpered to be protected. Usually, such feminine weakness brought out the best in a man. Look at Paulie—he wanted to tilt at windmills for the dancer. Hagan ought to be willing to level city blocks on her behalf. If anyone could save Serena from the downhill spiral, a police officer seemed the logical choice. Last night Hagan had been handy.

She turned the key in the ignition. For a change the car started without incident so she was not embarrassed among the clutch of true enthusiasts. She returned a few smiles and bumped over the grass toward the exit gate. The guard flagged her out ahead of a black Nissan with a smoked windshield and purple-tinted side windows. She waved her thanks and accelerated onto Military Road.

Growing up, Rebecca had cuddled up to her uncle and embraced his passion for racing. She'd been less in tune with her mother's passion for dance, or rather, her mother's insistence that Rebecca learn to dance. Looking back, she couldn't totally blame her mother. Rebecca had been a bony adolescent with legs that grew fast and weren't always in control. She had the scars from skinned knees to prove it.

Her mother had enrolled her in a string of dance classes beginning at age five with tap lessons. Initially, tap had been an exuberant free-for-all. That ended with the first recital. Swaying in a grass skirt and cellophane leis, sweating under hot lights, she saw the faces of her cringing, expectant parents and froze in sheer terror. The next day, her mother decreed that Rebecca's legs were too undisciplined. What she needed was ballet. It would teach her grace and poise.

What her mother needed was a three-hour respite every Saturday morning from her daughter, which the lessons ensured. While Rebecca endured dictatorial dance masters, Pauline Moore shopped, had her hair done or gossiped over coffee. Until the twins were born. After that she spent those precious hours bonding with her sons without having to deal with the silent criticisms of her too-observant daughter. As she told anyone who'd listen: Rebecca had developed an irritating habit of questioning everything, especially her mother's authority.

Ballet lessons had lasted until her sophomore year of high school, when puberty reared its ugly head. One wintry morning, Rebecca had thrown off her coat and stomped her pink satin toe slippers on the polished floor of the foyer. She refused to waste any more of her life in a musty old hall being screamed at in French by a prune-faced prima donna with a bun. Her father had been shocked; he thought Rebecca liked ballet. Her mother had frosted up faster than the window-panes. She intoned that Rebecca would regret her stubborn-ness, but she couldn't fight them both and swept from the room. Rebecca stared at her father, stunned that she'd won a battle of wills with her mother.

As an adult, Rebecca realized she'd lost the war.

The early dance lessons had given her good posture, a graceful stride and a pastime she genuinely enjoyed—once she no longer had to take lessons. She didn't care whether the music came from a jukebox or an orchestra, whether a man held her in his arms or she line-danced with a gaggle of girls. Hear the music, and she absorbed the rhythm, took it in through her pores like a heady aroma. Turned it to move-ment in every sinew of her body. Dance was her form of es-cape.

Usually.

Her gut told her that tonight was going to be more embar-rassing than exhilarating. A public reminder that she should have listened to her mother and continued the dance lessons.

Crossing Arkansas, Rebecca turned into a 7-Eleven. She snatched her purse before the car had rolled to a halt. The outside pay phone had gone the way of most urban phones—receiver ripped from the cord, missing the phone book. In-side, a clerk with dreadlocks and freckles was shaping her nails with a foot-long emery board. Rebecca asked if they had a phone she could use. The manicurist ignored her, talk-ing over her shoulder to someone named Bernice. Rebecca tried again.

The girl sighed. "We look like we working for mother f'ing AT&T?"

That got a chuckle from Bernice—bent over, back to her,

unloading cartons of cigarettes. She straightened, took in Rebecca's black denim, punk haircut, the circles under her eyes, and the exposed wound on the neck. Shook her head.

"Get it for her, sugar. It's behind them boxes what say napkins."

Miss Dreadlocks pocketed the emery board. She produced a beige push-button phone wired into a plug near the floor. She shoved it across the counter.

The older woman waddled over. "You looking for a shelter, we got that number. Battered women. Family assistance. We knows those numbers by heart."

Rebecca thanked her, said she was looking for an acquaintance who used to work in the area. "Patty Jenks, teaches dance, did an act at the Four Aces?"

"Why didn't you say so, girl? You about standing in her second office."

Bernice sashayed from behind the counter, pulled Rebecca outside by her elbow. She pointed to the alley between the parking lot and a soot-covered industrial building.

Rebecca only half heard her directions. A movement to her left grabbed her attention. A man was leaning over the door ledge of the MG, rummaging in the open glove box. Rebecca yelled "Hey" and ran toward the car.

Bernice swung around after her and let loose with a string of urban epithets. The man jerked upright, scowling. He was thin with a dark complexion, sunglasses and a white dress shirt. He clutched a crumpled scrap of paper in his right hand.

He bolted down the street, disappeared at the first corner.

Rebecca dismissed giving chase. He was too young and too agile to catch. Besides, what was there in her car worth stealing? She had her purse and cell phone with her. The radio was original, but hadn't worked in twenty years. It was still there. She peered into the glove box, shuffled through the papers. Registration, owner's manual sans cover, crumpled gas and fast food receipts. What could be missing?

Bernice plunked her hands on her hips. "Damn druggies. He get anything you value, girlfriend?" Rebecca said no. Bernice kept on. "What you think he took?"

Rebecca shrugged. Maybe nothing. Whatever the fleeing man was clutching might not have come from the glove box. Maybe he was checking her VIN number against one on a car he'd been sent to steal or repossess. It was that kind of neighborhood.

But the young man hadn't looked like a repo specialist. He looked like the younger man who had accompanied Sergio Dohlmani to the Grand Prix.

Bernice finished her diatribe against urban punks and repeated her directions to the dance studio. Rebecca asked if there was anywhere to park nearby.

"You mean safer than here? Hell, no. Just the alley. Won't be no tires when you come back. Leave the bug where it's at. I watch it much as I can."

Bernice sashayed back into the 7-Eleven ahead of a pack of boys from the hood in jailin' attire moving to the beat from a box like a ten-legged octopus floating through the deep.

Rebecca clutched her purse under her arm, jogged down the alley. She glanced over her shoulder more than once while struggling to recall anything that had been in the car that was worth stealing. She sincerely hoped that the perpetrator was some hophead, not Dohlmani's errand boy who had followed her from the race grounds. But she didn't believe it.

She looked both ways in the deserted alley before entering the fire door someone had wedged open with a brick.

According to Bernice, Patty's studio was on the third floor. The industrial warehouse looked like it had been built in the twenties. Its open spaces had been converted recently into smaller offices. Most were empty, if the hushed hallways were any indication. Rebecca climbed the stairs in preference to trusting the elevator. They were ill-lit. Twin odors of urine and perspiration cut through the scent of pine cleaner. The metal railing was clammy, in need of paint. No graceful wide wooden steps with a polished banister. Still, she experienced the same feeling in her gut as she had as a girl, climbing alone to face her dance teacher: anticipation laced with dread.

Not that Patty Jenks reminded Rebecca of any of her past instructors. None of them had been built anything like her. Five-nine, chest a forty DD and hips skinnier than Juanita's—everything from her walk to her teased hair and glued-on lashes—proclaimed Patty a stripper. And proud of it.

The two had met when Rebecca had been freelancing, submitting Sunday supplement articles to any paper that would pay. She'd done a piece on the gentrification of stripping. An ancient art inching its way toward respectability as bored housewives and professionals took it up as a form of exercise. Or therapy, getting in touch with their feminine sexuality in a look-but-don't-touch setting.

While Rebecca had marginal respect for the yuppies in search of safe fantasies, she did respect Patty. There was nothing fake about her. She was an uneducated hooker from Galveston, Texas, who'd followed the wrong man to Washington. Gave up on politicians, men in general and on hooking—after her second miscarriage. Started working out to get her figure to where she wasn't too ashamed of it and began stripping.

She'd confided in Rebecca that one night on stage she figured out it was what God intended for her. Had to be, 'cause she was real good at it. Felt almost spiritual when she was into her routine. So she decided to thank Him by helping other directionless girls choose getting naked over getting laid.

Thirty-six

Mick slammed the door exiting the captain's office. Being chewed out twice in one week was as tiresome as it was irritating. He was major-league ripped at being warned away from the club. Admittedly, Dexter's order made sense from a procedural standpoint. The Feds were still within their rights to threaten to shoot some Rambo cop jeopardizing an operation. He could take it. He might deserve it, but Moore and the little dancer didn't. They were civilians. They should not be allowed near the place when an undercover operation was about to break. Prime opportunity for innocent lives to get in the way of stray bullets. Moore attracted enough trouble on her own without the police setting her up. Where the hell was she, anyway?

He stormed out of the precinct wondering if Schneider or Llewellyn had been warned off as well. They had a legitimate and presumably unrelated reason to be nosing around the club. Feds might have given them a pass. Since he couldn't locate Moore, maybe he should go visit Schneider. See what he was up to on this fine Saturday. Offer to give him a hand with the case.

Schneider wasn't up to anything, at least nothing at District Six.

"Gone fishing," said the sergeant without looking up from typing her report.

Mick shoved his badge under her nose. "Lieutenant Schneider has the day off?"

C. Saunders looked up. She had slanted hazel eyes and one freckle almost dead center on her nose. "Gone fishing." Mick smiled. Saunders smiled back. "That's what he does on time off. You sure you're a detective?"

Mick nodded: a detective assisting Schneider on the dancing girl murder.

Saunders leered. "Lucky you. All the guys around here want to get their hands on the stripper case, if you catch my drift. If anyone but Schneider was working it, it would take six, maybe eight months of nightly investigations before they even thought about closing it out. Even if they never came up with a suspect."

Mick hoisted his thigh up on her desk, shoving the keyboard aside. "What's different about Schneider?"

"Different?"

Mick raised an eyebrow. "You said if anyone but Schneider was working it. What's different about Schneider heading up the case?"

Saunders rocked in her chair, backpedaled. "Schneider's okay. Just too many years working Vice, I guess. He's real sour on the fairer sex, at least those who make a living with their bodies." She swiveled closer. "My first day on the job, this tall knockout comes. Wants to see Schneider about her sister's death.

"I ask where and when did it happen? She says it's an old case, from the First, but they told her Schneider had been in charge before he moved over. I'm trying to put her off, save him the hassle, when the lieutenant walks in. He talks to her right in front of my desk. He can barely contain himself. Goes through the motions—case closed, nothing new or they would have been in touch, writes down her phone number. Gives her the get-on-with-your-life speech. Then shoos her out. Comes back in muttering, 'Sister was a fucking whore. What does she expect to happen?' Pitches her phone number in the wastebasket."

"Guess Schneider skipped the sensitivity training sessions."

Mick unwrapped a toothpick. Saunders shouldn't be telling tales on fellow officers. He probably should reprimand her. Instead he bent forward, gazed past the freckle into her eyes. "I heard the reason he transferred from the First had something to do with a hooker? He roughed one up pretty bad, as I remember."

Saunders straightened the papers on her desk and eyed Mick. She shook her head. She hadn't heard that Schneider'd done anything like that. Just that he'd burned out. Guys said his last investigation had gotten to him. A young mother had claimed that some ambassadorial type was raping her fourteen-year-old daughter. Before Schneider could investigate, the mother was murdered. That sent the girl over the deep end, total lunatic. Schneider didn't talk about it, but Saunders could see how something like that would mess you up bad.

"Remember the mother's name?"

"Nope. Don't think I ever heard it."

Mick slid off the desk, squared up her keyboard.

"Case like that could drive a man to drink. Or go fishing. You happen to know where Schneider drops his line?"

Thirty-seven

"Foreign sounding how? British? Eastern European? Asian?"

Jo reached for his pen. It eluded his fingers and rolled off the desk. When he leaned down to retrieve it he glimpsed Mrs. Wetherly's distinctive car pulling in to the curb in front of his office. *Damn.* He had to get off the phone.

Peter Hayes was still mulling over the question. "Middle Eastern? Very faint. Bullied the operator to be connected to Rebecca Moore. Refused to believe that she no longer worked for the *Post.* The operator passed him along to me to convince him."

"Did you convince him?"

"Probably not. When he asked if she was still a reporter, I muttered something flip about once one, always one. Guy sounded unimaginative enough to take it at face value."

After hanging up with the unidentified Arab, Hayes worried that there was a connection between the call and Becca's questions about Gentlemen Only. He figured he'd better warn her that someone was nosing around, but couldn't reach her. No answer at home. Not at the shop. Cell phone was off. Could Jo get a message to Rebecca, have her call him?

Jo agreed to relay the message. He tried to hang up.

Hayes stalled him. "Tell her that Dohlmani's party boat is moored somewhere in Virginia. The stringer can't remember which harbors it stops at. She caught it at the last pickup on the Maryland shore. She remembers it was a nice boat. But she had to wait for it at a creepy deserted ruin called Marshall Hall."

The instant Jo hung up, there was a knock on the outer door.

Had he turned on lights in Edna's area? He didn't think so, it had been bright outside when he arrived. His plan had been to research legal precedents for paternity testing, then take Rebecca to lunch. Unable to find her, he'd been filling time.

Now he was caught.

Jo slid a loose file into the drawer and locked the desk. He rationalized that since it was Saturday, no client should expect to find him at the office, nor be disappointed if he weren't. He slipped out the back door. He was not proud of evading Mrs. Wetherly. He simply was too frustrated to deal with her.

Rebecca was being stubborn about producing her birth certificate, which was surprising. Wetherly was being equally stubborn on the matter of DNA. She'd convinced Zimmer to aid her in obtaining a sample; how, Jo couldn't begin to fathom. If Rebecca squawked—as he assumed she would—Jo would fight it in court, though the whole debacle went against his sense of logic. If Rebecca simply would prove she was not related to Dorothea Wetherly, then the old woman would go away.

As would Zimmer. The sheriff had phoned Jo's office twice today. He threatened to have Deputy Olsen stake out the shop, waiting for Rebecca's return. You would have thought she was a felon on the lam instead of merely among the missing.

It didn't bother Jo that she wasn't answering her cell phone. To Rebecca, a phone was a tool of convenience. She would turn it on when she needed to make a call, oblivious of the fact that someone might be wanting to reach her at some other time. Infuriating, but not cause for worry.

What did worry Jo was Rebecca's spending the entire day in DC. She had not done that since taking over Walt's business. Once Rebecca had moved south, she'd cut herself off from her coworkers on the paper. True, the murders of Graham and Vera Stuck had forced her to reestablish some of those ties. So, perhaps Rebecca was in Washington rekindling old acquaintances.

He should be pleased that she was mending the bridges to her past.

Perhaps he would have been—if Michael Hagan wasn't in the picture.

And living in DC.

Jo took the long way around. Out of sight of his office, he slipped down the bank of the stream. He followed it away from Main Street, scrambled up to higher ground around the bend near the ruins of the mill. He wove a path through the vine-riddled woods, crossed the field behind Rebecca's house, entered the clump of fir trees shielding the rear of the shop. He stood in the shadows, invisible from the road.

There had been no sign of Rebecca at her house; he hadn't expected her to be there. The business looked more promising. Lights were on in the machine area. Jo could hear voices. Was it possible that Rebecca had returned, was ignoring her phone messages and going about her business as she often did on Saturdays?

He approached the back door. The knob turned beneath his grip. A frisson rippled up his neck as he recalled standing outside the shop the night Rebecca had been abducted by a deranged killer. Then, too, he had paused in the dark, willing her to be inside working, unharmed. Then, too, the door had been unlocked when it shouldn't have been. The shop had been empty except for the cacophony of running machinery and Rebecca's blood-soaked shirt.

Jo pushed his glasses higher on his nose and entered. He crossed to the double fire doors leading into the machine area. Through the gap he saw Frank Lewes hunched over a workbench worrying something with a small screwdriver. The voices he'd heard were coming from the radio tuned to a NPR marathon of *Car Talk*. Frank muttered "Idiot" as Jo approached, presumably annoyed with the current caller. He flinched when Jo said hello. Then reached up and turned down the volume.

"You looking for Reb, you get at the end of the line. I been taking messages all day."

"She hasn't called?"

"Did once before nine. Said she had errands to run in the city. Going to that damn club tonight. She's supposed to come pick me up. Look at the time. She doesn't get here soon, won't be able to turn around and drive back."

"Who called?"

"Who didn't? Customer at the Grand Prix called to thank her, got his picture taken with some politician and is proud, as if it meant something. Zimmer's looking for her. Says she's to call him ASAP. Then that reporter fellow called when I was at lunch, left a message. And Hagan called twice. He didn't leave no message."

"Hagan called for Rebecca?"

"Yeah. That's the only ray of sunshine. At least she isn't hanging out with him."

Thirty-eight

The halter top and tap pants revealed that Patty Jenks was just as voluptuous as Rebecca remembered. Her posture and the look in her eye elevated her from barroom floozie to no-body's fool. Standing just inside the bare room, Patty listened to why Rebecca had searched her out. She nodded in understanding. She invited Rebecca in.

Since she'd gone into a taxable business, Patty was firm about getting paid for what she did. No freebies. You pay her, she pays her taxes. Someone who needs help maybe gets it.

But this was a special case. Patty felt for the dead dancers in a way Rebecca never could. She'd danced in their shoes, faced their desperation, been tempted by the same evils, beaten by the same assholes. She'd gotten out; the dead ones never would. She suggested a compromise, a two-hour lesson for the price of one and a coupon for a free session Rebecca could pass along to some girl on the street. Rebecca agreed.

Patty crossed to a tall window embedded with wire mesh and coated with grime. She talked over her shoulder as she went. "Could be the murders have nothing to do with the guy who's getting them pregnant. I've known gals would knife a girlfriend over a used Wonder bra. Low self-esteem doesn't do much for self-control."

She fiddled with buttons on the boom box sitting on the window ledge. Slow, sultry jazz with a lot of bass took over the room. She turned to face Rebecca.

"Strip."

Rebecca blanched. "Just like that?"

Patty pointed. "There's a pole. Use the room. You want a chair, there's one against the wall. Show me what you've got."

"But—"

"Butt's what you wiggle, honey. Show me yours."

Rebecca's initial attempt at stripping leapt ahead of her first gang shower on her list of most embarrassing public humiliations. She wasn't ashamed of her body, exactly. She was just uncomfortable about flaunting it. Reticence, ingrained in her by generations of stern-faced Puritan ancestors, was harder to shake than her posterior. In a candlelit bedroom with the man of the moment, okay, she could be suitably provocative. In daylight, in the cavern of an empty room being judged by a sexy professional . . .

Mercifully, Patty stopped the music after two of the longest minutes of Rebecca's life. She was down to her bra, panties and red splotches of humiliation flushing her chest. Patty's only comment was that at least Rebecca could move to the beat.

Patty returned to the window wall. She bent to paw through a wooden toy chest crammed with gaudy outfits no bigger than a pair of socks. She selected a burgundy G-string and bra that would barely cover Rebecca's endowments, told her to put it on. Rebecca looked around for a dressing room.

Patty hooted.

"You've got nothing I don't have, girl. Nothing nobody at that club hasn't seen, pawed and soiled a million times. What you've got to have is attitude. When you strut your stuff, you're selling what's inside you. They can't touch that. Control it and you control them. And their fantasies. They'll love you for it and come begging for more."

She handed Rebecca a pair of spike heels shedding glitter.

So began Patty's lesson on the Zen of stripping. Rebecca wasn't convinced that she could ever feel isolated from a roomful of gawking men, but each time Patty coached her through the moves, she got closer to losing herself. The music carried her so far, then Patty's voice kicked in.

"This is about you, not them. You are the sensual beauty in all women. You are the wisdom of the mothers. The innocence of the daughters. The timeless mystery men can never fathom."

Patty circled Rebecca as she spoke, hypnotizing her with a soothing chant. When Rebecca moved to the center pole, Patty's voice floated over her shoulder, electrifying Rebecca's movements against the cold metal. She knew her pelvic thrusts were becoming more provocative, more erotic. She was able to slide her hands over her body without blushing, skim the swell of her breasts, the hollows of her hip bones, glide from cheeks to thighs. The freedom of not holding back was its own turn-on.

The two-hour lesson stretched into three. By two-thirty Rebecca was glistening with sweat, grinning like a Cheshire cat and feeling more relaxed than she'd been in a year. While she pulled on her jeans, Patty prepared a CD with some of the music she'd practiced to and a few more numbers that suited Rebecca's style—for the encores. She supplied a flesh-colored patch to put over the wound on Rebecca's neck and loaded her up with four costumes to try. She could return them when she came to tell Patty how the debut went. She reminded her to shave her bikini line. And not to use talc, since sweat makes it streak and blob.

* * *

Rebecca strutted down the alley to the 7-Eleven. She clutched the plastic shoe bag holding the costumes and wondered if she could ever perform like that for a man in private or if the old inhibitions would return as certain as the tide.

She wondered if the man would be Hagan.

Their relationship was as volatile as nitroglycerine in the back of a pickup truck. Knowing that Mick was equally confused about it was only a minor consolation. Seeing him again made her want to work it out, one way or the other. Last night, she'd sensed that he wanted her to stay. Why hadn't she? If he'd come out and asked her, would she have spent the night? Why had she dumped Serena and run? Why hadn't he asked her?

Rebecca shelved the questions and returned to the thrill of stripping. To some men, witnessing the routine up close and personal might be intimidating. As Patty had said, public stripping wasn't about them at all. They're hungry little boys with faces pressed against the window of the candy store, bellies aching. If you withhold the treats, they starve. Rebecca couldn't wait to share that bit of philosophy with Jo.

Jo. Shit.

She'd promised him she would call Mrs. Bellotti about her birth certificate. She hadn't. For no good reason. It was senseless not to. She could still see the forlorn look on Serena's face—frightened, alone and nowhere to go. Dependent upon strangers. Rebecca slowed as she approached the 7-eleven. At least she had family who cared about her and held on to mementos like her birth record.

The sports car was still in front of the convenience store. All four tires were still holding air. Rebecca stuffed the bag of costumes behind the seat and went in to offer Bernice the coupon for a free lesson with Patty. Bernice shook her head.

"Sweetheart, where you think I learned this attitude? That

woman's better than Preacher Johnson at making you feel good about yourself."

Rebecca bought a bottle of water, a Granny Smith apple and a twenty-minute phone card. Bernice placed the phone on the counter. Rebecca slid it closer. She dialed her parents' home. Mrs. Bellotti answered. She shrieked with delight, thrilled to hear from her little Rebecca. She was so bored with the folks away. What was her angel doing to stay busy?

The question was genuine. Mrs. B always wanted to hear everything, every detail: what was done or said, how Becca felt, how she responded. The housekeeper thrived on gossip and lived vicariously. She wasn't just being nosy. She cared.

Standing in the cluttered convenience store, watching Bernice pretend not to listen, Rebecca admitted to herself—perhaps for the first time—that while she was growing up, Mrs. Bellotti had been her only confidante in the house on State Street. Rebecca hadn't told her everything, but when she needed to talk, she shared her secrets with the squat woman who dressed in black and smelled of garlic and incense.

At the time, Rebecca hadn't questioned it. Few of her adolescent friends had opened up to their parents, either, though most parents tried to make them. Hers didn't. There were no afternoon sessions over milk and cookies where she talked about school friends and classes. As long as she was polite and on time for dinner, Robert and Pauline were content with her behavior. Not having to trouble with her, they could concentrate on the obstreperous twins. Her parents had relegated their daughter's emotional upbringing to the housekeeper, along with folding the laundry and taking out the trash.

Rebecca winked away an unexpected tear and turned her back on the curious Bernice.

"Trash" was what Mrs. B would have called her if she knew that Rebecca had spent the afternoon learning to strip because she was performing at a shady nightclub where young dancers kept turning up dead. She avoided the discussion by complaining that she couldn't chat, she was using someone else's phone. She asked Mrs. Bellotti to find her birth certificate and fax it to her lawyer. She fibbed, claiming that she'd misplaced her passport and needed to apply for a new one. The white lie led to a grilling about where and when Rebecca might be traveling, which evolved into a lament about how Mrs. Bellotti had never returned to the land of her birth, not in all the years she'd worked for Becca's parents.

Rebecca refrained from commenting. There had been many days she would have sacrificed her babysitting money to send Mrs. B back to Sicily—permanently. Today, she hated herself for ever having resented the housekeeper's well-intentioned meddling. She hung up feeling melancholic but virtuous. In a few minutes Jo would have a copy of her birth certificate for the misguided Mrs. Wetherly. One crisis dealt with.

She settled in the MG, opened the water and took a long swallow. Next crisis on the list: retrieve Serena. What had Hagan done with the girl all day—taken her to the National zoo? She couldn't imagine Hagan cooped up inside his condo with the sultry Serena. Or rather, she could. But if that were the case, she didn't want to know the details.

She bit into the apple. Juice trickled down her chin. Reaching into the cubby for a napkin, she wondered again what the intruder had been searching for. She pawed through the contents, idly looking for Hagan's business card that she'd misplaced. Ian's was still there. So, what wasn't? Something small and white. Something—

Damn. Something she didn't use anymore and had forgotten about. Something like her *Post* press pass. Credentials she should have turned in during her exit interview. The head of Human Resources had forgotten to ask. Perversely, Rebecca refused to relinquish it voluntarily. She didn't carry it. She'd left it in the car as a nostalgic irritant.

She searched again. The press pass wasn't there.

Maybe the searcher had been a punk after all and he'd snatched the press pass hoping he could use it to talk his way backstage at rock concerts.

She wouldn't bet on it.

Instead she'd put money that Dohlmani had recognized her at the Grand Prix. He'd followed her to the pit lane, watched her try to avoid him. Her evasive behavior made him curious, so he sent the young man in the white shirt to wait for her. Tasked him to follow her when she left the race grounds, to find out who she was when she wasn't Salome, the cocktail waitress.

Leaving the race grounds, Rebecca had been too busy looking for a pay phone to glance in the rearview mirror. She looked now. She scanned the sidewalks, the alley and nearby parked cars. She was suddenly anxious to get moving.

She tossed the apple onto the passenger seat. Started the car, exited the lot heading south.

She debated between going to Hagan's apartment or his precinct. She wasn't sure she could find his place coming from this direction, in the daylight. Besides, he wasn't likely to be there. The police station would be a safer bet and it would be listed in her atlas. She checked the map at the first stoplight. District Two was located at 3320 Idaho, NW. Not far at all.

Waiting for the green, she drummed her fingers on the steering wheel. How would Dohlmani react if he suspected, erroneously, that she was a newspaper reporter? Logically, he'd assume that she'd infiltrated the club hoping to investigate the murder of his dancer. After all, she'd shown up the day after the girl was found. Who wouldn't make the connection? Would he fire her? Probably.

Even if she convinced him that she'd been sacked by the *Post* and was working for tips to make the rent, Dohlmani wouldn't want her nosing around. That wouldn't mean he was guilty of anything, just protecting his privacy.

When she stopped at the next light, the MG sputtered. *Had to be the ignition.* She blipped the throttle, adjusted the rearview mirror for a better look at the cars behind her. The stingy mirror was missing much of its silver backing, but it showed one headlamp of a black Nissan peeking around the side of a minivan. The car's windshield was tinted, almost purple. It looked familiar. She'd seen it before—waiting when she exited the main gate of the Grand Prix.

Four blocks and three unnecessary turns later, the black car was still behind her.

She almost lost it on a left-hand turn with help from a rap-loving teen who pulled out from the curb without signaling or looking. After slamming on the brakes and making the requisite hand gestures out the window, the driver of the Nissan had whipped around the offending youngster and sped to catch up.

Rebecca wasn't being paranoid. She was being followed, tailed by someone she was convinced was Dohlmani's henchman.

Why was he after her?

He already had proof of her name and apparent occupation from the stolen press pass, and could have copied her current address from the MG's registration. Why chase her? What more could he want?

She checked the mirror again.

Her follower had tired of being cautious. Horn blaring, he forced a battered camper-topped pickup to ease over and let him by. The Nissan closed to directly behind her. He was riding her bumper.

Through the smoked windscreen Rebecca could see two heads above white collars. Not good. If they forced her to stop, she'd be outnumbered. One man she might be able to sweet-talk. Two wouldn't be inclined to listen.

Time to lose them.

She downshifted into third, tromped on the accelerator as she yanked the wheel hard to the right. The light car skidded down a side street lined with trash cans. The apple bounced off the seat.

Maybe it was the adrenaline pulsing through her veins into the steering wheel, zipping on through the drive train, but the MG seemed to perk up and decide to run. Rebecca leaned back, willed her shoulders to go loose, hands to rest lightly on the wheel. She accelerated through the gears. Breathed, full breaths in through her nose, out through her mouth. Eyes on the road ahead.

She steered around a truck backing from an alley.

Narrowly missed a teenage mother pushing a wobbling baby carriage out from between parked cars.

Clipped a trash can and set it spinning into the street.

She risked a glance behind her.

The Nissan braked to miss the mother, child and garbage can. The rear end broke loose, smacked into a parked car. They traded paint. The Nissan bounced off and kept coming.

Three right turns later Rebecca sped out onto Sixteenth Street, ignoring the stop sign and honking traffic. What was Painter's Rule of the Road? "Two wrongs don't make a right, but three rights make a left." She was now heading north.

Ahead the light turned red. A white hair in a Volvo slowed half a block back from the intersection. Rebecca thumped her hand on the wheel. *Move, you idiot.*

She feinted left, faced a steady flow of oncoming traffic— no room for three lanes. On the right was a deserted sidewalk. She gave it gas and steered the small car up the handicapped ramp and onto the walkway. Perfect fit.

Until someone pushed open the door to a bistro.

Rebecca squeezed left, scraped the length of the MG along a lamp post and upended a stone planter of red geraniums and purple petunias. The beautification committee would be pissed, but the Nissan was trapped four cars back.

Rebecca bounced the MG off the curb at the light and slid right. Down a short block she took another right, hoping to circle around behind the Nissan, then sprint in the opposite direction. She was giddy with the thrill of the chase; empowered by her session with Patty; amazed at the MG's handling and—and totally screwed.

Twelve feet ahead a trash truck filled the alley. Incessant beeping ricocheted off the cinder-block buildings as the truck backed into position and slid the forks into the handles of the two-yard Dumpster. Rebecca downshifted hard into second, letting the engine brake the car. The MG fishtailed on the street litter but managed to stop before hitting the truck. It swerved parallel to it, sideways across the alley.

Her heart pounded. Adrenaline raced through her limbs.

The driver engaged the hydraulic lifts. The arms began to hoist the trash container into the air over the bed of the truck.

Rebecca slammed the car into reverse. Backing to straighten it, she saw the Nissan go past the alley. Heard the squeal of tires as the driver hit the brakes and reversed direction.

She shifted into first, aimed the car at the Dumpster and revved the engine.

The container lid clanged open, spilling its load into the back of the truck. Empty, it started back down.

The operator noticed her waiting. Wagged his arm out the window in a cool-your-jets motion.

In the rearview mirror Rebecca watched the Nissan career into the alley, race straight for her.

She counted to five.

With the can hovering four feet in the air, Rebecca gunned the MG and scooted under it.

As she skidded around the next corner, she heard the crash.

She hoped they'd ducked.

Thirty-nine

Frank returned to tinkering with the rear coupling on a train car smaller than his hand. He grumbled that if his boss didn't care enough about her friends to show up when she promised, guess she didn't need them looking after her. Jo squeezed Frank's shoulder. Frank had been the first to dare Rebecca to go undercover, but Jo had not worked hard enough to discourage the folly.

Jo slipped out the back door, circled the shop to come out on Main Street, opposite the village grocery. Its bold black-and-white sign said simply "Deli & Market." It was much more. Just as his harlequin storyteller was more complex than it appeared. Two masks, one black, one white, facing in opposite directions. He'd bought it as a young man when he was in great need of clarity. The longer he studied it, the more the faces blurred into shades of gray.

But that was typical. Jo was good at seeing conflicting sides of an issue, bad at separating them. He couldn't decide if he had become a lawyer because he could debate opposing views with equal conviction, or had developed the skill gradually as he practiced law. While useful in court, it complicated life. Take Mrs. Wetherly's case. Viewed one way, she was an obstinate fool on a quest that would disappoint and maybe destroy her. On the flip side, she was a tenacious optimist searching for a hint of salvation. Or perhaps she was a little of both. Even though he was avoiding her, Jo admired the older woman's willingness to wrestle her demons. He shared her desire to go back and right the past.

Or did he?

Jo had never returned to Jamaica. Not since he'd lost his first murder trial.

He'd once been the island success story. He'd gone to Stanford University on scholarship, graduated from the law school. Then returned home to practice. Neighbors whispered that he'd gone all superior, looking down his nose on them whose lives consisted of fishing, rum and too many children. Maybe he had. Proverbs XVI applied to every generation: "Pride goeth before destruction, and a haughty spirit before a fall." Within a month Jo had been thrown into a case he should never have accepted—the brutal murder of the woman he'd loved. Weeks later Jo had lost the case, his home and his homeland.

Inside the deli, Jo selected a chunk of smoked provolone, another of extra-sharp cheddar and a wedge of brie. Half-sour pickles from the barrel, tomatoes, green grapes and a fat loaf of olive bread.

When he left the deli, he would go to the office and call the repair shop, guilt them into loaning him a car if the Saab was not finished. Tonight he needed to be at the club, sipping watered drinks, listening to hackneyed music and watching over Rebecca.

Just thinking of her in that place caused Jo to smile and frown simultaneously. And not pay attention. He wandered into traffic.

A heavy blue car slowed to a stop inches from his thigh.

Before the driver exited the car, Jo knew it it was M. L. Talmadge. It had to be, since the car was the Rolls-Royce that had brought Mrs. Wetherly to his office. Talmadge nodded, held the door. Jo accepted defeat, greeted Mrs. Wetherly and joined her in the back seat of the Silver Cloud.

She did not return his smile. Her lips were clamped tighter than a Sunday school teacher confronting a miscreant.

"Where is my granddaughter? No one will tell me."

Jo sighed as he removed his glasses.

"I can't help you, but I can be frank with you. Rebecca has involved herself in the unexplained deaths of teenage dancers at a strip club. She has gone undercover to learn what she can about the girls, the owners and potential murderers among the customers. She drove to Washington early this morning. She called Frank before nine. No one has heard from her since."

Mrs. Wetherly squinted at a slender wristwatch. Her frown deepened, a horizontal line appeared between her brows.

"Should I be worried, Mr. Delacroix?"

"I am."

"I see." She considered the back of Talmadge's head. "Do they permit matrons of my years in this club?"

"The only age restrictions, I believe, are for those too young."

"Good. We have nothing more interesting to do tonight, do we, Talmadge?" She sat back against the padded leather and patted Jo's knee.

"Care to ride along, lawyer, for an evening of sin and excitement? Who knows, before it's over we may need your services."

Forty

Once the Rolls was gliding along the freeway, Jo placed his groceries on the floor. He rested his head against the blue-gray leather and inhaled the pervasive aroma of the hide conditioner worked into the skins. It was not a bad place to be held captive. A most civilized way to travel. As he closed his eyes, Mrs. Wetherly resumed her daughter's tale as if it were a tape she'd paused after their last meeting.

At the news of Nicole's death, Mrs. Wetherly's heart had betrayed her. She'd collapsed and undergone a triple bypass. By the time she was home, Leon had buried their daughter. Several cousins attended, but no attempt was made to reach old school friends. Those few acquaintances in Massachusetts who knew where Nicole's remains had been taken sent flowers or cards. It was a pitiful send-off. Before she'd regained enough strength to berate herself, her husband was diagnosed with prostate cancer. With chemotherapy and radiation, Leon had survived for almost three years.

"I bore you with all this so you'll understand why it took me five years to begin asking questions. By then I was fueled by dual obsessions: a fear of dying, and a fantasy that my granddaughter had survived the storm. I clung to the hope of progeny, fully aware that I was being foolish. What eventually induced me to hire an investigator, though, was a note I found."

She adjusted her body against the armrest and wiggled to face Jo. "It was among a stack of sympathy letters Leon had left for me to read when I recovered. I hadn't looked at them earlier, but I forced myself to before I consigned the carton to the attic.

"The letter was from a man named Walter Moore or Morris—the signature was difficult to decipher. It was a very formal note from a person not comfortable expressing emotions. Yet the words he chose were more evocative of Jamie than any description I'd heard. Pain was evident in every line. The man had cared deeply, more deeply than a casual boating acquaintance or a friend of the family. He hadn't supplied a return address, which made me curious. The postmark was smeared, though I thought it might have been from Massachusetts. It could have been Maryland. On impulse, I placed the letter in a drawer instead of boxing it with the others. There it remained for the next twenty-three years, while I resumed my life."

Mrs. Wetherly coughed. A faint rasp deep in her throat. She asked Talmadge to keep alert for a restaurant. She was feeling peckish.

Jo indicated his purchases and his willingness to share.

Mrs. Wetherly's dimple appeared. "Cancel the restaurant, Talmadge, find us a shady picnic spot instead."

Again, she paused the tape of her quest for a granddaughter. While Talmadge scouted side roads, she rooted through the bags from the deli. She peeled away plastic wrap, sniffed the cheese, prodded the pickles for firmness.

Talmadge found a turnoff at an historic marker. Just a patch of dirt surrounded by scrub pines, but wide enough for the Rolls. They opened the doors, lowered wooden picnic trays fitted into the seat backs and divided the spoils. From the trunk, Talmadge produced a bottle of champagne and three flutes. They had nearly finished the bottle when Mrs. Wetherly picked up the tale.

In 1999, some months after Talmadge had come to work for her, Mrs. Wetherly removed the letter from her dressing table and showed it to him. Reading it for the first time, Talmadge agreed that it sounded as if it had been written by someone related to Jamie, or someone who had cared for him while he was growing up. Someone who might be able to tell Mrs. Wetherly about the young man's character. Or would know if his infant daughter had survived.

"Yes, I was clutching at the straws Talmadge handed me, and using them to whip myself like a flagellant from the Middle Ages. If I had really thought the letter would lead me to my granddaughter, why hadn't I followed the lead thirty years earlier? Why had I needed Talmadge to confirm my suspicions?" She shrugged as if she knew the answer and it wasn't worth the breath to explain it.

At her insistence, Talmadge contacted the investigative firm that had located Nicole in the sixties. He instructed them to search for birth records under the surname of Moore or Morris. The original searches using Nicole's maiden name and Jamie Roberts had failed. As did this one. The youngster who was assigned to the investigation spun his wheels for months and uncovered nothing.

"Two summers ago, out of patience, I decided to put it to rest any way I could. I thought a pilgrimage might help. Talmadge drove me to southern Maine, to the coast near where the bodies had been found. The town is essentially a summer colony with few year-round residents. The only public buildings are the fire station, a general grocery, a kayak and boat rental facility and the post office. No one in the store could help me; they were new owners. They sent me to the post office.

"The one-room building was manned by an elderly woman whose husband rocked on the porch out front. Postmistress Winslow remembered the drowning incident. Said she wouldn't be likely to forget it. Not a lot of excitement around those parts. She knew where the bodies had washed up and sketched us a map of how to find the spot. She'd warned us that we would have to drive onto private property to get close to the water, but said that was okay. Folks who owned the property rented it out. There wasn't anyone staying there at the moment. She complained that it had gone to seed. She remembered when it was a fine place, with nice plants, always spic and span.

"The woman leaned tight against the counter, lowered her voice. 'Of course, that was when the Moores owned it. They sold it off not long after the bodies washed up. Must have spooked them something awful. Else why would they part with that place?' "

Mrs. Wetherly emitted a deep sigh as she relived that day standing in a dusty post office gossiping with a woman who should have retired twenty years earlier.

"Can you imagine how her words struck me, Mr. Delacroix? My heart started pounding as if it would burst. I feared I had misunderstood her. But I had heard correctly. The connection had rolled right off her tongue as if it were common knowledge. Which it was in those parts. The reason no birth record was found in Massachusetts was transparent. As I learned that day, my granddaughter had been born in Maine, not far from where her parents perished. Nicole and Jamie weren't fleeing me for parts unknown. They were sailing home to be harbored by Jamie's relatives."

In a matter of days Talmadge had obtained a photostat of the birth record made out to James Moore and Nicole Marie in Georgetown, Maine. It had been filed by the midwife who delivered a baby girl, Elizabeth, at home in the cottage.

That record confirmed that Nicole and Jamie had been kindred spirits, determined to escape the lives their parents had planned for them. Nicole had dropped her surname, wishing to disassociate herself from her already distant parents. The young man had assumed Roberts as a stage name while he was performing in bands to scrape out a living. Or, perhaps, he'd changed his name so as not to embarrass his conservative family. Or to prevent them from finding him. With the birth of his child, however, he'd owned up to his family name.

Through the postmistress's records, Mrs. Wetherly located Pauline and Robert Moore, who had owned the cottage at the time of Nicole's drowning. They still lived in Boston on State Street at the same forwarding address they had given thirty-four years earlier.

They were stunned to hear from Mrs. Wetherly, but agreed to see her.

"The husband was at work the day I visited. Pauline spoke with me for some time. She was gracious, gave us tea. She admitted that James had been Robert's brother. The black sheep of the family. They knew he'd fathered a child, but had never seen the baby, nor met the mother before the family was lost at sea. She apologized for not attempting to locate me, but they had known nothing of Nicole's relatives. They wanted to put the tragedy behind them.

"I did not embarrass myself by insisting that the infant called Elizabeth was still alive. I'd met the family and learned a bit about the man my daughter had chosen. I might have approved of him if things had turned out differently. It was painful facing what might have been, but it gave me some peace. That seemed to be the best I could do."

Mrs. Wetherly asked Jo if he was planning to pour the rest

of the champagne before it went flat. He splashed the last inch in her glass. She sipped, smiling like an imp.

"Then, lawyer, Pauline Moore made a kind-hearted mistake. She pointed to a shelf containing several scrapbooks. She generously asked if I'd like a photograph of Nicole and Jamie. It was an offer that she appeared to regret immediately, but she was too well bred to take it back. She hesitated, then rose and fetched a leather-bound album of keepsakes from the early years of their marriage. She located a page with several black-and-white snapshots of her brother-in-law and Nicole and placed the album on my lap.

"Mr. Delacroix, the happiness on my daughter's face was too much to bear. I had never seen that joy. I felt my eyes tearing. My grip loosened on the stiff sheets; several escaped my fingers, flipped forward. To buy time to regain my composure, I glanced down at the newly revealed page. I expected to see vacation shots of places unknown, family parties of people I wouldn't recognize."

She shook her head. Years later she still couldn't believe what she'd seen.

"The page held snapshots of a toddler. In one she was riding a tricycle, hunched over like a racer, large light eyes staring straight into the camera. She was grinning, her full bottom lip pursed forward. There was a Band-Aid on her knee. My heart stopped. I started to choke. I shut the album, begged Mrs. Moore for a glass of water. When she left to fetch it, I did something reprehensible. I stole that photograph, slipped it into my purse. By the time Pauline returned, I was examining likenesses of Nicole and Jamie, trying to decide between two. I made my selection, which she removed from the album. Talmadge and I left the house on State Street almost immediately."

She tapped on the back of the front seat. "Talmadge, hand me the notebook."

Talmadge passed back a cloth-covered journal, perhaps four by six inches. Every page was covered with well-formed script. Occasionally, a loose sheet had been slipped between the pages. Mrs. Wetherly struggled with stiff fingers to remove an ivory envelope from next to the back cover. From it she extracted two photographs.

She laid them on the picnic table in front of Jo. She compelled him to look, dared him to argue with her deduction.

How could he?

Though of different vintages, both photographs showed a child on a tricycle: an imp with tangled chin-length hair, knowing eyes thickly lashed. In one picture, the girl had a small mole on her left cheek, just below the bone. Other than that, they could have been of the same child.

Jo turned to Mrs. Wetherly. He pointed to the first picture. "Nicole?"

Mrs. Wetherly smirked. "Of course, my daughter, age five."

She tapped the second photo. "And this one's Rebecca Elizabeth Moore."

Forty-one

"Yeah, Salome? Well I don't care what Dohlmani told you." LeClerc was at his pugilistic best, beating a finger into her chest, centimeters north of her breastbone. "He's not here. I'm in charge. You waitress in the lounge like always. You want to dance for Dohlmani, do it at the party. You got a special invitation to the *Floating D*."

He locked stares with her for a count of twenty.

Party? On a yacht? Rebecca broke away and sashayed toward the dressing room.

He trotted after her. He wrenched her elbow, flung her around to face him. "Don't you ever take one of my girls away again without clearing it with me first. Never."

Inside the tangerine room, Serena was changing into her costume, slowly. Her movements were jerky, her face pale. Rebecca handed her the red shoes Paulie had bought. Serena took them listlessly. She'd said she understood the reasons why she had to return to the club, but she wasn't happy about it. Neither was Rebecca.

* * *

After escaping the Nissan, once her heart rate had returned to normal, Rebecca had crept to the Second District in third gear, scanning for cops while considering her predicament.

Undoubtedly, the garbage truck driver could identify her car as a sports job, maybe even as an MG, but what were the chances he got the license number? Would the police be on the lookout for any woman in the vicinity driving a battered sports car? If they stopped her, could she be charged for leaving the scene of an accident? *What accident?* She'd swear she hadn't witnessed an accident. She was fleeing from a couple of lunatics chasing her for no reason. Frightened, she'd darted through the alley to lose them.

The story sounded reasonable to her, but her lawyer would know best. At the next light, she'd reached for the cell phone to call Jo. Then remembered it was dead.

She hoped the occupants of the Nissan weren't.

If they were conscious, would they give her name to the police? To do so, they'd have to admit they were chasing her, wouldn't they? And come up with an explanation the cops might buy. She didn't think Dohlmani would like them blabbing to officials.

At Connecticut Avenue, she'd considered turning around, driving to Head Tide, letting the whole thing blow over without her. She would have, if not for Serena. Someone had to take care of the girl and by now Hagan must have run out of his limited patience. That might work in her favor. If she took the girl off his hands, he might be willing to put in a good word for her relative to the car chase. At Porter Street she turned left onto Idaho.

Hagan hadn't been at the precinct, but Serena was. She was glued to Sergeant Batisto, pulling on his arm, having hysterics over being forced to return to the club.

The sergeant declined to explain. He'd sent Rebecca to talk with the captain.

Captain Dexter shook her hand with one that reeked of cigar spittle. He told her to sit and scowled like a doctor who'd seen your X rays and didn't want to discuss the large shadow on the left lung. He calmly explained that there was a federal sting in place at Gentlemen Only. He'd only just learned about it. The authorities were requesting that everything appear normal, which meant having Serena in place. She would be needed there only through the weekend. After that, the dancer could go home to her family, to Hollywood, or wherever.

Rebecca pressed him for details.

He shook his head, clamped his lips shut.

Rebecca complained of a sore throat, said she'd better not work tonight. She'd need Serena to nurse her. Dexter threatened charges of obstruction.

Rebecca folded her arms across her chest and told him to go ahead. "Throw me in jail, then I won't have to drive Serena to the club. The girl is terrified, perhaps with good cause. I won't place her in potential danger without knowing more about the situation."

Dexter started to scold her with a long, thin cigar. Then he stood and circled around the desk. Leaning over her shoulder, he aimed for her Achilles tendon—appealed to her journalist's instincts, stressed the critical importance of timing.

Direct hit. Timing was something Rebecca understood. She'd been undercover enough times to know how fragile investigations became as they reached the boiling point. Like a distillate in a centrifuge, gaining momentum, spinning faster and faster. Introduce an unknown substance into the mix, or take one out, you risked it bogging down or disintegrating too soon. She'd seen it happen. It wasn't pretty.

Serena was the unknown in a screwball experiment. Dexter insisted she'd be all right if Rebecca took care of her. Rebecca wasn't so sure, but acquiesced. She would return the girl to the club and watch over her *if*, in return, Dexter would take care of one small traffic infraction.

Rebecca yanked open her locker, threw in her purse, kicked off her shoes. She reached for the Gypsy costume before remembering that she'd ditched it in the washer at home. After two nights, it already smelled of sweat, smoke and spilled drinks and was dabbed with blood. She lifted out Kathleen Hagan's harem outfit.

Rebecca was irked that LeClerc was making her wait tables. After the two hours with Patty, she was pumped, ready to start stripping tonight. Even if it proved embarrassing, it was her best chance to inspect the audience from the dancers' perspective. Search the salivating faces for signs of a murderer.

She shook Patty's costumes from the bag and hung them from the metal hooks in the locker, decorating the interior with risqué bits of cloth. Juliette whimpered from across the room, tiptoed over to investigate.

"Oooh, let Julie see. These are quality, girl. Double stitching. That's important so's the seams don't give." Juliette held a red-fringed number up against her chest. "Where did you get? Tell me, tell me."

Rebecca admitted to taking a refresher lesson with a stripper friend who had loaned her the costumes for tonight's debut.

"Only Ozzie says there's been a change of plans. I'm back on tables."

Lucy sat up from lacing her shoes. "Count your blessings, doll face. Dance pay's no better and the tips come with strings of I-don't-know-what attached. Shoveling drinks, you know it's your feet that are going to be sore in the morning." Lucy straightened her apron and jiggled out of the room.

Rebecca slipped into her heels. "LeClerc says I'm going to

Dohlmani's party later. What's the *Floating D*—a restaurant? Where is it? Are you going?"

"Mr. D's party yacht. You going to his private gala?" Juliette held up inch-long eyelashes dyed purple, judged their effect in the mirror. "He never asked me, but I've heard. You can't not go, girl, but you can say no once you're there."

Too bad. Not going sounded like a fine idea.

Rebecca hesitated only a second before lifting an ivory-colored outfit from the hook. She slipped out of her bra and fastened the satin top around her. The reinforced sides pushed her breasts inward and up, threatening to fall out of the skimpy fabric. She wiggled into the matching G-string.

Juliette turned, ruby nails gluing a fake lash to her eyelid.

"Way you go, girl. Nothing wrong with a silky surprise under your frock. Just don't get carried away. You go to the party, you stay with the other girls. All leave together. And you remember every single, special detail to impress little Julie tomorrow. Promise?"

"Promise."

Rebecca leaned across the bar and stole a maraschino cherry from the stainless steel bin. Vince watched her do it. His eyes lingered too long on her chest. Maybe the stripper's bra was more obvious than she suspected. She smiled to herself, chewed and swallowed the cherry. Held the stem in her mouth.

"Hey Vince, watch this."

Rebecca pushed the stem between her teeth to show him, then sucked it back into her mouth. She pursed her lips and began tying the stem into a knot with her tongue. She hadn't done it in years. Not since graduate school, where she'd perfected the talent, winning scores of drinks off gullible strangers. Tying the knot wasn't the impressive part. She'd met others who could do that. Tying and untying it in fewer than ten seconds was the real trick.

Sort of like being a reporter. To be really good, you had to stay flexible. Be able to leap to the wrong conclusion and back across the chasm in one breath. She hoped she was wrong about the *Floating D* and it was simply a pleasure craft.

She displayed the tied stem for Vince to inspect, then popped it back in her mouth. Next time she slid her tongue forward, she pulled out the straightened stem. The bartender's smile said he'd seen it before. He poured her a ginger ale.

"Quite a talent, Sal." He slid the glass in front of her, lightly touched her arm. "That's not your only one from what I hear."

Rebecca raised her eyebrow.

Vince lowered his voice. "LeClerc gets a call earlier. Makes him madder than a pit bull at a drug bust. He's spitting into the phone. I hear phrases like 'knew the bitch wasn't no dancer,' 'teach her to snoop around here,' 'she'll be out on her skinny ass so fast she'll get nothing.' He'd calmed down to a low boil before he hung up."

Rebecca could guess who'd been on the other end of the phone. Dohlmani's boys must have survived the car crash and handed over her press pass to their boss. She snatched another cherry.

"You think LeClerc was referring to me?"

"That's a fact. You're his 'bitch du jour,' as they say." He topped off her drink from the multiple spigot and replaced the soggy napkin. "You just watch where you're treading in them fancy heels, Salome. I'll cover your back if I can, but I can't be everywhere. Too many of you girls are ending up dead."

Forty-two

Mick drove to his mother's house on autopilot. He navigated the narrow streets half empty of cars. Families away for the weekend or out enjoying Saturday outings. He pulled to the curb, shut down the car and sat with the keys in his hand, lost in thought. Not lost, really. More like bouncing between thoughts, a Ping-Pong ball in a closet.

Quandary number one was Schneider. He'd been the officer in charge of the Sanchez case. A case involving a teenage girl sold to an embassy pervert, and her mother, the stripper, who had her neck broken. It could have been a ball-buster of a case, one that led to nightmares, encouraged an officer to switch departments. One minute you've got solid evidence on a guy, next minute the witness is dead. Case closed.

Did it mean anything in the context of the present investigation? Probably not. That was five years ago. Probably just another coincidence. If he hadn't been nosing around in the past for similar cases, he wouldn't have stumbled on it.

It was a lucky find but it did not excuse his behavior; he should not be checking out a fellow officer. He might think Schneider was a lazy louse, but that could be Mick's lack of perspective. He was too close to some of the players. He had no concrete reason to tail the guy.

But he had.

He'd gone to the marina where Schneider anchored his boat. He'd parked in the lot across the street, taken out his binoculars and located Schneider's slip. The fishing boat was a humble fiberglass number, maybe ten years old, thirty-six feet, with a pilot house and open stern. Antennas proclaimed it ready for foul-weather trips.

Schneider had been on deck, in a stained T-shirt and cut-off jeans. He held a spray bottle of cleaner in one hand, a beer in the other. He halfheartedly attacked mildew on the captain's seat while ogling the cuties in bikinis two boats over. An average slob relaxing on his day off.

Bored with housekeeping, Schneider had set down the bottle of spray and picked up a cell phone. The call didn't last long, but he was fuming by the time he hung up. Even from forty yards Mick could tell that crumpling the beer can and pitching it into the bay hadn't helped.

Mick left before Schneider decided to come ashore for more beer.

Moore was problem number two. From Sal, Mick learned that Moore had resurfaced late afternoon. She'd strolled into the station house to claim Serena. Before she could slip away, the captain had convinced her that Serena had to return to the club. The captain hadn't forced Moore to take the girl. Didn't have to. Of course not. Moore had gone willingly once the captain explained the situation. What natural snoop would pass up the opportunity to get herself in trouble? Trouble that hadn't ended well for at least three dancers.

The police photos still haunted Mick. Shauna's eyes mildly surprised as her life drained away through the slit in her belly. Karin's dark hair drifting through empty sockets, her flesh eaten away by predatory fishes. He couldn't stomach seeing Moore's face in the next set of photos. She'd looked suitably horrified when he'd shown her the pictures. He thought she comprehended the seriousness of the game being played at Gentlemen Only.

Not for the first time, he questioned what drove Moore to walk through fire for others. She was bright enough to recognize the dangers, brave or foolish enough to ignore them. Reckless behavior in the line of duty he understood. It was what he was paid to do. Moore did it for free. He hoped she didn't have a death wish.

The captain had said much the same thing about him, followed by the threat that if he showed his face at the club, he was finished. He could turn in his badge, his gun and find an alternative career that didn't require taking orders.

Mick got out of the Jeep and locked the door, then remembered Hayes. The reporter had called twice. First time, he was looking for Moore. Second time, he'd left a message.

Unfolding the pink memo sheet and flipping open the phone, he dialed Hayes's number. He leaned against the SUV, playing tic-tac-toe in the grit on the fender while he counted rings. Fifteen and still Hayes didn't answer.

Mick checked the memo slip. He'd punched in the right number; guy must have a life after all. He shut down the phone wondering what it felt like to go out on a Saturday night like normal people.

He read Sal's scribbles aloud.

"Tell, Bec—bad time, floating dee, last sat, every mth, stay dry."

Gibberish.

Forty-three

Rebecca's tray clattered on the bar. It was her second screw-up in a row.

"Table twenty-one wanted vodka tonics, not gin. Sorry."

Lambesco shrugged as he whisked away the glasses. He was unflappable. And possibly a nice guy, despite the jail-house tattoos. He'd told her about the phone call that riled LeClerc. He'd offered to protect her. Could he work for the Feds?

He set two fresh drinks on her tray. As she reached for it, he touched her wrist. "You okay?"

"Truthfully? I'm worried about Serena. Have you talked to her lately?"

Vince plunged the dirty glasses into the sink of soapy water. "Not since she came off stage at ten. You check the lounge?"

She had. Serena wasn't there. Nor was she in the rest room. Or backstage. Rebecca had snuck up to check the dormitory. Two large rooms with four beds each, all empty.

Rebecca delivered the drinks to the party of four, gave the change to the accountant type. He pocketed the money without leaving a tip. She turned away.

Lucy was just coming in from a smoke break. Rebecca blocked her way. Lucy stashed her pack of cigarettes and straightened her apron.

"Serena? Yeah, I seen her. She left a while ago with some guy."

Rebecca's pulse quickened. How could Serena have left? Why? The girl was supposed to stick close to her. She grabbed at Lucy's arm. "But she has another set to dance."

"Whatever. Could be she's doing the guy in the lot. Though he didn't look the type, even if she was willing. Pretty sure he's the cop was here a couple of nights ago."

"What cop?"

"One that dragged out that softie that likes shoes. You know the one I mean."

Rebecca nodded. Oh, yes. She knew the customer who had been dragged out. And the cop who'd done it.

She responded to a signal from a table near the wall. Two more Cosmopolitans and a Planter's punch; they were going to feel bad in the morning.

Why would Hagan pull Serena from the club? He knew what was coming down tonight. He'd been warned to stay away. Why would he jeopardize the operation and his tenuous position on the force? Why the hell hadn't he alerted her if the game plan had changed?

LeClerc was waiting for her at the bar. He clamped a hand on her forearm and chewed her out over the botched drink orders. She took his bitching, then shook off his hand.

"You're so on top of things, LeClerc, do you know where Serena went?"

"Yeah. With the cop. I let her. He came to the side door, asked permission to question her again about Antrim. It's a slow night. I did my civic duty."

Rebecca fretted and fumed through two more drink orders, then told Vince she was taking a break. She went to the dressing room, fished out her bag. She sat cross-legged on the floor rummaging in it for Hagan's business card.

Juliette swept through the door. "Will you look at my nails, girl? Two chipped and it's not eleven. Will this night ever end?"

"Fair question, Julie."

Rebecca gave up the hunt. She could probably dial his cell number from memory. "Julie, you have a cell phone I could use? I'll pay."

Juliette blinked, shook her sequined head. "Don't do technology. There's a phone in the hall. Who you calling?"

Rebecca stuffed the paraphernalia back into her purse and mumbled, "My mother. I'm worried about my little girl. She's got a cold." She crammed her bag into the locker.

Juliette's head bobbed. "Knows what you mean. I worry about all little girls, especially Serena."

Rebecca jerked around. "Did you see her leave tonight? You know where she is?"

The performer was at the dressing table, fussing with a bottle of sparkly gold nail polish. She shoved her gym bag out of the way. It gaped open. Something small and silver, which looked suspiciously like a cell phone, was visible inside.

Before Rebecca could question it, Juliette plopped into a chair and continued. "No, and it's got me worried. The Oz says she went off with that cop. Why'd she do that? Oz never lets a girl go off during her evening gig. You know what she's up to?" Juliette blew on a nail, babbled on. "Never liked that cop. He's got a mean streak. You catch my drift?"

Rebecca didn't. Hagan had negative qualities, but he'd never struck her as mean.

Juliette smoothed on more polish.

"Oh, that's right. You wasn't here Wednesday when he came to drag little Paulie away. One cold fish, let me tell you.

Enjoyed roughing him and his friend up. Bet he be a card-carrying sadist."

Now Juliette's description sounded even less like Hagan.

"What did the cop look like?"

"Tall, beefy, hair thinning, going gray. Not somebody you'd want ringing your bell for a date."

Schneider? That made no sense.

Rebecca left Juliette air drying her nails.

Forty-four

"Moore? Hey, what do you know, a five-letter word for a pain in the ass. Thank you for not returning my calls."

Moore whizzed by his sarcasm. She spoke faster than she normally did. "Around ten-fifteen Schneider came to the club and took Serena away. Do you know why? Your Captain Dexter ordered me to keep an eye on the girl until she left with LeClerc. If plans changed, I should have been told."

Mick ditched the crossword puzzle on the floor. "Schneider removed Serena?"

"That's what I said. She's not here, so she's not going to be anybody's bait."

Shit. "Moore, nothing changed that I know of. I'll alert the Feds. We'll find her. Be careful, please. Are you listening? Don't do anything to attract suspicion."

"*Moi?* Oh, brother. Hold on."

Moore must have clamped her hand over the mouthpiece. Mick could make out muffled voices arguing. Something about "fuck" and "date," followed by "hang up."

Then Moore's voice came back, low and placating.

"Thanks, Mom. Gotta go. Getting off work early. Got an

important party. No, not at the club, some fancy boat, the *Floating D*. The manager's taking me. Yeah, right now. The owner himself will be there. This may be my break. Wish me luck."

Mick was cursing when she hung up.

Idling in front of his mother's house, Mick had decided Dexter was one hundred percent correct—he was not good at following orders, and he was too old to start.

He'd locked the car, gone to greet his mother and begged her for dinner-to-go. He'd planted a kiss on her forehead, raced up the stairs two at a time. He came back down with a black chamois shirt that had belonged to his father. Decidedly better for night excursions than the pasty yellow Italian knit he'd bought to impress Moore. On the way out he borrowed black, paint-speckled Nikes from the hall closet.

Thermos of coffee, two ham sandwiches and the surveillance kit he kept in the car—what more could a maverick cop want? *Maverick.* He had always liked the sound of the word. Some stubborn cowboy who refused to brand his cattle but still shot at anyone messing with them. The term was starting to fit him like a kid glove made from a free-range heifer.

He'd driven from Arlington to Gentlemen Only, parked on the sand shoulder of the entrance drive. The scrub vegetation and the bend in the road helped obscure the SUV. He wasn't invisible to cars exiting, but wouldn't be noticed immediately. And, technically speaking, he wasn't on the club's property—though the captain might not be impressed by a quarter-mile distinction. With his infrared binoculars he could watch cars leaving, check out the occupants. Between car sightings he'd struggled with a *New York Times* crossword puzzle and hashed over pieces that didn't fit the investigation.

Then Moore had called.

Her babbling at the end of the conversation had made sense of Hayes's earlier phone message. The *Floating D* was apparently the name of Dohlmani's party boat. The reporter had discovered that it went out the last Saturday of the month—tonight. He was warning Moore to stay dry, which sounded like a fine idea that she was being forced to ignore.

Mick cursed his imagination as it rolled out full-color footage of a white yacht cruising the Potomac on a spring night, everyone on board partying in the main cabin. A faceless man throttles a girl at the stern of the boat and slips her body into the water and nobody sees. He calmly watches her disappear under the foam from the wake. How hard would it be?

Mick pitched tepid coffee out the window and dialed the precinct. He was patched through to the captain.

Dexter couldn't explain Schneider's actions. He'd see what he could find out.

When Dexter called back he was still in the dark. According to his department head, Schneider had the day off. No, he hadn't been warned away from the club because no one expected him to go there. Schneider rarely worked when he wasn't on duty. Maybe he was following up on a loose end? Or taking the girl out for ice cream? Schneider's captain would try to reach him, send a car looking if necessary.

The Feds were less charitable, screaming that Schneider had picked a piss-poor time to start investigating. They wanted him found and fast. And what in blazes was Moore doing going off with LeClerc? LeClerc was supposed to be escorting Serena, falling into the trap they'd so carefully laid. If Moore screwed up the operation, she'd be twisting wrenches in the auto pool of a federal pen.

Mick clicked off while Dexter was delivering one more warning to stay away from the club.

Sure thing, go home, paint shutters, get the update Monday.

Too much was coming unraveled. Instead of delivering Serena as scheduled, the little snit of a manager was dragging Moore to Dohlmani's private party. Why? If the Feds were correct, LeClerc should have been handing Serena over to the pervert tonight. According to the inside man, LeClerc had been sweating bullets over making the arrangements. What had induced him to blow it off?

A bigger threat.

Dohlmani.

Mick didn't swallow Dohlmani's pure and sensitive act the way Moore did. The man was too smarmy, too successful to be holy. Mick sure didn't trust him around Moore. Even if Dohlmani was a saint, after a couple hours trying to talk sense to her in a confined space, any man might be tempted to throttle Moore and toss her overboard.

Mick pounded the steering wheel. Screw the captains, every blasted one of them. He was going in.

He started the ignition and hit the gas. The rear tires spun in the sand. The back end lost grip. He gunned it, countered the skid. The tires caught, pulled the Jeep onto the highway. Mick wrestled the steering wheel to put it straight on the road.

A car approached, exiting the club. The Cherokee was only inches over the center line, but so was the other car. It was black, solid and speeding. Mick swerved to avoid contact—not far enough, not fast enough. The speeder clipped the Jeep's rear fender as it whizzed past.

The wheel was wrenched from Mick's grip. Top heavy, the SUV skidded off the side of the road, onto the soft shoulder. It tipped, landed, lunged across the drainage ditch and smacked into the trunk of a pine tree. The radiator burst, sending billows of steam into the branches of the tree.

Mick snapped back from the steering wheel, clutched at his neck. He grabbed the binoculars from the floor, jumped from the car, scrambled up onto the highway.

The boxy vehicle was disappearing fast.

Mick trained the glasses on it. The license read "Gents." Two occupants. The driver was short, his head barely cleared the headrest. Not Dohlmani. It was LeClerc. Mick didn't recognize the passenger, didn't need to.

He slipped down the embankment and reached into the car. He pulled his gun from the glove box, pocketed his cell phone. Someone in the club had to know about the party boat—where it was docked, where it picked up passengers. They would tell him—bet on it.

He scrambled onto the tarmac, began jogging.

The trees opposite him suddenly lit up as headlights streaked around the curve. Another car was approaching, this time heading toward the club. *Great.* Maybe he could hitch a ride. Mick stopped in the road, turned.

A heavy car careened into view. He raised his arms to flag it down. It was traveling much too fast, listing on two wheels, tires groaning on the pavement. Mick froze in the beams from the headlights, too startled to move, ears deafened by the squeal of rubber as the driver tried to brake.

Forty-five

"Bleeding, fucking idiot." LeClerc had been addled by the close call leaving the club, but he didn't slow down. He hitched forward in the seat, scrutinized the left front fender, looking for dents in the Shadow's paint job. He couldn't tell the extent of the damage without stopping. No time. They had to reach Marshall Hall by eleven. He'd announced that the second before they clipped the SUV.

Rebecca was shocked and relieved to see the Jeep. Hagan had to have been already on his way to the club when she'd phoned him. But why?

Despite his feigned ignorance on the phone, something major must have gone wrong—wrong enough to prompt Hagan to show up against direct orders from at least two law enforcement departments. Unless they'd sent him? If so, it could not be good news. Come to think of it, whenever Hagan showed up—

LeClerc slapped at her elbow. He was pouting.

"So? What, no comment? I said, you should be fucking honored. Dohlmani ain't free with invites to his boat parties. This is my first. You're working, what—three days? You get to come along. 'Course, you're a broad." LeClerc swiveled his head in her direction, fleshy tongue wetting his lips.

His leer made Rebecca squirm. She shifted the hard-wired bra digging into her side. When Dohlmani had told her she'd be dancing for him tonight, she'd foolishly thought he meant on stage. Pity about Patty's lessons going to waste.

LeClerc noted her fidgeting. Joined her, adjusted the seat belt pinching his stomach.

"Sal, I'm psyched to get on board. Check out the players. Eat dinky hors d'oeuvres instead of pork rinds. Smell women who aren't for sale. Sounds grand, doesn't it?"

Just making it to the boat alive sounded grand to Rebecca. If LeClerc didn't keep his eyes on the road, they might not. He couldn't steer and talk at the same time. True, she knew from experience that if they hit anything smaller than a semi, it would come off second best to the Rolls. What was the quip about the Silver Spirit in the early eighties? "So sturdy you could run over a Toyota without spilling a drop of your martini." She really wished she had one—a martini, not a Toyota.

LeClerc was as garrulous as if he'd downed three. He lowered the leather armrest between them, leaned in her direction.

"Yeah, this could be good, Sal. Me being invited tonight. Dohlmani let slip that he may go back to Egypt. Gonna need someone to take over the club. Tonight's probably a test. He's going to see how smooth I handle myself with the heavy rollers." LeClerc dimpled at the windscreen as if posing for a photo op with Nicole Kidman.

At least he was facing forward, eyes on the dark road. Since they left Route 210, the highway had become narrower and more sparsely lit. Fewer cars approached. No one was following them. When they'd first picked up the newly paved freeway, Rebecca had hopes they were heading toward civilization. Fifteen minutes of deserted road dispelled that idea. At the junction for Waldorf they stayed on 210 going west to

Indian Head. After several miles the housing developments were replaced by an occasional tobacco barn or sporadic clusters of buildings. Areas too unpopulated to rate town names. The only sign she'd recognized was for Accokeek. That had been a good five miles back.

LeClerc was relaxed, like he knew where he was going. One hand on the wheel, the other stroking the leather next to her thigh. Then he grimaced.

"But if I'm coming along just to babysit you, I'll be pissed, love, real pissed." He grabbed her knee. Twisted his head to glower at her. The thick lenses masked his eyes. "My luck hasn't been real good ever since you showed up."

"Don't you mean since Shauna was killed? I thought you were supposed to protect the girls?"

LeClerc squeezed hard just above the kneecap. "Christ. The little twit wasn't killed. What's wrong with everyone? She offed herself. I saw her do it. Rambled on about sending her unborn to Allah or some such crap."

Rebecca pried at his fingers on her knee. "You were there? You let her stab herself?"

"Let her? I couldn't stop her." LeClerc yanked his hand away.

Shauna had cornered him in the hallway behind the bar. She'd learned she was pregnant, and was not keen to play Mommy. She begged LeClerc to do something. Find her a husband. Punish the man responsible. Get money for the baby. Housing. Help her. He told her the only thing he'd get her was an abortion. She freaked. Screeched it would be better to end it herself.

"She pulls out the damn letter opener. Got it hid in her waistband. I think she's coming for me and back up. Just then Lambesco yells from inside that Dohlmani wants me. I turn my head. You know, to tell him I'll be there in a jif. When I look back she's standing in the doorway moaning, eyes big as saucers. The knife's stuck in her gut. Before I can move, she lurches into the alley. Dohlmani bellows. I go to stall him, keep him from seeing the girl. I'm not losing this job because of some hysterical cunt.

"I'm back in a heartbeat but she's gone. She's not outside. So I run upstairs figuring she's popped into her room for a Band-Aid. Not there. I start thinking maybe I've been had, the knife's a prop and she's fine. She'd have to be, right? How else could she run away and hide?"

Rebecca didn't bother enlightening LeClerc about the power of adrenaline. Or the difference between a bullet to the heart and a blade slicing through less-vital tissue. If his story was true, Shauna had stayed upright long enough to stagger into the parking lot and crawl onto the flatbed and into the Bentley.

"Why didn't you tell the police?"

"You think they'd believe me, even if they'd listened? They had a suspect. They were happy."

LeClerc gripped the steering wheel, two and ten o'clock, hunched over like a geezer. "I'm not so dumb as I'd fess up if I don't have to. Dohlmani finds out one of his girls is knocked up, he'll have my balls."

He hit the brakes too hard to avoid a fallen tree branch. Rebecca snapped forward. In the glow from the instrument lights she saw that his rising anger was laced with fear. His frustration and the story both seemed real. For a few days the blinders had worked. LeClerc had put off the police, avoided Dohlmani's finding out, was ready to start peddling another girl.

So what changed?

The clock on the dash said 10:48. If they had to meet the boat at eleven, they must be close, but close to where? Rebecca couldn't recall a marina in this area. There must be a new harbor club. Hopefully one open late with lots of revelers strolling on the piers. LeClerc turned right at County Place Liquors, Route 227. A brown National Park Service sign said they were heading in the direction of Marshall Hall, four miles.

Charles County hadn't wasted tax money on streetlights. Not much point. There was only one house every half mile. A smattering of trailers off a side turning. Hand-painted sign for hot crabs. No traffic. No lines in the middle of the winding road. No shoulders. No people.

Why had LeClerc told her about Shauna's death? For the same reason he was driving her to the boat? Because what she knew no longer mattered? Because after tonight she would no longer be a threat?

She moistened her lips, glanced at the speedometer: thirty-five. She tried to remember if LeClerc had activated the power door locks. The door would be heavy, but at the speed they were traveling, she could force it open. She might survive the fall onto the pavement.

The last house was behind them. The night was pitch.

LeClerc muttered, "Creepy." Then, as if reading her mind, he hit the master button on his door. The locks on all four doors clanged, buttons snapping down, like cell doors at lights out.

He turned into the property designated as Marshall Hall, crept down a one-lane drive hemmed in by a few trees. After a hundred yards a second lane branched off to the right. LeClerc stayed straight.

Rebecca strained to see out the side window. A quarter moon illuminated a stone building the size of an ice shed. Farther away it shone on the ruins of a large gutted building, perhaps once the main house. Roofless, one end was still standing, its point stretching into the empty sky. The other walls were of varying height, rubble heaped against them. The entire structure was surrounded by chain-link fence to keep out kids, the curious, or desperate lovers looking for a trysting spot.

When the car braked, Rebecca turned front. Her gaze followed the headlamps. Ahead, through a swath cut in leafy trees, she saw moonlight on water, presumably the Potomac. The road sloped down, disappearing into the river, a minimal boat launch facility. One weak light swayed on a weathered post.

There was no yacht waiting offshore.

She wasn't surprised. It had all been a sham.

LeClerc backed the car close to the trees at the perimeter of the parking area and shut it down. The headlights remained on, cutting dual paths in the dark. He remained staring ahead, both hands gripping the wheel.

He wasn't taking her to the boat, or to a party. He was finishing the job the two in the Nissan had botched this afternoon. He'd been instructed to get rid of her somewhere unconnected with the club. Somewhere her body wasn't likely to be discovered immediately, if ever. Somewhere like the isolated shores of the Potomac.

Forty-six

Mick raised his arm to block the glare of the lights, dropped his gun hand to behind his thigh. The car stopped inches from him, a wall of curved metal and radiator slats. The front doors burst open. Two men scrambled from the car, ran toward him. Mick eased the gun forward. Squinted as a voice called out.

"Christ, Hagan, you've chosen an inconsiderate means of committing suicide. Have some pity for the poor driver who hits you."

Delacroix was in shadow, but Mick recognized his voice. Recognized the smirk as well when the lawyer closed in. He seemed relieved that the Rolls had stopped in time. Definitely a good thing—the damn car could have doubled for a tank. A very refined, baby-blue tank, but one capable of doing serious damage.

The driver was more solicitous. He asked if Mick was hurt. Did he want to go to a hospital?

Delacroix grabbed Hagan's arm. "There's no time for that, Talmadge. Hagan—is Rebecca at the club, do you know?"

Mick hesitated only a second, then told the lawyer what he

thought was going down. He linked the drowned dancer to Moore's being dragged to the party aboard the *Floating D.* He imparted enough information to justify commandeering the hefty Rolls-Royce. It couldn't handle any worse than the Jeep and it had a sound radiator. Delacroix had witnessed Moore's innate talent for getting into dangerous situations before. Mick counted on his putting Moore's best interests above all else.

What he hadn't counted on was the octogenarian who crawled out of the back seat of the car.

"I am Dorothea Wetherly, Rebecca's grandmother. If you require the use of my car, you shall have it. However, we're going with you."

There wasn't time to argue. Mick briefly considered raising the gun and shooting her. He was sure the world would be better off without another headstrong female, whether or not she was related to Moore. Instead he produced his badge.

Delacroix distracted him from pulling rank. "You need us, Hagan, I know where the boat picks up on the Maryland side. It's not far."

Mick snarled. "Where and when?"

Smug, Delacroix indicated the car. "Get in and I'll tell you."

Mick started around the front of the grille, stroked the Flying Lady in passing.

"I'm driving."

A resounding chorus screamed "No!"

If he weren't paranoid about Moore in the clutches of LeClerc, Serena going off with Schneider, and the probability of losing his job, Mick might have given in to hysteria. It was ludicrous. Floating along in the back seat of a Silver Cloud, surrounded by soft leather, burled wood, the strains of Mozart or some other dead composer wafting from the rear speaker en route to chase down the bad guys and rescue the fair maiden. He was trapped in a demented fairy tale.

Delacroix, like the scheming wizard, knew the magic word, and he refused to give it up. Well, at least to Mick. The driver had to know. He exited the freeway, turned down deserted side roads without asking directions. The roads were not encouraging. Each one was narrower and less traveled than the last. Mick started to squirm.

Mrs. Wetherly tapped his knee.

"It's not fair to keep you in the dark, officer. We're going to Marshall Hall. It's the ruin of an eighteenth-century estate that once belonged to William Marshall. It's on the water. There's a boat ramp and a dock. It's closed after dark, but the locals don't obey the signs. Fishermen launch runabouts there and fish in the shallows. Talmadge knows all about it."

Talmadge demonstrated his knowledge, prattling on for the next few miles about the manor's history. Delacroix appeared to listen. Mick tuned it out.

He extracted his cell phone from his pocket and called the captain. He kept the conversation brief to avoid complications. He volunteered that LeClerc's destination was a party boat, the *Floating D*. It picked up passengers at Marshall Hall, Maryland side. Mick would try to board there. *Yes*. He'd wait for backup before doing anything stupid. Mick hung up feeling more optimistic. Dexter would call the Feds and have them alert the Coast Guard. Good to know people in high places.

He leaned forward and ordered the driver to goose it. Talmadge chose that moment to make an abrupt right turn at the sign for Route 227. Mick was thrown sideways. Tires squealed, the back end threatened to lose touch with the road. When Talmadge stood on the brakes, the nose of the Cloud dived toward the pavement. Mick swore he could smell brake dust and burnt rubber. Maybe the beast wasn't such a hot chase car. Talmadge apologized. Mrs. Wetherly forgave him.

Delacroix muttered a prayer.

"Five more miles. Let's hope the boat's still there."

Hope, is right. LeClerc couldn't have more than a ten-minute lead. Mick guessed that the *Floating D* had too much keel to come to shore for passengers, so they'd send a tender. Would the captain wait until he saw car headlights, then launch the smaller craft to pick up the customers? Or have the ferry boat waiting at the dock? If they'd already picked up at Marshall Hall, would they return for more guests? If not, how the heck would he get on board?

Forty-seven

Rebecca eased her hand toward the door. She pulled at the chrome lever knowing escape was a fantasy. She doubted she'd be quick enough to exit the car before LeClerc grabbed her. If she did get out, where would she run? The ruins offered no safety. Even if she could make it to the highway, the closest house was a half mile back. She wasn't going anywhere near the water. She was trapped in the dark, locked in with LeClerc, waiting for his next move.

It wasn't what she expected.

He unstrapped the seat belt, smoothed the bunched sides of his polyester blazer, said, "You think I look okay?"

She blinked. Okay for what—throttling her?

He pulled down both sleeves. They cascaded over his knuckles. "I don't want to embarrass Mr. Dohlmani. He's real particular about what people think. Cares way too much. If he didn't—"

What? If he didn't care, you wouldn't have to kill me?

LeClerc scowled, annoyed at the thought of Dohlmani's power. "Why does Dohlmani care if the girls have some fun? He treats them like furniture you need to move to sweep around. Forgets their names half the time. But if a girl wants to have a bit on the side, he gets riled."

Rebecca was a tad riled herself.

"You think Shauna was having fun, that's why she killed herself? You were selling her for sex, weren't you? You call that fun?"

LeClerc chewed at his lip, like a man who wants to unload but won't out of habit. "Karin was into it. They all got presents, attention, time away from the rattrap."

"The girls liked it so much, how come they kept disappearing?"

LeClerc hit the steering wheel. "Just three." He poked fingers in Rebecca's direction. "Martine. Karin. Shauna. And they didn't disappear. Shauna killed herself. Karin drowned."

"And Martine?" Rebecca knew she shouldn't push, but couldn't stop herself. If he was going to throw her in the Potomac, she wanted to go with her curiosity satisfied.

LeClerc slumped. "I don't know. I was told that she married some guy, moved. But no one ever heard from her. Never heard from Karin, either. I should of guessed about her. That bitch would've called to gloat if she'd made good. He said they'd left because they wanted to. I had to believe him."

Softly Rebecca asked, "Who said?"

LeClerc didn't answer. He picked at a hangnail with his front teeth.

The whine of a motor cut through the silence. LeClerc sat up. A light bounced over the water, the beam from a searchlight mounted on a motorboat, coming closer. Rebecca could make out the low boat by its wake. It was angling for the dock.

Relief seeped in. Maybe her imagination was out of whack, the victim of too many recent murders. Maybe there really was a party boat, LeClerc would take her aboard and the most she had to fear was Dohlmani's anger over her snooping in his private affairs. Sounded doable.

LeClerc grunted, shut off the headlights and hit the switch for the locks. He hoisted himself out of the car, pulling at his blazer to get it to hang straight, then spoiled the effect by dropping the wad of keys into the pocket.

Rebecca scrambled out her side. She hurried toward the boat, but stopped short of stepping out onto the dock. It was nearly indistinguishable from the shadows of the overhanging trees and the murky water below. Reeds floated near the shore. She glanced over her shoulder, gauged the distance to the woods, to the ruins and back to the car.

LeClerc pushed past her as a motorized Zodiac maneuvered into position perpendicular to the end of the wharf. He took hold of the mooring line. Motioned Rebecca to get in.

The skipper was in his late thirties, blond with a beaming smile. BRIAN was embroidered on his starched white shirt, along with the red-and-gold logo for the *Floating D*. He greeted them by name and helped Rebecca aboard. As she settled on the seat she saw an enormous yacht, emblazoned with lights, hovering in mid-river.

Part Four

Adrift

Forty-eight

Dohlmani posed on the deck of the yacht, one hand on the railing, watching as the motor launch covered the short distance from shore. Above his head were strings of lights that reminded Rebecca of those her mother had draped in the garden for an eighth-grade party, minus the paper lanterns. Beside him was a slim blonde in a tight white skirt and a pressed shirt with the ship's logo. Salsa music was playing. Someone laughed. It felt like a party.

Dohlmani leaned down, offered a hand to help Rebecca aboard. Her thin heels slipped on the moist deck and she slid into him. He held her for a second before helping her to balance. His cologne smelled a lot better than she did. He turned his attention to LeClerc and gestured to the blonde.

"Lisa will show you around. There are refreshments and, as you know, gambling. I expect all good guests to lose substantial sums, since it is for charity. I make no exceptions for employees."

His grin dared LeClerc to try his luck. LeClerc wasn't the type who liked to lose, but if he won, Dohlmani would be displeased. Better he should just drink and not gamble at all.

LeClerc chewed his cheek as he considered his options. He followed the attractive mate inside, eyes glued to the movement of her buttocks.

Dohlmani took Rebecca's arm and wrapped it through his.

"The *Floating D* is a most impressive craft. Where would you like to begin the tour, Salome? Or should I call you Rebecca? Unless, of course, you prefer Ms. Moore?"

She hesitated. He sneered at her indecision. She maintained eye contact.

"Rebecca's fine. Thank you for asking."

By showing his cards, Dohlmani had elevated the game from employer and waitress to something else. But what?

Dohlmani pulled her arm closer. "From the first it was obvious that you were more than a nightclub employee. I'm not surprised that you're a reporter, though I am disappointed by your approach. You should have come to me for an interview. I have nothing to hide."

As he steered her past the main salon, Dohlmani kept up a steady patter about his charities and the amount of money that changed hands each month. Through the curved bank of windows she saw LeClerc in a familiar pose, leaning against the bar, drink in hand. Lisa was talking to a table of men in designer sweaters playing poker. Two men and a woman in a halter top were intent on a round of blackjack. A bald man in a tight suit played backgammon opposite an elderly matron wearing ruby silk pajamas. More guests were drinking in groups or clustered near a portable piano, goading each other into playing a tune. One wore the collar of a cleric. Lots of colorful material if she'd been covering the event for the society page.

Once on the starboard side, Dohlmani motioned her aft and up a flight of narrow stairs, cutting the tour short. The engraved sign on the door at the top side PRIVATE. It opened into Dohlmani's stateroom. Like his office at the club, the room was tasteful and opulent. Deep blue tones, befitting a ship; poplin instead of silks. The music here was orchestral. The surroundings should have been soothing.

They would have been if the vessel hadn't swayed.

They were under way and she was alone with Dohlmani.

Rebecca hated being on the water. She wasn't sure whether she was on a ship or a boat. Anyone else in her family would have known how long it was, how heavy, how many knots it could run full out. Her brothers could have accounted for all of the antennas and explained the navigation system. Rebecca couldn't get past the fact that it was condemned to float on cold, deep water.

At Dohlmani's insistence, she sat in a padded seat near the wall of windows. She could see the lights strung on the lower deck and Dohlmani's reflection in the glass watching her. She swiveled inward, away from the dark night and the darker river.

Dohlmani offered her a drink. She declined. He opened a latched cabinet and selected a bottle of red from a wine rack. He uncorked the bottle and brought it and stemmed glasses to the table beside her, in case she changed her mind. Ever the perfect host. He placed one glass on either side of a riding crop.

She expected him to grill her about why she was spying at the club. She'd rehearsed her story. She was down on her luck, needed more cash. Thought it would be a novel experience. Possibly work up material for a book. He could check with the *Post*. He would find out she had been fired a year ago. She was no longer an investigative reporter. They wouldn't accept an article from her if she paid them.

She expected him to question her until satisfied with her answers. Then fire her and let her go.

She did not expect him to lean over her chair and kiss her. Not a gentle lingering kiss like she'd experienced in his office but an open-mouthed fervent one. Hot and rough, teeth on teeth, forcing his tongue into her mouth. She couldn't break away. He straddled her legs, his weight heavy on her thighs.

With one hand he gripped the back of her neck, holding it still. With the other he picked at the bandage on her neck. Without warning, he ripped the patch loose. The dried blood had stuck to the gauze. As the scab was torn away there was a sharp sting, then the warmth of fluid running down her neck.

Dohlmani eased his mouth off hers, slid his lips sideways to the wound and began licking the blood from the cut.

Rebecca sucked in air, shivered. She pushed at his chest.

He sat back far enough to focus on her face. "How rude. I have made you bleed." He kissed her lightly on the lips. She could taste her own blood.

Then he was standing. He turned his back to her and poured wine, two inches in each glass. He handed one to her. "Forgive me?"

Rebecca accepted the glass but did not drink. Dohlmani laughed, fluttered his hand.

"Blame it on your attire. You are so provocative. Much more so than in jeans, with hair cut short like a boy. Your costume shows you know what men like, yet in everyday life you deny us. Why is that?"

He set down his wine, watched her face intently, waited for a reply.

What was his game? She refused to believe that he'd commanded her presence on board merely to seduce her. What did he want?

She had nothing to lose by asking. Which question first?

She twirled the wineglass. A drop splashed on the bodice over her heart. She frowned at the red splotch. Better than blood, but she should wipe it off before it stained.

It seemed like too much work. *What was wrong with her?*

She leaned her shoulders against the chair back, gently swiveled from side to side. Her neck burned where the scab had come loose. Stung where she'd felt the sting of a—a what? Dohlmani was still watching her, watching like she was a laboratory animal. Waiting. For what? She didn't really care. She was feeling relaxed. Too relaxed to concentrate. Perhaps she should skip the preliminaries. Start with the big one: Did you kill Karin Petra? Or Martine? She giggled softly.

Dohlmani smiled like the Cheshire cat. He was proud of her. He patted her knee. He told her that he would ask LeClerc to join them.

Rebecca wanted to protest, but Dohlmani had disappeared. When he rematerialized, he was speaking into the intercom. She tried to concentrate. She couldn't. She focused on the wine sloshing in her glass. It looked untouched. Why was she so mellow? Why was the slender stem so heavy? What was . . .

The glass slipped from her grasp.

"Rebecca, open your eyes, please."

Dohlmani was leaning over her. His hand cradled her cheek. It was warm and smooth. He moved her chin so their eyes met.

"Ozzie has joined us. We'd like to ask you some questions. Speak to us, Rebecca. Ozzie wants to know why you came to work at the club."

LeClerc stood in the center of the room, slurping a drink, a belligerent schoolboy called to the principal's office. His eyes flitted around looking for a way out.

Good idea. She wanted to go, too. If only her legs weren't so wobbly. Why was that? She should ask Dohlmani. Instead she slid forward in her seat and answered his question.

"To investigate the deaths of the dancing girls."

"Very good, Rebecca." Dohlmani stroked her cheek, her neck. He licked his finger. "What do you know about those poor girls?"

"They were being supplied as prostitutes to some dignitary. Man liked virgins. Once pregnant, they were killed. No further use. Disposable dolls."

"Really?"

Dohlmani wasn't touching her anymore. He sounded far away. She twisted her head until she spotted him at the bar. He had set down his glass, carried the riding crop instead. He circled behind LeClerc. The short pudge looked seasick. Dohlmani hissed like a viper.

"Is that true, Ozzie?"

Dohlmani's voice was pitched low. LeClerc's was falsetto. He stammered that there was only one customer. Very discreet. Not often. Nothing that would embarrass Mr. Dohlmani. Girls wanted it. They got gifts. The man was generous to them.

Dohlmani stopped a yard away. "And to you? Was he generous enough to induce you to murder my dancers?"

He slashed the crop against the manager's thigh.

LeClerc shrieked.

"I had nothing to do with their deaths. Shauna did it herself. Ask Moore. The kid was screwed up about being pregnant. Kept muttering that she'd send the unborn to Allah. I tried to stop her, get the knife away from her. She was too quick."

LeClerc raised his hands as he stepped back. He knew what was coming. Dohlmani's whip caught him across one palm and his cheekbone. He squeaked. His hand flew to his face. Blood dripped down his wrist, stained his shirt cuff. Dohlmani closed in, yanked LeClerc's hand from his cheek.

"You let her leave my club and bleed to death among strangers. And now you foolishly have confessed your guilt in front of a reporter."

Rebecca corrected him automatically. "Ex—."

Dohlmani dismissed her. He paced. In a professorial voice he asked LeClerc how they could solve their mutual problem. He prodded LeClerc for the best way to assure that the deaths, and the pandering of young girls, would cause neither of them embarrassment or worse. He assumed that the man with the taste for young flesh would not talk?

That left only Rebecca Moore, the reporter.

What could be done?

Dohlmani didn't need to be more explicit. He'd drawn a line in the sand broad enough for LeClerc to stumble over. The two of them could escape public censure *if* Rebecca never told the story. All LeClerc had to do to be safe from prosecution, and back in Dohlmani's good graces, was take care of the reporter.

Not good. Time to leave.

Rebecca struggled to stand, wobbled, pushed off and lurched toward the door.

Dohlmani grabbed her around her waist and pulled her against him.

"Ozzie, it appears that Ms. Moore is very drunk. Or rather, is about to be. She should know better. It is so dangerous, staggering on a slick deck. Especially in flimsy footwear. So easy to lose one's balance and fall overboard."

Dohlmani shoved her toward LeClerc, who lurched under the unexpected weight. He eased her back into her seat. A drop of sweat fell from his forehead into her lap. Rebecca fingered the damp splotch. So like the drop of blood that fell from Shauna's lifeless finger.

Dohlmani handed LeClerc an open bottle of liquor, then reached behind the bar. He came up with a gun, checked that it was loaded, tucked it into LeClerc's jacket pocket. He patted it like a talisman.

"For backup."

LeClerc averted his eyes, straightened and faced Dohlmani.

"I won't need it, boss. I can handle it. You're right. Accidents do happen."

Forty-nine

Jo leaned over the front seat as Talmadge brought the Cloud to a halt. Ahead, black water lapped a boat ramp. The river seemed abandoned. No sign of a yacht.

Hagan bolted from the car and sprinted toward a vehicle parked near the tree line. He felt the hood, he tried the doors, looked inside for bodies. He pounded on the trunk.

Jo slid from the Rolls, loped in the opposite direction, toward the water. A lone fishing boat was tethered to the side of a short pier. From the end of the wharf he could see a large, festive ship disappearing around the bend, moving upriver. It had to be the *Floating D*.

Jo called out to Hagan, gestured toward the battered skiff drifting beside the dock. "Can you start one of those without a key?"

"Boston whaler? No problem."

Hagan yanked on the line, caught the side of the boat. Before he could swing his leg over the gunwale, Mrs. Wetherly and Talmadge descended on him, both full of suggestions. Hagan held up a hand to forestall them.

"The Feds will be here soon, along with the Coast Guard.

You tell them where I've gone. I'll call you once I'm on board *if* you need to send in the calvary. Otherwise have them stay put."

Talmadge protested. He would go with Hagan. Wetherly shushed him. She recited her cell phone number.

Jo wrote it down. He was definitely going with Hagan.

"How do you plan to get aboard?" Mrs. Wetherly addressed the detective as if he were a schoolboy who'd forgotten his lesson.

Jo stepped in front of Hagan and answered her. "We'll pose as invited guests, late for the rendezvous. Explain that we had to borrow a boat to catch up."

Hagan paused, checking his gun, annoyed by Jo's use of the plural. He clearly envisioned a one-man show. Jo argued that the deception would be more believable with two stragglers. He'd been thrown out of the club recently. Someone on the staff might remember him as a customer. Besides, two could search faster.

Wetherly nodded. The teacher's pet had come up with a bright answer.

"In that case, Talmadge, give Mr. Hagan your blazer so he looks more presentable."

While Talmadge held out his coat for Hagan, Mrs. Wetherly tottered to the car and returned with something in each hand. She tried to pass Jo a gun, short-barreled and ugly. He refused it.

She insisted. "Mr. Delacroix, you should not go without protection. There are some situations not even a lawyer can talk his way out of. Take it for Rebecca, if not for you."

Jo eased her hand aside. He wouldn't know how to use it, it would only get in the way. She relinquished the revolver to Talmadge, handed Jo the flashlight instead. He could always use it to brain the villain.

She directed Talmadge to lose the tie, roll up his sleeves

and try to impersonate a boat hand. He would skipper the two men to the yacht, then return to wait with her. The idea didn't set well with Talmadge.

Mrs. Wetherly didn't care. She had one more order.

"Fetch them a bottle of champagne from the car. It will add to the illusion of the partygoers. And get the bourbon. The boys should smell the part and I could use a nip myself."

Jo directed the flashlight up under the dash. Obviously Hagan had stolen boats before. It took just minutes for him to fiddle with wires and make the connection. The motor sputtered to life. Hagan adjusted the choke as it warmed up. Jo moved aside some fishing rods. He motioned Talmadge onto the boat and helped him into the captain's seat. Hagan was ready to cast off.

Talmadge swallowed. Sotto voce, he admitted he'd never driven a boat before.

From the dock came Mrs. Wetherly's voice. "Nonsense, Talmadge. You can do anything you set your mind to. Ferry them out and come right back."

Jo patted him on the shoulder. He stood behind him and showed him how to shift out of neutral and advance the throttle. Hagan cast off the line, shoved the boat away from the pier.

Once they were a short distance from shore, Jo eased Talmadge's hand forward. The boat accelerated smoothly through the calm waters. A light spray came from port as they turned upstream. Jo flexed his knees, reveling in the motion of the waves. He felt his face relax as the wind cooled his skin, as he breathed in the openness of the river. He embraced the illusion boats offered: that you were leaving all your troubles behind. Island mentality. Escape was all around you, if you could walk on water.

In ten minutes they'd caught up to the *Floating D*. It was

ambling up the Potomac, with no apparent destination and in no hurry to reach it. Jo leaned over Talmadge's shoulder, covered the man's hand with his own and pulled back on the throttle. The Whaler slowed.

Jo took control of the steering wheel. He maneuvered the craft alongside the stern of the yacht. He started laughing, lurched, pretended to have fallen against the skipper. As the aft wake raised the boat and slid it toward the larger craft, Jo leaned dangerously far over the side to grab for the yacht's ladder. A mate—fearing a crash, or man overboard—trotted to their rescue. He tossed a line to Hagan and used a hook to swing around the rear of the motorboat.

Jo stumbled as he grappled for the bottle of champagne rolling from side to side. He hissed his esses.

"See, Michael. I told you Oz wouldn't leave us behind." Jo thrust the bottle at the mate. "For you."

Without waiting for Hagan, Jo scrambled up the ladder and boarded the *Floating D.*

Fifty

Rebecca's spine was liquid. She oozed farther down in the chair, closed her eyes. The lights were too bright. She ached to sleep. Why wouldn't they leave her alone? She parted her mouth to ask the question. Tepid liquid flowed down her throat. It trickled on her chin. She choked, sputtered. Her eyes shot open.

LeClerc was bending over her with a bottle of scotch. She hated scotch. She tried to push him away but her arm flopped, numb at her side. Behind thick lenses, LeClerc's eyes shifted from side to side like fish floating in an aquarium, lots of slithery fish. His voice was gruff. He ordered her to drink up. Dohlmani hovered behind him, leering. LeClerc pinched her chin. Poured more liquor in her mouth.

She spat it out. *Enough.* She needed air.

She struggled to stand. Her ankles buckled. A buzzer sounded repeatedly, like an annoyed gnat.

"Get her up." Dohlmani faded from the picture.

LeClerc pulled Rebecca to her feet, turned her around. The gnat stopped buzzing.

Near the door, Dohlmani listened at the intercom. He frowned. "Keep them with you until I come down."

He asked LeClerc about inviting guests. LeClerc denied it. Dohlmani reached for the crop.

"Yet somehow they knew to board at Marshall Hall. I'll deal with them. Take your date down the starboard side. Make certain there are witnesses to her drunkenness. I'll have the mate bring our guests forward, leaving the stern unattended. Go now."

Rebecca's head lolled on LeClerc's shoulder. She wanted to straighten, make the world level again like a gyro, gyros, gyre and gimble in the wabe. She giggled. Her feet kept tripping. How many were there?

The manager gripped her waist, pudgy fingers biting into her bare midriff. He struggled to keep her on her toes, moving forward. Stairs—much easier. Gravity was her friend. Until her left foot slid off the step and she pitched forward. LeClerc was thrown off balance. They bumped down two steps before stopping.

He pressed her against the wall in a crude embrace as a couple went by on the outside deck. They glanced over, sniggered. Rebecca tried to call out. He covered her face with his, hissed at her to be quiet, stop squirming. He smelled of onions and sweat. The beautiful people moved on.

LeClerc dragged her with him. The night air was heavy with humidity, as dense as her head. But there was a breeze. Rebecca tried to gulp in air.

They were at the bow now, into the lights. Too bright, it hurt to look. She squinted. Behind the glass, guests were drinking and gambling. A few stared at them, ogled her, the bundle lolling against Ozzie's hip. Rebecca tried to call out but her tongue was too swollen. She licked her lips. He whipped her around, she skidded on the deck. Someone inside laughed, called her a souse. LeClerc bent down. He dragged her up by her elbow, then scooped her up in his arms, like the groom on his wedding night. There was jeering and clapping. A red-faced duffer chanted, "Stateroom, stateroom."

Rebecca struggled, squirmed, slapped at his face.

LeClerc held on, lugged her doggedly toward the rear of the ship.

There it was darker. Quieter. No music, no laughter, no talking. Just LeClerc's labored breathing and the pulse of the engines.

Rebecca forced one eye open. She was looking up: sky, a smattering of stars. Her head sagged, her view did a one eighty. Below her, dank water lapped against the hull. She imagined she could see strands of seaweed floating, beckoning. Feel the cold tentacles on her skin. Her head was too heavy to lift, so she shut her eyes.

She was so sick of being haunted by water.

Fifty-one

Mick lurched away from the first mate.

"Sure thing, skipper. We get it. Dohlmani doesn't like unexpected guests. But, hey, that's no reason to make us feel like criminals. We jus' want to party. Which way?" He spun around, aimed for the hatch.

At the word "party," Delacroix launched into what sounded like a college drinking song. He gave Mick time to cross the room, then stumbled in his wake, placing his rangy body between Mick and the mate. Good defensive move. Mick wondered if the lawyer had ever played football. And for what college.

Right now Delacroix was playing drunk with real finesse. Mick was going along. Anything to make them appear harmless to the guys with braid on their shoulders. But he was getting antsy about Moore. Where was she, and with whom? He wouldn't find her hanging out in the pilot house or whatever. When the captain had reported them, Dohlmani said he would be down, which meant his office was up. Couldn't be too hard to find.

As Mick staggered through the hatch, he nodded to

Delacroix. The lawyer winked. He had his arm around the mate's shoulders and was singing the refrain loud enough to wake the fishes.

Mick sprinted forward on the gently swaying deck. Twenty feet ahead a narrow metal stairway went up. He took the steps two at a time. The door at the top had an engraved brass sign, PRIVATE, and a recessed door handle. Good place to start.

The door wouldn't budge. Mick started pounding.

"Hey, Mr. D. Open up, it's me." Not original, but drunklike.

When the lever started to turn, Mick braced his weight against the door. As it swung in, Mick's heft went with it, forcing Dohlmani to back up. Mick slammed the hatch behind him and grabbed at Dohlmani's shirt front, wrinkling the starched linen.

Dohlmani regarded the fist at his chest as something unholy. He raised his hand. He was holding a gun—a shiny Beretta.

Mick slowly unclenched his fist, patted the silk shirt front to smooth the fabric.

He pulled out his identification. "Lieutenant Hagan, Mr. Dohlmani. Sorry about barging in. We have reason to believe that one of your staff abducted a woman and brought her on board tonight."

Dohlmani considered the statement, eyebrows raised. He retreated, circled behind the varnished bar. The Beretta disappeared from view.

"You're here after one of my employees? Who?"

"LeClerc."

Dohlmani picked up a glass half full of deep red liquid. He sipped. He admitted that LeClerc had asked, almost begged, to be included at the festivities this evening. It was an unusual request. Reluctantly Dohlmani had agreed.

"You say my manager forced a woman to accompany

him. And you suspect this woman is in danger? Why? Who is she?"

Mick studied Dohlmani's smooth face. His expression said that he was perplexed, ignorant of the deceptions being perpetrated all around him.

Mick enlightened him.

"A woman named Rebecca Moore is posing as a waitress at your club, using the name of Salome. She's a reporter working on a story about the dead dancing girl."

Dohlmani looked shocked. "Does she suspect LeClerc of having caused the unfortunate girl's death?"

Mick shrugged, he didn't really know her suspicions, but it was possible.

Dohlmani poured himself another dollop.

"Oswald has not been himself lately. He has been excessively nervous. Flying off the handle. It's most distressing. Now this."

Dohlmani sighed as he sat near the window, crossed one knee over the other, letting his ankle dangle. Silk socks so smooth he had to be wearing suspenders. His demeanor was starting to annoy Mick.

"It will be a lot more distressing if we don't find her soon. Have you seen them?"

"Actually, yes. They were here when the captain announced that you had stormed aboard. LeClerc took Salome, ah, Ms. Moore, outside for a bit of fresh air. She seemed inebriated."

"Christ." Mick wrenched the wineglass from Dohlmani's hand and slung it toward the windows. Merlot sprayed across the white carpet and deck chairs. Matching red flashed on the boat owner's cheeks. Mick dragged him to his feet.

"Show me where they went, Dohlmani. Now."

Fifty-two

Rebecca tried to shake her head. It listed left and stayed there.

The nightmare had always been gentle, lulling her into a feeling of calm, until the end. Tonight it was rough. She wasn't floating. She'd been tossed facedown onto something hard. Instead of water she smelled vinyl, musty with mildew. The pulsing of engines throbbed beneath her. The sea swelled. The boat lurched. She started to roll onto her back. Her hips slid over a sharp edge before being stopped, braced by a warm thigh. Half on, half off.

Someone swore.

Who's there? Should she know? Yes, she should know her date. Rebecca giggled. *Mother said you are always courteous to your date, until you get home. Always go home with the boy that brought you. Who brought me?*

She really should open her eyes.

Someone was removing her shoes. The freedom would be delicious if she could feel her feet. She thought about wiggling her toes. No response. She tried her fingers. She wasn't sure where they were. Under her? No, one hand was on her hip. She felt it being gripped as she was pulled around to sitting.

She cajoled her right eye into opening.

She was staring at a white . . . what? Wall? No, fabric, stretched tight. She brightened. A shirt worn under a blue blazer. She should know the wearer. If she could open her other eye . . .

The man yanked her upright. The boat swayed. She swayed with it, a reed tossed in a storm. No balance. Her anklebones were strapped together. She took baby steps like a geisha. Started to slide.

Her admirer pulled her close. *Shall we dance?* He stank: sweat, gin, onions. Where had she smelled that combination before? He lifted her into his arms. A breeze toyed with the fabric covering her legs, raising goose bumps on her thighs. It lifted a strand of hair, drew it across her face, across her closed eyes. It snagged on the mole on her cheek. She groaned.

A man was yelling. Calling her name. Someone she knew? Did he have her sweater? She hoped so, she was starting to shiver. He yelled louder.

"LeClerc. Stop."

The clerk stops what? The clock stopped? At what time? She giggled. Her head rolled forward. She drifted, so relaxed.

Then there was an explosion.

Shit. This wasn't in the dream. Her head snapped back. Sizzling stench. So close. Fireworks?

Another explosion.

Rockets red blare? Nope. Water balloons.

Splat.

Warm fluid bathed her chest, face. Glued strands of hair to her cheeks.

She must open her eyes. They'll be stuck shut. She must—
The arms holding her let go.

Set her free, left moist palm prints of flesh exposed to the night.

She was falling.

Arms flapped, touched nothing.

Falling.

Legs tight together. Straightening, heavy, pulling her down.

All wrong.

She never fell. She floated.

She was falling.

Her feet smacked the water.

Eyes popped open. She faced the engulfing blackness.

Rebecca opened her mouth to scream.

Fifty-three

Mick did not see Moore go overboard. Legs splayed, both hands gripping his weapon, he'd witnessed LeClerc wrestle her limp body into his arms. He'd seen Dohlmani's first bullet tear through LeClerc's neck inches above her face. Heard the second shot: It had smacked into LeClerc's back. Mick prayed it had struck bone, lacked the velocity to penetrate through his body and into Rebecca's.

Holding his gun level, Mick swung toward Dohlmani. The arrogant ass was leering, adjusting his arm for another shot. One eye closed, Dohlmani sighted on LeClerc as he tottered under Moore's weight.

Mick fired. He meant to knock the gun from Dohlmani's grip. Instead he shattered the man's wrist. Blood, tissue and the handgun flew across the deck. Dohlmani was too stunned to scream. He grabbed his lifeless hand and stared at Mick.

Mick swiveled to find Moore.

She was gone.

LeClerc lay crumpled—half on the deck, the rest of his torso hanging over the gunwale. Mick felt for a pulse in the side of the neck that was still there. Faint, getting fainter.

Mick screamed at a guy in a white shirt running toward them. Told him to get medical help. The kid nodded and went to the intercom.

More running feet slapped the deck, other voices added to the confusion. Mick ignored them. He raced to the port side, leaned over, scanned the water. It was a sheet of black. Only the wake from the boat marred the surface.

Delacroix's voice boomed through the din: "Hagan. Where's Rebecca?"

The lawyer was on the second deck leaning dangerously far over. Mick pointed toward the water.

Delacroix screamed, "Where?"

Mick didn't answer; he didn't know where. He raced to Dohlmani, grabbed him by the arm that wasn't bleeding and dragged him to the intercom.

"Have the captain turn the boat. Now. Call out the crew. Get lights, whatever you need for a search. Then S.O.S. the Coast Guard."

Dohlmani glared at him, but he hissed the orders into the speaker.

Mick returned to the side, returned to scanning the water. He heard the engines moan as the power was eased off, followed by a reverse thrust. The vessel began a slow arc to starboard, changing direction.

He saw a small light flickering in the dark at the same moment Delacroix yelled again. It was a flare, sputtering about forty yards in back of the turning boat. Next to the flare the Boston Whaler bobbed in the water. Talmadge was at the helm. Mrs. Wetherly clutched the windscreen for balance. She held a snub-nosed Smith & Wesson in a frail hand, used it to point at the flare. Mick signaled back that he'd seen her, but the old woman wasn't looking. Her gaze was focused on the upper deck.

As the bow swung perpendicular to the channel, Mick

looked up, perplexed at what held her attention, until he saw the lawyer. Delacroix had shed his jacket and shoes. He stood poised behind the aluminum railing gauging wind and distance. He retreated from the rail, paced out of sight. In his mind's eye Mick saw the lawyer regulate his breathing, collect his energy, focus his concentration.

Then without warning, Delacroix burst through the air above him.

Running strides had taken Delacroix to the mark where he launched himself up and out. He cleared the upper railing. His chest forward, arms akimbo, back arched, pants flapping, toes pointed. Damn tie flipped over his shoulder. Delacroix seemed to hang in the air, an archangel frozen in mid-flight.

As he started to descend, he folded into a jackknife. Twelve feet from the surface he cupped his body outward. Eased his legs back. His toes just skimmed the railing on the lower deck. His arms and torso sliced into the water with barely a ripple.

Someone on deck gasped.

Mick realized he was holding his breath. He would later admit that it was one of the most impressive feats he'd ever witnessed. At the time, adrenaline pounding in his ears, every detail seemed painfully slow and deliberate. Suicidal.

Mick moved. He scurried forward along the deck, wrestled a life preserver from one of the crew, pitched it at the hole in the water where Delacroix had vanished.

Fifty-four

For a nanosecond, hanging in the night air, Jo had been transported back to Jamaica. The breeze on his face. The lapping of the waves below him. His muscles remembering the moves with perfect coordination. On the island he had been clad in skimpy trunks, surrounded by friends, showing off for a beautiful woman. Not one who had been sent to a watery grave, one who had died another kind of horrible death.

He hit the water. He let the dive carry him to a depth of twenty feet, then opened his eyes and swam forward until his lungs screamed for air. Surfacing ten feet to the near side of the flare, he jerked water from his face, sucked in air and disappeared again.

When he next broke the surface the *Floating D* had edged closer. Searchlights played on the water. Mrs. Wetherly balanced in the fishing boat, gestured to the sparkler. Jo prayed the flare was accurate. He filled his lungs and dove.

The river was relatively clear of silt. He could make out an occasional fish, shafts of light filtering through the murky depths. He circled the target area. Widened his search with each arc.

No sign of Rebecca.

His chest craved air. He burst to the surface again. A spotlight hit his face. Talmadge was shouting, his arm pointed left.

Jo filled his lungs. Dove.

He stroked in the direction Talmadge had indicated. Nothing. He forced his body deeper, turned, began a slow circle back. More nothing.

Then, in his peripheral vision, the ghost of a movement. Jo backpedaled. He swung around. Off to his right, five feet below, a white arm floated.

He'd found Rebecca.

Jo wiggled through the water toward her. Her chin sagged against her chest. *How long had she been in the water? Two minutes? Four?*

He clutched her wrist and pulled her upward. Her body resisted. The diaphanous skirt wafted around her legs, obscuring her feet. He felt down her body until he located her bound ankles, lashed together, with an anchor line attached. The barbed anchor wasn't heavy. It was stuck on something out of sight.

Jo clawed in his pants pocket, dug out his whittling blade, flicked it open. He sawed back and forth through the nylon line. It gave up its hold strand by strand. Finally it split apart. He grabbed Rebecca's hips, propelled her upward, his body close below.

Their heads broke through the surface together.

Jo gasped in air. He reached for Rebecca's inert form. He tipped her head back on his shoulder, forced her mouth open, breathed his air into her.

Voices called out. Jo didn't look up. There was only one voice he wanted to hear.

He gulped in more air, forced it into Rebecca. *It had to work.* He could not lose her.

He tried to feel her neck for a pulse. Her head lolled forward, nearly slipping again beneath the water. The long tresses of the wig drifted around her like an oil spill.

He clutched her chin, bent her head back. Sucked in air, leaned toward her face.

It jerked from his hand.

Rebecca coughed. Eyes huge, she gasped, choked. She clawed at her face. Sank, sputtering. Resurfaced, spewing water. She emitted a high-pitched keening through pursed lips. He reached for her. She struggled away. Her hands wild, batting at her head, her face, her neck.

Jo paddled closer. She slapped him away, screeching. He saw the horror in her eyes.

Oh, God—the nightmare.

Jo gripped her arm, yanked her toward him. With his free hand he ripped the wig from her head and flung it. It sailed about ten feet, stalled, plopped on the surface, where it floated—a harmless pelt.

He cupped Rebecca's cheek and forced her to look at him, making inane sounds as one does to an infant. She was gulping air. Tears were running down one side of her face, but her arms ceased flailing. She swallowed hard and bit her bottom lip as she finally returned his look.

Jo smothered her lovely face against his chest.

"Sssh, Rebecca. It's over. Over. This is how it ends. You are saved."

Fifty-five

We have lingered in the chambers of the sea
By sea-girls wreathed with seaweed red and brown
Till human voices wake us, and we drown.

Rebecca couldn't shake the verse. The closing stanza of T. S. Eliot's "The Love Song of J. Alfred Prufrock." It echoed in her soggy, drug-fogged brain. She hadn't intentionally memorized it. The words had insinuated themselves in her subconscious. More water imagery, more seaweed.

She was awake. She hadn't drowned.

She was sitting cross-legged on the wharf at a Coast Guard station. All around her human voices were comparing notes, asking questions. Every few minutes someone would squat down in front of her and walk her through the story again. Police, Coast Guard, federal agents.

Hagan gave her space.

Mrs. Wetherly had wrapped her in a blanket, patted her hair awkwardly with a towel that smelled of gasoline. Someone had brought the older woman a folding chair. She sat stiff-backed, holding her purse on her lap. Waiting, in case Rebecca needed her. Waiting for Talmadge to return.

Talmadge had maneuvered the Whaler next to them as they floated in the river. With Jo handing her up, Talmadge had pulled Rebecca onto the small boat, then helped Jo onboard. Mrs. Wetherly directed Talmadge to take them to the safety of the Rolls. But the Coast Guard showed up and pulled rank. As bidden, Talmadge followed along in the wake of the cutter.

Once Rebecca, Jo, and Mrs. Wetherly were safe on the pier, Talmadge had returned to Marshall Hall to return the Boston Whaler and retrieve the Cloud. A cop of some description went along. He would bring back the Silver Shadow that LeClerc had parked there. The club manager wouldn't be driving ever again. He had bled to death on the deck of the *Floating D*.

The party boat was docked behind the Coast Guard vessel. The lights were still blazing but it was nearly deserted. The guests had left their names, addresses and statements before being allowed to call for rides home. The skipper and crew clustered on the pier near the ship, waiting to give their statements.

Jo sat beside Rebecca, thigh close even after she'd pulled her hand away to warm it under the blanket. He had saved her life. He wasn't ready to relinquish her to anyone else's care.

A paramedic had checked her over, announced that Rebecca was in shock. She insisted that she was just cold, dazed from the water. Hagan got in the act, saying it was the drugs. According to Dohlmani, LeClerc had drugged Rebecca's drink.

Rebecca shrugged. She remembered refusing a glass of wine, but not much else. Hagan asked if it could have been in the whiskey LeClerc had poured down her throat. She didn't think so, she'd been dopey long before that. She thought she remembered being pricked in the neck. It could have been the scab breaking loose, or an insect bite. The medic located a puncture mark at the edge of the wound, which looked like it had been made by a needle. She hadn't seen Dohlmani with a syringe, but he could have palmed it. She asked about the drug. From her symptoms, the technician assumed it was a fast-acting barbiturate. Possibly thiopental. Good old sodium Pentothal. Truth serum. The whole truth and nothing but. What had she said?

She shivered. What had they thought she'd say?

Hagan wandered away to do official things, like have Dohlmani searched for a hypodermic in case he hadn't had time to pitch it overboard. Then have him taken into custody for shooting LeClerc.

Dohlmani admitted that he shot his manager to save Rebecca, but claimed it was self-defense. Naturally, several mates were backing up his story. They all maintained LeClerc had brandished a gun, then put it back in his pocket—his left pocket, which was a peculiar move for a right-handed man. Dohlmani planned to sue Hagan and the department for the excessive force used when maiming his hand. His lawyer was rushing to the scene.

That wasn't Hagan's only concern. Dexter had sent a message via Schneider that he wanted Hagan to report to his office at eight A.M. tomorrow. Something about countermanding orders.

Schneider had stopped by to apologize to the Feds for screwing things up. His captain had reached him and told him what was going down. Took his head off for blowing the sting. He felt terrible. He'd just wanted to interrogate Serena again. Figured she'd open up if away from the club and LeClerc. Like everyone else, Schneider was eager to finger the former manager, now conveniently dead. Schneider insisted that LeClerc had been his number one suspect all along.

None of that mollified the Feds. They'd lost their one known link joining the girls to the procurer and the middleman. They had yet to locate the money. They had a likely name for the guy diddling the girls, but so what? He was protected by diplomatic immunity. Worst case, he'd be sent home before his term ended. Months of quality work down the drain. Thanks to Schneider.

When he ran out of officials to apologize to, Schneider strolled over to Rebecca. She sent Jo to scrounge up a cup of coffee. Schneider squatted in front of her. He said he would release Paulie in the morning. He admitted that maybe he hadn't had enough solid evidence to go after her guys the way he had. But it had seemed pretty substantial at the time.

"And now it doesn't? Why not, the killer's still out there." Rebecca clutched the blanket closer around her shoulders.

Schneider looked perplexed. "Hagan said LeClerc claimed the Aziz girl offed herself. It was suicide."

"True. But LeClerc also insisted that he had nothing to do with two earlier deaths. He blamed those on his partner. It was his accomplice who said that Karin had gone to dance at a club in Baltimore and that Martine had gotten married."

Rebecca huddled her knees in closer. "LeClerc was skeptical of those stories from the first. He accepted them because it was easier. He deluded himself that he was running a simple prostitution scam. His hands were clean of murder. At the end, he knew better. He's dead, Lieutenant, but the accomplice isn't. You still have work to do."

Schneider scowled. "Don't suppose he gave you a name?"

Rebecca didn't answer. She was distracted by a movement in the distance as a long-legged woman slipped from the back seat of a gray sedan. Her head was nearly shorn, dark with tight curls. She wore jeans, gold hoops and an armful of bangle bracelets.

Schneider repeated his question. Rebecca shook her head. *Who was the woman?*

Schneider prodded, asked if LeClerc had said anything else, anything at all that would help identify the man. Rebecca sighed, pleaded that she was too out of it to answer more questions. She blamed her fuzzy memory on the drugs traipsing through her bloodstream. She'd already told the officers everything she could remember. She'd be more cogent later.

Jo returned with a cardboard cup of acrid coffee and resettled beside her. She leaned into the shelter of his arm.

Schneider closed his notebook and walked away, hands thrust deep into his pockets. The tall woman watched him as he got in his Buick to leave, then turned to consult a clipboard left perched on the hood of a car. Neither she nor anyone else thanked Schneider for coming. He'd be persona non grata with the Feds for years to come.

Serena, on the other hand, had become the darling of the investigators. She'd answered their questions solemnly, thanked them profusely. Made them feel the job had been worthwhile if it prevented such a sweet girl from ending up on the streets or dead in a gutter.

In truth, the girl seemed unfazed by her field trip away from the club, though she'd clung to Hagan until he promised that he would drive her to his condo when the Feds released them. He'd mumbled something noncommittal and passed her off to wait with Mrs. Wetherly. Serena snuggled against the older woman's chair, content as the frail white hand caressed her hair. Rebecca watched, letting herself be mesmerized by the movement. When the hand stopped, she looked up—the Silver Cloud was pulling into the lot. It was time to go home.

Jo helped her rise.

Hagan stood outside the huddle of cops and watched as they walked to the car.

Rebecca was unaware she had dozed off. She was jarred awake when Talmadge braked for a red light somewhere on Route 4. She was in the back seat of the Cloud, legs curled under her, leaning on Jo—something she had been doing a lot lately. She clutched two photographs, sticky between her fingers. In the dim light of the car they looked like duplicates of the same snapshot.

Mrs. Wetherly checked on her from the front seat with concerned eyes. She looked alert, as if energized by the night's events. Content that everything had turned out well, she'd finally stowed her handgun in the glove box.

It occurred to Rebecca that the elderly woman was someone she might like being related to. She had spunk and determination. The ability to see herself clearly in the mirror, examine the warts, regret them, yet still accept the reflection as her own. And go on. Rebecca knew the fortitude that last step took. She smiled as she handed her back the snapshots.

"If you still want me to have the DNA test, I will."

Mrs. Wetherly's bottom lip quivered when she said, "Please."

Rebecca wasn't sure whether the old woman was afraid the blood test would prove they were related or that they weren't. Either way Mrs. Wetherly needed to find out for sure. So did she.

On the ride home Mrs. Wetherly and Talmadge had recounted the highlights of their investigation to find her missing granddaughter. Rebecca admitted that the trail of evidence was compelling. Reporter or not, she would have followed it without hesitation. She asked only one question.

"How did you locate me in Head Tide? What led you from Massachusetts to here?"

Mrs. Wetherly grinned as she slipped the photographs into an ivory envelope.

"You mean how, without your mother's help, did I make the leap? Your mother—Pauline, rather—neglected to mention Walter Moore at all. Or the fact that her daughter had lived with him most summers of her adult life. That omission made me very suspicious. You see, I'd compiled the genealogy, I knew there was a third, older brother.

"And then there was this." She handed an envelope to Rebecca. "Do you recognize the stain?"

Rebecca fingered the envelope. It had been addressed to Mr. and Mrs. Leon Wetherly in her Uncle Walt's crabbed handwriting. In the lower left corner there was a dark spot, the size of a pencil eraser. Rebecca sniffed at it. She slid out the pictures and examined the inside for bleed through.

Mrs. Wetherly was grinning like a child expecting to pull off an April Fool's Day coup. Even Talmadge was leaning to catch Rebecca's facial reactions in the rearview mirror.

Rebecca hazarded an educated guess. "Brake fluid?"

Mrs. Wetherly tittered and clapped her hands with delight.

"Castrol RR363 to be precise. We had it analyzed. The brake fluid used in post-war Rolls-Royces. No other cars. Your uncle must have had the note around when he was adding fluid to a car and it got splashed. Not enough to necessitate rewriting the envelope. Or perhaps he didn't notice it. Anyway, Talmadge searched for Rolls-Royce repair shops throughout the country until he located Vintage & Classics, owned by one Walter Moore. My deepest regret is that by the time I'd worked up my courage to approach him, your uncle had died. I cursed the Fates and myself repeatedly. I thought I was back at square one. When Talmadge could no longer stand my moaning, he attacked the Blue Marsh County probate records. There he learned that you—Rebecca Elizabeth Moore—had inherited the repair shop. And it seemed my journey would have an ending after all."

Fifty-six

Jo walked Rebecca to the house. She asked him to leave, she wanted to sleep. He stood outside and listened for the sound of the dead bolt. He waited for lights to go on downstairs. Satisfied, he walked slowly back toward the idling Silver Cloud.

Rebecca had been returned home safely.

The sky was tinged with gray, dawn was still two hours away. Tomorrow they would talk. Tomorrow they would work through all that had happened. Right now he was too tired. So tired he had stopped walking, stood swaying on the flagstones. A night predator wiggled through the grass, stalking an unseen rodent in the flower border. Jo marveled that it could have the energy at that hour.

Talmadge drove Jo the short distance down Main Street and left him in front of his office. Jo would spend the night in the room on the top floor. He often did during the week. Had been doing so more often since Rebecca came into his life. He stood on the stoop with his jacket over his arm and his shoes in his hand, trying to wave as the Rolls drove away.

The effete gesture reminded him of the animal hunting in the lilies.

What would be nosing about so close to the house? Not a fox. The tail was too thin, the fur too dark. It didn't bound. It moved more like a cat. Like a plump cat. Like a black cat named Maurice, which should have been inside the house.

Rebecca never let Moe out at night, there were too many predators. She lived in dread of something happening to him. Partly because she loved animals, but more because Walt had entrusted the cat to her care. She'd instilled her paranoia in her workers and friends. None of them would have let the cat out to roam.

How did it get out?

Was he certain that the animal rustling through the fronds was Moe? Could it have been some neighbor's cat? A raccoon? Jo closed his eyes and revisited the scene.

No. The animal definitely was Moe.

Jo pitched his shoes and jacket at the sidewalk. He raced back to Rebecca's.

On the rise in front of the house he paused. Everything looked normal. Lights were on in the house, upstairs and down. The shop was dark, as it should have been. There were no unexplained cars parked out front or on the path separating the properties. Across Main Street the storefronts were blank, empty. No stranger loitered under a lamppost. Two cars were parked against the curb, but that was not unusual. There were apartments over several of the shops.

No noise other than night insects.

Jo studied the silent house. He couldn't see the cat from where he stood. Could he have imagined it after all? Or, in her fatigue, had Rebecca left a window open, allowing the cat to sneak out?

It could have happened. Why was he so rattled?

Jo removed his glasses and rubbed his eyes. His imagination was getting the better of him. He had been dwelling in darkness lately. Time to welcome back the sun. No one was after Rebecca. Not now. She had survived another trial. She was finished with the strip club. LeClerc was dead. Dohlmani and his lawyer were negotiating with the police. Tomorrow Rebecca would return to fretting about over-engineered luxury cars and their owners. Right now she was sleeping.

Probably. Hopefully. But he wouldn't believe it unless he saw her face sunk deep in the pillow.

He'd heard her lock the front door. There was no reason to suppose she had opened it again, so he circled around back. He skirted the lily border, stepped over the herbs and stood on the cool flagstones of the patio. The sky was lighter at the rear of the house, over the open field. Light enough for him to see that the door to the kitchen was ajar. Six inches, plenty of room for a fat cat to wiggle through.

Jo tiptoed up the brick steps and eased the door open.

Inside, the kitchen was dark. The dining room as well. In the living room a table lamp by the door was the only source of illumination.

He stood on the threshold, listened.

He heard water running, pulsing through the old pipes in the ceiling. *Excellent.* Rebecca was showering, washing away the horrors of the last few hours. Cleansing herself of the river algae, makeup, scotch and the scent of fear.

The corner of Jo's mouth lifted as he imagined soapy trails of lather dissolving down her body. He could offer to scrub her back.

Perhaps not. Footsteps sounded overhead, too heavy to be Rebecca's. They crossed the hallway heading for the guest bath.

Hagan? Was that possible?

Jo pressed his hip against the counter, relived the scene at the docks. He was positive that Hagan had been standing near the building, haggling with the federal officers when Talmadge drove them away. Hagan could not have beaten them to Head Tide. Could he?

Besides, if Hagan were inside, where was his car? He would have no reason to hide it. Nor would he have snuck in the back door and left it open. Jo would have been dismayed but not surprised if Hagan had a key for the front door. He would be surprised if Hagan had let the cat out.

Jo quickly crossed the tile floor. He padded down the pine hallway, past the dining room, and entered the living room. He paused with one hand on the newel post. A soft glow spilled from the bathroom into the hallway above.

The water taps squeaked as they were shut off. The pipes clanged.

The bathtub? Had someone filled the claw-footed monstrosity that Walt had refused to replace with a modern fixture? Rebecca never used it. She showered. She hated baths. Too much like swimming in a coffin.

Jo rounded the newel post. He started up the stairs.

His foot was on the first step when he was grabbed from behind. A hand clamped over his mouth, strong fingers bit into his cheeks. Off balance, he was yanked backward, twisted around and pushed against the wall, pinned there by a body stretched full length against his. He stared into the dark eyes of an angry woman.

She pressed hard against his mouth as she fished out identification. The badge she flashed open said FBI. She mouthed the word *Okay?* Slowly, she lowered her hand, dispensed with the badge and pulled a gun from a holster at the small of her back. She motioned for Jo to remain where he was, frozen against the wall.

She, too, was barefoot. She strode up the stairs, two at a time. She paused when she reached the turn at the second floor. At the sound of footsteps, she ducked back down the stairwell, hugged the top step.

This close, the tread seemed inhumanly heavy—until Jo considered the possibility that the walker was weighed down with a second body.

Jo heard the splash.

The agent sprinted for the bathroom. A shot sounded before Jo could ascend the stairs.

The second shot came as he careened into the agent blocking the doorway to the bathroom. He couldn't see past her. He heard the body fall. It hit hard against the edge of the tub before smacking onto the floor. Before blood oozed into the grout separating hundreds of one-inch tiles.

Jo didn't care about the body or the blood. He pushed past the agent, her gun still poised. He stepped over the man's legs to reach the bathtub.

There, Rebecca floated as peacefully as if she were asleep. She was naked, her head resting against the slope of the porcelain, one hand flopped over the rim. A water nymph, slender and inviting. Her perfect whiteness marred by old scars, the discoloration of new bruises just forming. Guiltily, he drank in the view of her body, then moved to her face. Her eyes were closed, her breathing shallow, but at least she was breathing.

"Jesus Christ. Out of my way." The FBI agent nearly elbowed Jo into the tub. "I have a prisoner to restrain. Lucky for you he hit his head and got stunned. Else I'd be arresting you for interfering."

"He's not dead?"

"I look like I'm a bad shot? I wanted him incapacitated, not dead. Though preferably in a whole lot of pain."

She cuffed Rebecca's assailant with his own handcuffs.

"The detective's not getting off that easy. He's got too much to answer for."

Shaking open a towel to cover Rebecca's body, Jo finally looked at the unconscious man crowding the bathroom like a sack of discarded laundry. Bloody, bent, and splashed with soapy water, the unconscious Lieutenant Theodore Schneider had definitely seen better days.

Fifty-seven

Mick pulled up in front of Vintage & Classics and slammed to a stop. Off to the left Moore's house was lit up like a grand opening. Zimmer's patrol car was parked on the bridle path. The ambulance was loaded, engine running, ready to leave. The EMTs weren't racing. Either the injuries were minor or they'd been fatal. Schneider's Buick was parked in front of the newsstand.

The final act had been played out and Mick had missed the curtain. He dropped his forehead to rest on the steering wheel.

He had stood on the wharf, stared at the water, trying to erase visions of Moore drowning. He'd sensed Schneider's car pull away. Noticed it the way you see a kid cut through the yard. Benign movement that only takes on meaning when you discover the broken window.

But he hadn't added it up soon enough. Why not? The clues had been there.

Because Schneider was a cop?

Or because he never trusted his instincts when Moore was in the picture? He didn't like Schneider much. He liked

Moore too much. Fearing he was being irrational, overly protective of Moore, had he shied away from seeing Schneider's complicity?

Or did it defy belief that someone like Schneider, who had a solid twenty-year record working some lousy details, had veered from the path and ended up a murderer?

Mick could cast Schneider as the greedy, amoral go-between. The man who obtained girls from LeClerc, then supplied them to perverts and pocketed the money. That fit. Years working Vice could sour a cop on women as fast as a vicious divorce. You figured they were going to screw around anyway, you might as well profit from their behavior. You met so many lowlifes, they became the status quo; aberrant behavior became the norm.

Then an outsider, a predator, senses your disgust, makes you an offer too sweet to ignore. Some smooth ambassadorial type willing to pay big dollars to indulge his particular taste for olive-skinned virgins. What better arrangement than have a local cop supply his needs?

So how did it escalate to murder?

Mick was willing to bet the Sanchez case was the beginning.

It seemed probable that Schneider had hooked up with the perp when he was working Vice. Maybe even arrested him, or answered a call, met him at the scene. The men could have struck a deal, and Schneider began searching the streets for girls who would satisfy.

Schneider had needed them fresh. Schoolyards would have been too risky. So he'd have hung out around shops where teens frittered away babysitting money on trinkets. One day he spotted Angela Sanchez. Perfect: lovely and a loner. Maybe he figured there was no family keeping an eye on her. Or maybe he knew the mother was a stripper, assumed she wouldn't care what happened to the girl.

Schneider had been wrong about that. Anita Sanchez had cared. She'd made her daughter talk to her. Then, being a good citizen who believed in the system, she'd gone to the police for help.

She might not have recognized Schneider the day she originally reported her daughter's rape, but she had to have seen him on her last visit—the day she came with a clear description of the man who had forced her daughter into a car and had taken her to a hotel for another man to abuse. Either Anita had confronted Schneider, or he'd recognized her. Same result. By the next morning, her neck had been snapped and she was rotting in an alley with three-day-old garbage.

Mick pulled himself out of the Jeep, started up the slope.

He wondered if Schneider had gotten off on the rush. Felt a surge of power as he wrapped meaty hands around a delicate throat, watched the face suffuse as the oxygen was cut off, heard the cartilage crunch as he snuffed out a life.

Or had it begun as simple lust? Maybe after years of fantasizing about the girls he delivered, Schneider decided to take a taste for himself. Approached Martine, said he'd drive her home. When she didn't give him what he wanted, he found choking her almost as pleasurable.

Then Petra. Did she catch him waiting in the shadows? Confront him over her unexpected pregnancy, whine about her condition or lack of money? Or did she somehow learn he was a cop? Karin might have been stupid enough, arrogant enough, to threaten to turn him in.

But that was after he'd moved to the Sixth. Before that, a superior in the First must have suspected that the years in Vice were taking their toll on Schneider. Someone had recommended he be transferred to homicide, where the crimes involved more men than women. And the victims were already dead.

Schneider should have welcomed the change, taken it as a

gift and a warning. Instead, he'd taken his bad habit with him. He'd stayed in contact and kept supplying the goods. In fact, he located a reliable source in Oswald LeClerc—a nothing, determined to become a somebody. Tapped into his steady supply of young innocents, brought in from other countries with no family members to look after them.

Must have been a hell of a shock for Schneider when he faced the dead Aziz in the Bentley. No wonder he'd conducted the initial interviews at the club alone. Not because his partner was laid up, not because he disliked working with cops from other jurisdictions, but because it gave him and LeClerc a chance to square their stories. Together they'd decided that suicide was too unbelievable, better to steer the investigation away from the club.

So Schneider didn't find the blood. He didn't interview the dancers. He kept the spotlight focused on Antrim as long as he could.

He must have nearly pissed when he found Mick at the bar flapping photographs of the drowned Petra at anyone who'd look—pictures of the dancer he'd killed, who should have been reduced to a skeleton on the bottom of the river. LeClerc had helped him out then, using the necklace to throw suspicion back on Antrim.

But Hagan wouldn't go away. So Schneider complained to Dexter, got him pulled back.

Then Moore showed up asking questions.

Mick walked slowly through the grove and up the stone walkway. He paused outside the screen door. The living room was empty. He could hear subdued, late-night voices coming from the dining room, people talking farther along in the kitchen. Upstairs was quiet, crime tape draped on the bannister. Nothing to give him a clear picture of what had happened inside her house.

He expelled a breath he didn't know he was holding and let himself inside. No one ran to question his presence.

Mick climbed the stairs, ducked under the tape.

The light was on in the bathroom. Tub was full; some water had sloshed on the floor. A discarded towel lay half under the old-fashioned tub. What seemed like a gallon of blood stained the tile grout pink. No body.

The room across the hall was empty. Wooden table held a laptop, phone and desk light. From the windows the typist could see town, once the summer leaves dried up and fell off.

Mick backtracked to a hall running perpendicular. Door on the right opened into a guest room done in shades of blue. View of the shop beyond the grove. Bed neatly made. No signs of male habitation. *Good.* None of Delacroix's toiletries cluttering the bureau. *Even better.*

Moore's bedroom faced out back, spanned the width of the house. Walls sponged in pale peach and gold mimicked the sunrise beginning to flood the fields with color. Low bookcases ran under the windows; bureau with an old beveled mirror up against the wall to the bathroom; louvered white doors on the opposite wall hid the closets. On the nightstand was a hardback, her lawyer's business card sticking out from between the pages.

The damp outfit she'd worn earlier, the harem costume his mother had made, was dumped on the polished wood floor. Didn't seem like a thing Moore would do, but she'd had a bad night. He ran his hand along the curved foot of the sleigh bed and took in the view Moore woke to every morning, God willing. Nice way to start tomorrow.

He went downstairs.

Zimmer was in the dining room grilling a tall woman with kinky black hair and an attitude. A semiautomatic handgun lay on the dining table between them. She was punching the buttons on a cell phone. She handed the phone to the sheriff just as he noticed Mick in the doorway.

Zimmer nodded. "Wondered when you'd get here, boy. Go wait in the kitchen. Be with you in a sec."

The woman batted her eyelashes at Mick. She looked familiar.

So did the scene in the kitchen.

Moore was sitting at the table with a towel wrapped around her shoulders. A medical technician was shining a flashlight in her eyes. She was in a worn terry-cloth bathrobe, her hair was wet, there were circles under her eyes and a frown on her face.

She was a beautiful sight.

Mick sagged against the doorframe. He felt his neck muscles release. He hadn't allowed himself to imagine that Schneider had succeeded in killing Moore. Still, the worry had been there like a shred of meat lodged between back teeth.

The med tech stood, started packing up his tools. Mick shot him a quizzical look. Before he could respond, Delacroix's voice answered Mick's unasked question.

"She'll be fine. Schneider surprised her, hit her skull just hard enough to disorient her. He planned for her to drown. The blow, however, did not knock any sense into her. She's refusing to go to the hospital."

"Always in water over your head, aren't you, Moore?" Mick said it gently.

The left side of her mouth lifted in tepid response. It was better than nothing.

The lawyer was near the sink, fiddling with the coffeemaker. Mick had to ask, "Schneider alive?"

Delacroix said yes. They'd patched the gunshot wound in his leg, put ice on his head and taken him to the county jail.

Mick nodded. *Good thing.* If he saw Schneider right now he might have to kill him.

"Who foiled Schneider's plans?" Mick needed to know who'd saved Moore's life for the second time in one night. If Schneider had been shot, Mick guessed it hadn't been Delacroix pulling the trigger.

The lawyer placed a cup of coffee in front of Moore. He handed a second one to Mick and grinned.

"The FBI. Special Agent Teresa Kendrick, a.k.a. Juliette."

Fifty-eight

It was Tuesday. Rebecca had slept through Monday. She should be at the shop, but she had loose ends to tie up. And a few knots to try to unravel.

She selected a short navy skirt and peach linen blouse, which might brighten her complexion. The nightmare had left her alone the last two nights, but she still looked a wreck.

She liked Jo's theory—that since she hadn't drowned, the dream had lost its power.

The therapist suspected that Rebecca was just too numb at the moment to let its horror wake her. The demons would return with a vengeance. Rebecca prayed he was wrong. He could be: He was working with incomplete data. He still thought the nightmare had been triggered by her watching a murderer go up in flames, then trying to soak her burnt skin in the cold bay.

Rebecca was beginning to suspect that her fear of drowning was far less symbolic. That it was an infant's repressed memory of being abandoned at sea during the storm that claimed her parents' lives.

She dabbed makeup at the circles, gave up and reached for

her sunglasses. She pulled blue pumps from the closet knowing she couldn't depress the clutch if she wore them. It wouldn't be the first time she'd driven the MG barefoot.

She was in DC before ten. Her first stop was the impound lot. There she signed the release form for the transporter and provided the name of the firm that would be coming for it. She'd hired a bonded driver to bring the Bentley safely to Head Tide. She couldn't stand any more screw-ups with that car. The paperwork had been well-organized and was waiting for her. It hadn't taken long to complete, so she had time to kill.

She sat in the idling car, debated over meeting Peter Hayes for coffee or hounding Hagan for information. Hagan hadn't returned her calls; she wanted to know why. Peter had called every two hours.

She drove to the Second District, parked and entered through security.

Captain Dexter nodded to her in passing. Sergeant Batisto grinned at her, then shook his jowls. Said Hagan wasn't in the building. He couldn't say where the lieutenant was. He offered to give him a message for her. She told him not to bother.

At the Federal Building, she read and signed the typed statement regarding her involvement at Gentlemen Only and the attempt on her life. The bland agent admitted that Sergio Dohlmani had been in and signed his statement earlier but he could not discuss the contents. Rebecca wondered if the two versions had anything in common.

Special Agent Kendrick might know, and might be persuaded to tell her over a plate of pasta. Rebecca had arranged to meet the agent for lunch. They'd settled on a neighborhood trattoria that vented garlic onto the sidewalk.

Teresa was already seated when Rebecca arrived a few minutes before twelve. The agent was dressed in dark polyester trousers, matching jacket and bright white tee. Gone were the spindly heels, false eyelashes and sequined turbans of her Juliette persona. The woman was still imposing, taller than the average male, with a well-honed body and hooded eyes the color of Hershey's chocolate.

Her smile was dazzling. "I ordered champagne. We've got lots to celebrate."

"It's my treat, you saved my life."

Teresa shook her head, claimed she almost didn't.

"When Schneider split early from the Coast Guard station, I was afraid he was fleeing the country, going to wherever the money's stashed. It wasn't until he turned toward Head Tide I guessed he was going after you. I'd seen him reading the witness accounts; knew they gave your address.

"Once we got onto secondary roads, I had to hang back so he wouldn't spot the tail. By the time I located his car, he'd disappeared inside. But where? You county folks don't put numbers or names on your mailboxes. How's anybody supposed to find you? Good thing I spotted your lawyer sneaking through the shrubbery, so I knew which house to enter."

Good thing indeed.

Rebecca cringed, realizing that she might have been killed for no reason. She'd never been a threat to Schneider. She hadn't been clever enough to figure out who was pulling the strings, to figure out the tawdry *why*—that young girls were being killed simply because they got in Schneider's way. And because he enjoyed the power of killing. She hadn't been perceptive enough to notice him hiding in the shadows of the dining room. She'd walked right by, intent on finding a packet of hot chocolate mix to warm herself.

Schneider had hit her with a makeshift sap: a roll of pennies inside a napkin. Her pennies; her napkin. He'd caught her on the nucal ridge, according to the medic. Enough force to knock her out without breaking the skin. Inflicted the type of bruise she could have gotten falling in a tub, where she would have drowned. She bent her neck away from the lump and shivered.

Teresa touched her hand. "Wish I'd arrived sooner."

"Why did you arrive at all? How did you know Schneider was the killer?"

She laughed. "Two many questions. You decided yet?"

They ordered an antipasto to share, followed by pasta puttanesca in honor of strippers they'd met. The champagne arrived. Teresa tasted it and smacked her lips. "Don't beat yourself up, Sal. I had a five-year head start. And insider information, thanks to my niece."

Between bites of warm bread dipped in olive oil, Teresa talked about her sister: Anita Sanchez. Anita was eight years older. They'd squabbled growing up, grown apart when Anita had thrown away her future by getting pregnant. Turned to stripping, maybe hooking, to support her daughter.

Teresa was away at college when Anita had been murdered. After the tragedy, Teresa transferred to American University to be closer to her niece. For a while the girl lived with her in her apartment. But the kid was so deeply disturbed by the rapes and her mother's death that eventually she had to go to a supervised home. That was when Teresa decided to try for law enforcement.

"I needed to be able to make things right. I got nowhere trying to make sense of my sister's death. And I was useless in soothing Angela's torment. I felt so powerless."

Teresa had spoken with Schneider at the time of Anita's murder. She hadn't liked him, but she hadn't suspected him of anything more than incompetence. She'd tracked him down again after graduation to see if there'd been any progress. He'd switched precincts, but he was the same surly brute.

She poured more champagne, watched the bubbles break for the surface. "When the Bureau stumbled on LeClerc's hobby, and I heard that the girls being prostituted were so young, I volunteered to go undercover. It was a chance to help Angela by proxy, even if I was years too late."

The Bureau wasn't really interested in LeClerc. Mainly, they wanted to keep an eye on Dohlmani. They suspected he was using his party boat to reroute funds from sympathetic U.S. businessmen to terrorist cells. That was the reason they allowed her to go undercover. Her big mistake was the transvestite act. Dohlmani was such a prude, he wouldn't let her near the boat. Might offend his good customers. The Feds probably would have ignored the prostitution angle if the ladies hadn't sashayed a little too easily across the Canadian border. Since 9/11, everyone had been real antsy.

Then the girls started going missing, and the Bureau finally sat up and took notice.

Teresa shook her cropped head and took a long swallow. She reached out to touch Rebecca's hand.

"Can you imagine what I felt when first Martine, then Karin, vanished? Then poor Shauna. We had so many of the pieces of the puzzle, but couldn't connect the dots. We knew Ozzie received phone calls in the afternoon telling him the girl was wanted. We knew about the limo service. We knew there was a shadow man keeping an eye on the girls at the hotel, but never caught him in the act. We assumed he also received the payment for services rendered. God, I didn't want more girls to die, but we were too close to shut down."

She swigged from her glass and tried to smile. "Then you showed up, nosy reporter bitch."

"You were suspicious right from the beginning, weren't you?"

Teresa batted her eyes à la Juliette. "Honey, you ain't no hard-luck lady looking to make spending cash the lazy way. You got style."

"You snooped in my purse."

"Guilty. And I pressured them to get you pulled. By that time, my boys claimed you were instrumental to their plan. Best I could do was have lover-boy Hagan yanked back so he didn't spoil things trying to pull a Don Quixote."

"He's not my lover."

Teresa slid Hagan's battered business card across the table toward Rebecca. Winked. "Sure thing, hon. Whatever you say."

The waitress brought the salad. Teresa loaded hers with pepper and Parmesan. She wrinkled her forehead when she complained that, speaking of persistent men, Sergeant Brian Llewellyn was making a pest of himself, pretending to be helpful. Her eyes were twinkling.

Llewellyn had told her that Dohlmani planned to keep the club open. He was convinced the publicity of his trial—an innocent businessman wounded and wrongly accused by inept police—would be beneficial. Maybe, maybe not. But Llewellyn would watch the place. Then he carped that since Teresa's cover had been blown, he guessed she wouldn't be going back to the club.

"You should have seen the boy, hangdog and drooling. Sorry he'd missed my act. Ain't that a hoot?" Teresa finished her salad.

"He's working hand in hand with the DC cops on Petra's murder. Seems that Schneider's hobby is fishing. He and his ex-brother-in-law own a short, fat boat. Schneider likes to go out on it before first light, when the fish are biting and the fog is thick. Sometimes guts the catch on board. Only not all the blood the cops found was from fish. Forensic guys removed the railing around the bow and discovered dried blood in a screw hole. AB negative, same as Petra's. Rare. There might be enough for a DNA match."

Schneider's brother-in-law was being oh, so helpful, too. He mentioned that Teddy had stashed financial records in a beat-up tackle box in the garage. That was right after he'd returned from a vacation, bragging about the colorful fish and clear aqua waters off the Caymans.

Brother-in-law was also miffed at Schneider for using the cell phone he kept on board the boat for emergencies. Apparently, Schneider refused to pay for the calls, claimed they weren't his. Brother-in-law started keeping track.

"Don't you just hate it when big brother starts spying on you?"

The pasta arrived. Rebecca lifted a mouthful, blew on it.

"Do you think Schneider will be convicted of anything?" *Or moved to another jurisdiction? Please.* She couldn't stand the idea of having him so close. A reminder of her vulnerability.

Teresa ripped off a hunk of bread and attacked the sauce.

"Other than the attempted murder of sweet little you? Could be tough. The phone records will tie the cell phone to the club, but we can't prove Schneider made the calls. The Cayman bank account helps. As does the blood trace on Schneider's boat. And there's an underambassador from Finland who left his post early. Very suggestive, but he's not talking and no one on this side of the ocean can make him. Lots of soft proof. Nothing to make a D.A. cheer when you're talking about taking down a cop."

Teresa wolfed down a forkful, patted her lips with a napkin. "But . . ."

Rebecca grinned. "But what?"

"Did I mention that my niece, Angela, is much stronger now? She's been working through the trauma of the rape with art therapy. Real talent for faces. In a recent session she was able to draw a portrait of the big guy in the gray suit who delivered her to the nasty man. Guess who it's the spitting image of?"

Fifty-nine

After lunch, Rebecca stopped at a lab outside the beltway to have blood drawn for DNA analysis. Mrs. Wetherly had been there ahead of her. She'd given them her sample and provided a braid of Nicole's hair. At thirteen the girl had reached behind her back and hacked it off with embroidery scissors. She'd felt it was time for a more sophisticated hairdo.

Rebecca asked how long the test would take.

The chubby attendant told her a few weeks. There was a rush order on it. The results would go to Mrs. Wetherly. Rebecca would have to contact her.

She folded the receipt into eighths, pocketed it. If the test proved they were related, the very foundation of her life would change in less than a month. That would take adjustments she was too tired to think about. More challenging even than fretting over Hagan and his current disappearing act.

When she arrived home it was after five o'clock and still over ninety. The air was thick with humidity. Every inch of Rebecca was sticky. She peeled off her skirt and blouse, traded them for shorts and a sleeveless cotton top.

In the living room, she rewound the messages on her answering machine.

The first one was from Jo. Val had been given six months of community service for the parole violation. He'd agreed to spruce up the plantings in the park opposite the police station two days a week after work. Zimmer and Val were both pleased with the arrangement. Zimmer got cranky staring at weeds.

"There's more good news. Mrs. Antrim's arthritis is impeding her ability to get around. And she's developing a cataract in her left eye. Sensibly, she has hired Serena to be her companion. Paulie is beside himself and all over her. This weekend he will move Serena out of the club and into their home."

Rebecca wondered about the long-term ramifications of the job offer, but would say nothing to Jo. She'd let him have the illusion of a happy ending.

The second message was a long one, from Frank.

"Some fellow named Ian called. Said you gave him your card. You must have 'cause he had the number and I've never heard of him. Hope you didn't meet him at that nightclub? He said for you to call soon. He's got a race car he needs ready for Indy in September. I told him we don't do race cars. He laughed. Said you should call."

Rebecca grinned to herself. *Who says we don't do race cars?*

Frank's voice droned on. "Other call was from your father. Says you need to have a talk, something about a new passport. Why? You ain't going noplace. He wondered when you could plan a long weekend to go to Massachusetts. I told him never. You so far behind now we're working six days a week. He said you should call him."

Frank snorted into the answering machine. She could almost see his mouth clamp shut as he paused, unsure how to continue. That was usual. Frank didn't talk a lot, but when he opened his mouth he had plenty to say.

"But those ain't why I called. They came in early, during work hours. I guess I shouldn't have stayed late." Another pause. He lowered his voice.

"Don't want you to be surprised tomorrow, but Mr. Todd Shelley just walked through the door. He wants to know where the hell is his 3-Litre Bentley. What in blazes do I tell him?"

Rebecca grimaced as she hit rewind. She made a mental note not to answer the phone for the rest of the night. Explaining the Bentley's involvement in the dancing girl's death to the hyperactive Shelley would take way too much energy.

Moe was in the kitchen staring at the back door. That was his idea of begging—he shouldn't have to ask, she should be bright enough to open it and let him out.

Two days ago Rebecca had discovered the source of Moe's fascination with the perennial border: a tiny black-and-white kitten. There weren't any houses close by; she couldn't imagine where it came from. She was sure where it wanted to be—inside, every time the door opened. That seemed to be all right with Moe. Maybe he was lonely in the house since Juanita left. He was definitely out of sorts since the Doberman was claiming attention at the shop.

Rebecca opened a bottle of Shiraz, grabbed a glass and carried both out to the patio to watch the sunset. Moe ran to the border, stuck in a paw and hopped back when the kitten emerged. Both sprinted in her direction.

She bent down to wiggle a stick for the kitten. He pounced, then darted around the chair leg. She switched the twig again. Bright eyes bulging, his head wobbled back and forth following it. He pounced. Hopped back, hind quarters wiggling. She laughed. Switched the stick again.

She heard footsteps on the flagstones a second before the smell of sesame oil registered.

"Chinese?"

Hagan stood with his toes in the oregano, holding out the thick brown sack like a prize-winning fish. His eyes were masked by sunglasses. He was in ripped jeans, sneakers and an electric blue polo shirt. Head cocked to one side.

The kitten spun around, saw Hagan, puffed out its tail, arched its back and hopped sideways under the table.

Hagan burst out laughing and stepped across the herbs. He began unloading cartons of food.

"Who's the pint-sized rodent? Moe okay about him? Probably the weather's too hot for this spicy stuff. But man, I've been smelling it coming, going, and in my sleep. It finally got to me, so—"

Rebecca sat up. "You're staying at Lu Chan's?"

Hagan licked a trickle of Szechuan sauce from his thumb. "The marina's too pricey. Besides, it's fully booked into October."

"Why?"

Hagan shrugged. "Tourists like it? It's the only motel with a water view?"

"Why are you here?"

Hagan pulled out two more white cartons and set them on the table. "My buddy Schneider's being held in the Blue Marsh County lockup. Remember?"

"So what? You're a DC cop."

Hagan remained with his back to her, rearranging things on the table. "Actually, I'm not at the moment. I'm on ninety days administrative suspension. Captain thinks I have trouble following orders. And minding my own business. And he suspects I might be trigger happy." He turned and removed his sunglasses. "I've got chopsticks. We need spoons for the hot and sour soup. Which drawer?"

Rebecca flipped the twig toward Moe and held up a hand. "Hagan, are you working with Zimmer?"

"He thought we might try it out. Since he's got a criminal and I've got time on my hands. Napkins? Hell, paper towels will do."

He tried to cross by her en route to the kitchen. Rebecca uncoiled one bare leg, swung it out and tripped him just below the knee. He toppled forward, caught himself on the back of her chair, hands straddling her shoulders. She let her leg drop.

"Michael Hagan, are you planning to move to Head Tide?"

He tilted his head. Lowered himself slowly until their noses touched.

She had to close her eyes to keep them from crossing. She could smell him, feel his breath on her cheek. Feel the pulse under her collarbone speed up. She knew without looking that he was grinning.

His tongue ran across her lower lip. Then his lips brushed hers, less a kiss than an exhalation as he breathed, "Maybe."

PERENNIAL DARK ALLEY

Investigate the Hottest New Mysteries!

Sign up for the FREE HarperCollins monthly mystery newsletter,

The Scene of the Crime,

and get to know your favorite authors, win free books, and be the first to learn about the best new mysteries going on sale.

To register, simply go to www.HarperCollins.com, visit our mystery channel page, and at the bottom of the page, enter your email address where it states "Sign up for our mystery newsletter." Then you can tap into monthly Hot Reads, check out our award nominees, sneak a peek at upcoming titles, and discover the best whodunits each and every month.

Get to know the magnificent mystery authors of HarperCollins and sign up today!